Melanie Myers is a Brisbane-based writer, academic, and occasional actor. She has a Doctorate of Creative Arts. Her short fiction and articles have been published in a variety of publications, including *Kill Your Darlings*, *Overland*, *Arena Magazine*, *Griffith Review* and *Hecate*. In 2018 she won the Queensland Literary Awards Glendower Award for an Emerging Writer. She is the former artistic director of Reality Bites Festival, a non-fiction writers' festival based on the Sunshine Coast. Details about her work can be found at melaniemyers.com.au.

MEET ME

AT

LENNON'S

MELANIE MYERS

First published 2019 by University of Queensland Press
PO Box 6042, St Lucia, Queensland 4067 Australia

uqp.com.au
uqp@uqp.uq.edu.au

Cover design by Christabella Designs
Cover photograph by Lee Avison/Trevillion // orangecrush/Shutterstock
Author photograph by Glenn Hunt
Typeset in 12/16 pt Bembo Std by Post Pre-press Group, Brisbane
Printed in Australia by McPherson's Printing Group

 The University of Queensland Press is supported by the
Queensland Government through Arts Queensland.

  The University of Queensland Press is assisted
by the Australian Government through the
Australia Council, its arts funding and advisory
body.

A catalogue record for this book is available from the National Library of Australia

ISBN 978 0 7022 6261 6 (pbk)
ISBN 978 0 7022 6375 0 (pdf)
ISBN 978 0 7022 6376 7 (epub)
ISBN 978 0 7022 6377 4 (kindle)

To my grandmothers who both served

Audrey May Toomey (1914–1952), WAAAF
Marjorie Agnus McMinn (1922–1978), AWAS

- 1 -

Ribbed glass windows flanked with flower boxes of ribbed glass strike an unusual note in the Wintergarden ... to create a harmonious room which is a distinct asset to Brisbane's social life. Music each evening adds a tuneful accompaniment to this ideal cocktail rendezvous.

—Lennon's of Brisbane brochure, 1941

When an unpublished manuscript by Gloria Graham was discovered, three things happened: there was a minor bidding war to publish it (generating sufficient interest to be reported on in the mainstream press); the discoverer of the manuscript – a disheartened and disillusioned PhD student examining women's wartime writing about Brisbane, with a particular focus on Graham – obtained a scholarship; and a revival of Graham's long-forgotten satirical play, *Tie My Apron Strings, Would You?*, was mounted at a popular theatre venue.

The problem for Olivia Wells was that only the third thing was true – along with the part about her being disheartened and disillusioned. There was no unpublished manuscript by Gloria Graham. Having devoted the last two and a half years to the subject, Olivia should have been happy about the renewed interest in Graham's work, but she was frankly annoyed that some upstart little theatre company no one had heard of was earning the kudos for rediscovering Graham and her plays. The arts writer from *The Courier-Mail* even declared that 'Retrorep TC have single-handedly revived interest in Graham – the mid–twentieth-century feminist writer of poetry, plays and several works of short fiction from Brisbane – who has lingered on the edge of obscurity for the last forty years.' Olivia wanted to throttle her.

The company had, at least, offered her two opening night tickets when she called the producer and explained her interest in the work, and she, in turn, had promised to review it. He had not asked for her dramaturgical input, however, even though she'd done a drama minor as part of her undergraduate degree. So much for being an expert, she'd thought.

Olivia never did fit with the drama crowd. They were too spirited, too social, too inclined to think highly of themselves. The solitude of research suited her. She loved the quiet purpose of the State Library, in particular. Here, looking out over the cinnamon expanse of the Brisbane River, she could dip into the city's past. The light, spacious interior of the John Oxley Library was the perfect place to time travel: a liminal space of sage-coloured lounges and chairs, smooth maple desks, and green bankers' lamps that straddled the comfort of the present with the neatly catalogued past. She'd spent the better part of the day in the JOL, as she called it, looking through World War II ephemera and related fiftieth-anniversary commemorative material, much of it of only passing relevance to her research.

A recorded message announced that borrowing would cease in fifteen minutes and the library would close in half an hour. It was time to put the photocopier to work. She'd been reading personal stories, small memoir pieces by women that had been collated in a few different remembrance publications, she could potentially write a chapter on. Most were fairly mundane accounts about austerity measures ('making do'), working long hours at tedious jobs and waiting for menfolk to come home. If they noticed the bougainvillea and poinciana trees cheerfully decorating their streets and gardens, they didn't mention it. But what could you expect? These women weren't writers. They were simply telling it like it was. Those who brought up 'the Yanks', who were 'everywhere', did so from the perspective of observer. It was always *other girls* who were mad for them, not the person telling the tale. Olivia would love to know where all those 'fast' types had left their stories.

One woman, a waitress at Lennon's, claimed to have bought a coat from McWhirters with the generous tips she received waiting on American brass. She thought she looked quite smart in it, before realising fur coats were the gift of choice for women whom American servicemen 'favoured'. She then promptly burnt the thing, 'without regret', but not without having her picture taken in it first. Olivia considered the poorly reproduced photo: though only about twenty, the girl was painfully matronly. The long boxy coat didn't help; she looked about as fast as a snail.

Olivia glanced up from her desk. The creamy afternoon light, so settled only an hour before, had all but disappeared. The sun had drifted west, taking with it the warmth that had made sitting by the window so pleasant. The chill of the air conditioning and her goose-pimpled arms could no longer be ignored. The river was like ribbed glass, crudely reflecting the cityscape on the other side.

She returned the items she'd borrowed and left via the automatic doors. The war-brides documentary on VHS had been interesting, but was only tangentially related to her research project. The humid February air outside was a welcome embrace coming from the chill of the library. After collecting her bag from the locker room, she took the lift to the ground floor and walked out onto the Breezeway: an understated moniker when a gusty August wind whipped through the atrium. The show started at eight, and she wasn't meeting her boyfriend, Sam, until seven. Her indecision as to how to fill the next hour disconcerted her. The building had shut down for the evening and an air of desertion skulked through the pale-green concrete structure, despite the handful of students, mostly internationals, seated outside the library's cafe and bookshop with laptops. Not wanting to overthink it, she headed towards the Kurilpa Bridge, past GOMA, with the vague intention of walking along the river.

The sun sank with one last eye-pinching flare behind the hills, turning the sky a luminescent inky blue. Olivia had gone further than she intended, almost as far as Davies Park where the West End markets were held on Saturday mornings. Screeching bats rose like a black cape from a grove of Moreton Bay figs. It was time to head back. The river was now slick as obsidian. Mangroves in silhouette crouched at its edge, protecting new roots that poked through the mud like fingers. The smell of river muck was sharp but not unpleasant.

Olivia pulled out her phone to text Sam she'd be late and saw she had an email alert. It was from her mother, the subject: *Your Father*. She needed to sit down to read it. There was a park bench, she remembered, down by the Go Between Bridge. She walked briskly. Only half an hour earlier there'd been a few joggers and cyclists, even a young family with a toddler in a stroller. Now, oddly, there was no one. She often walked alone at night when she didn't finish teaching until 9 pm. It was just a matter of keeping that ball bearing of fear on an even track. She supposed all women carried it around with them, it was in their DNA, but if you didn't dwell on your vulnerability then that little sphere of

4

cold steel couldn't multiply into uncontrollable terror. The trick was to hold your head up, keep your gaze straight and steady, let each stride strike the pavement with your right to be there: heavy, insistent.

She was anxious by the time she reached the bench: put it down to the email. Why did her mother have to use such a melodramatic subject line?

> Hi Sweetheart,
> Your father called me (yes, I know, I went into shock afterwards). He wants to get in touch with you and asked for your email address. I said I'd check with you first. He found a half-sister or something and wants to tell you all about it. That may well be true, but I get the feeling it's more an excuse to make contact with you. Perhaps it's time?
> Love, Mum.

Olivia read it twice more, then put her phone in her bag, noting that Sam hadn't replied to her text. The twilight had shifted to a darkening amethyst. The moon, a Cheshire Cat smile, had just crested the horizon. Olivia stood up and began walking. She passed the old Foggitt, Jones & Co. warehouse and the rear end of the milk factory with a dim sense of their stubborn hold on the landscape in an area undergoing aggressive urban renewal. It was easier to concentrate on the Moreton Bay figs and their hidden spaces along the riverside than on her mother's email.

A man in work garb approached from the opposite direction. As he got closer, he gave her a weak smile, as though aware of her scrutiny. The place was known to be a haunt for drug dealers and unsavoury types once the sun went down, and even if she wasn't terrified she had every reason to be vigilant. The memorial plaque for the poor French girl who was raped and murdered in the park not so long ago was not far behind her. Olivia remembered the bright cornflower blue of her eyes in the photographs published online.

She was almost back at the library precinct when Sam replied.

> Sorry babe not going to make it tonight. On a roll with this piece.

Even though she had half expected him to cancel, the disappointment whirred through her like an angle saw. She was tempted not to reply, but couldn't bear the thought of him knowing she cared. Better to be blasé, but most of all understanding that artists need their space. Genius doesn't accommodate social engagements – or a girlfriend, for that matter. Olivia had accepted that at the outset. The attraction, if not exactly instant, drew her in like a force field only science fiction could conjure. They'd met at a house party in Paddington, a thirtieth birthday with a 'lost in the forest' theme; she'd gone as Snow White.

She saw him first, doing that thing: his party trick where he rolled his stomach in a grotesque exaggerated wave. He wasn't particularly good-looking: impish, devilish, maybe – that could have been the satyr costume – but he was different, and she had gone to bed with him that night with no hesitation. She tried to recall that first attraction: the way he zeroed in on her, claimed her with his eyes, and then his hands. She had never felt so *desired* before and had reciprocated with something as equally ferocious.

The next day he showed her his studio. She'd been prepared to write off their encounter as a one-night stand. Although she didn't indulge in them often, she was pragmatic enough to do so without regret, providing the sex was decent. Then she'd seen his current body of work: a series of mythic animal sculptures made from recycled metal. The concept itself was hardly new, but what he could do with old car parts, bedframes and all manner of discarded bits of iron, steel and copper was intricate and magnificent. Some were abstract, hybrid creations, others more conventional and realistic, but all were exceptionally detailed.

The piece he had been working on was a python made from mismatched spoon heads coiled around an actual tree branch, with a literal fork for a tongue. Again, not the most original image, Olivia accepted, but she was still convinced of his talent; and that, she had enough self-awareness to understand, was her downfall. She couldn't let him, or at least the idea of him, go.

There was still time for her to get a pre-show drink, and maybe a sandwich for dinner. She took the stairs that connected the library to the art gallery and museum. It was silly, childish, but she liked the Whale Mall: looking up at the humpbacks dangling in barnacled parabolas overhead and listening to their mournful, strangled moans on auto-loop. Her father had taken her to the museum once as a child to see the dinosaurs. She did the maths; it had been seventeen years since she saw him last.

She'd never once blamed her mother for leaving him, but the reasons for his gradual disappearance from her life in the years afterwards still made no sense to her, even when she was old enough to understand what was really meant by 'a drunk and a gambler'. His reason for contacting her now seemed odd. She'd wondered about her father's 'real' mother; perhaps he remembered her well enough to suspect curiosity would get the better of her.

A man she'd seen earlier at the library was standing on the walkway that connected the museum to the performing arts centre, looking over at the forecourt below. The year before there'd been a ten-metre animatronic baby brachiosaurus on display there. Olivia had been disappointed when it was removed. The man turned and caught her staring, and smiled before she could pretend they hadn't made eye contact.

'Hey, you mind if I ask you something?' His accent was American, with the hint of a drawl.

'Um, sure.'

'You wouldn't know where the Carver Club used to be, would you? It was a jazz club for African-American servicemen during the war. It was supposed to be around here somewhere.'

'I do actually. It was just over there.' She gestured with a flick of her wrist at the beige brutalist structure ahead. 'Where QPAC is basically, maybe a little further down Grey Street.'

'QPAC?'

'The performing arts centre.'

'Of course. Well, damn. I was close, then. I'm Tobias. Pleased to meet you.' He held out a hand for her to shake.

'Olivia. Where are you from?'

'Originally? Louisville, Kentucky. My family lives there. But I've been in LA for over ten years.' He faced her square on. 'I don't suppose you'd like to come downstairs and have a drink with me?'

She hadn't expected that. If it was a pick-up technique, at least it involved the personal touch; the intermediary crutch of a smartphone dispensed with. She would like to know about his interest in the Carver Club.

'I suppose I could. Why not.'

The forecourt outside the Lyric Theatre was busy. For musical theatre types, *Cats*, Olivia assumed, was the catnip of Broadway musicals. She spotted an empty table and claimed it before someone else could while Tobias went to the bar. She'd requested a white wine, anything except a chardonnay. A frazzled woman nearby was attempting to round up four girls in furry ears and tails embodying their feline spirits in the most literal of ways. Tobias almost tripped over one pouncing on a mouse as he returned.

'My apologies,' said the cat's mother.

Tobias gave her a 'no bother' wave.

'Mikaela. Sit down and finish your pizza. *Now.*'

'Cats don't eat pizza.'

'Pretend it's a bowl of Whiskas, then.'

Olivia exchanged an amused smile with Tobias as he handed over her glass of wine. She thought about offering him the spare ticket. Though logical, she concluded, it was also inappropriate. And it reeked of desperation. It was a moot point anyway; as he sat down, he announced he was going to a play 'about apron strings somewhere round here'. Olivia told him the entrance to the Cremorne Theatre was around the side of the building.

'My friend Clio is in it. We used to hang out in LA.'

'You're an actor, then?'

'Was. Past tense. These days I'm an acting coach and occasional director. You could say LA finally wore me down. There are only so many bit parts playing drug dealers, petty crooks and violent thugs you can do before that shit gets to you. Plus, I enjoy teaching.'

He asked her what she did. She said she was a university tutor. History and literature courses. She found it difficult to explain her doctoral research. Apart from it sounding about as useful as a deckchair on a submarine (as her grandmother would say), she wasn't sure herself some days. What did studying a minor literary figure from Brisbane contribute to the world? She gave him the short, vague answer she gave most people, hoping he wouldn't ask her to elaborate.

'So why the interest in this woman, this writer, this Graham lady ...'

'Gloria Graham.'

'You're writing a PhD on her, so her work must mean something to you.'

'I don't know. Her work interests me, that's all. She wrote about things few other people wanted to write about at the time, with an unconventional take. There's not a great deal in the way of scholarly analysis or research on her writing, or her life in general. I'm curious about what informed her fiction and poetry, I guess. Who she was. But what brings you to this little corner of the world? Brisbane's a long way from LA.'

'I've got a ten-month contract working with student actors at a university here. Clio set me up with some contacts of hers. And, to be honest, I've always wanted to see where my grandfather spent his war years. He used to talk about Brisbane a bit.'

'Ah, yes, the Carver Club.'

'Yeah, he spoke real fondly of that place. Anyone would think he built it with his own two hands.'

'The nostalgia of youth?'

'No doubt, but it was more than that. It was Brisbane itself. He was lucky, I think. He met some real nice people. The sort that didn't mind having a black man over for Sunday dinner.'

'Oh.'

'I know what you're thinking. Look, we don't have to pretend we don't know black servicemen were kept over this side of the river away from white people on the other side. We both know that, right? You're the history expert here, after all.'

Olivia nodded.

'No point in pretending it didn't happen then. A place has got to come to terms with its ugly history, is what I think. Otherwise it metastasises like a cancer cell. And from what I understand, ugly history goes back a lot further here than just the war.'

She wanted to say something, but the impulse died on her lips. He seemed to expect her to have some particular insight on the subject. Of course she agreed with him. She picked up her glass and drained the rest of her wine.

'You want another one?'

'I think we'd better get going.'

~

Olivia lurched from the entrance of the Fox Hotel and into the pedestrian rail that ran along its Melbourne Street frontage. The rail's purpose, she supposed, was to prevent patrons like herself from stumbling straight onto the busway. She thought going outside might straighten her out, but it only made her more aware of how drunk she was. If she'd eaten more than a quiche the size of a fifty-cent coin and two mini spring rolls that had been served up as opening-night fare, she would have been fine. She'd only had a few glasses of wine. And, at Tobias's insistence, a Kamikaze shot.

She'd been enjoying herself, too. How long had it been since she let herself go on a dance floor like that? Probably the last time a DJ had played Madison Avenue's 'Don't Call Me Baby' without irony. It didn't help that Tobias and Clio didn't seem to know the meaning of the word *inhibition*. Or *restraint*. Or *embarrassment*. Which encouraged her to also forget such concepts existed.

'Hey, there you are. You okay?' Tobias put a hand on her shoulder.

'Not really.'

'You want to go for a walk? Maybe that would help.'

'I should probably drink some water first.'

'Wait here. I'll go get you a bottle.'

He returned with a chilled bottle, and her bag. 'You want me to get you a taxi?'

She took another sip and shook her head. Getting into a car, even for the short ride home to Highgate Hill, would be more than she could stomach.

11

'I think I just need to walk for a bit. I don't live far from here, like twenty minutes away.'

'I'll come with you, hey. Just want to make sure you're okay, that's all.'

'Sure. I actually wouldn't mind going by the river.'

'I'll just let Clio know we're leaving.'

Olivia had expected Clio to be standoffish and 'actressy' when Tobias introduced them over champagne, but she was disarmingly friendly. It was Clio who insisted she come along afterwards for drinks at the Fox with the cast and crew. Olivia had been relieved to have only nice things to say about Clio's performance. She had, in fact, been moved to tears by her portrayal of Graham's unhappy 1950s housewife, Irene, but she'd need to find a less clichéd way of expressing that in her review.

'So, where to?' Tobias asked.

'This way.' Olivia headed off, pointing in the direction of the city, and stumbling on a kink in the footpath. 'Ouch … You know,' she said, checking her stubbed toe for blood, 'there used to be this grand old dancehall called the Trocadero next to the hotel, which was also called the Terminus back in the day.' Pointing up, she added, 'There's a train overpass here now, as you can see.'

'I'm guessing that's why this big old sign says *Trocadero Dansant*. You're quite the history buff, aren't you? A verbose one when you're drunk.'

'I'm a rambling bore.'

'Not at all.' He was inspecting the adjacent glassed-in display of sepia photographs that had been hung to jazz up, along with a coat of red paint, the column beneath the overpass. The selected images were a montage of the dancehall, outside and in, during its heyday. 'Don't know about you, but I always wanted to sit in

12

a big moon crescent myself and get my picture taken with a hot date. Instagram fodder, that is.'

She steadied herself against the concrete wall, hoping the sensation of trying to stand in a dinghy on choppy water would go away.

'Come on, let's keep walking.' Tobias took a hold of her hand.

By the time they'd reached the cultural forecourt beside the river, she felt a little better. There was a bench, but the grass looked more inviting, even if the earth beneath it was still damp from recent summer downpours. Tobias wandered across the lawn and over to the giant letters spelling out *BRISBANE* by the wall that overlooked the path parallel to the river. Olivia watched him rather than lying down and closing her eyes. She could have so easily yielded to the warm night, the faint breeze, the star-freckled sky overhead, that grinning moon. But the pinwheel would start if she did that: first it would just be the stars spinning above, then, if she didn't pass out first, it would be the problem of her father and what meeting him would mean. Was he seeking forgiveness? Would she have to pretend to understand? Probe him for explanations and answers? Was there some kind of etiquette for this kind of thing? Where would they meet? Would she greet him with a handshake or a hug? Should she be cool, but polite? Or prickly, perhaps even hostile?

She tried to picture what he looked like now: a man in his late fifties to whom time was unlikely to have been lenient. He hadn't quite been forty when he'd disappeared for good from her life, but the image of him that lingered most was a photo her mother took of them at the beach when she was eight. What she hadn't appreciated then was how preposterously good-looking he was, but not in his features alone. He'd always been tanned from a life carried out in the sun. His eyes, a dark, moss colour with glints of copper, were perpetually restless. The joke's on

13

you, they seemed to say. If his charm could be pinpointed, Olivia would have said it was in his smile, which somehow gave the impression he was winking at you – a 'larrikin's grin'. Women, she worked out later, had fallen at his feet like tin soldiers.

Olivia had closed her eyes while her head engaged in pirouettes. It would take some effort, she conceded, to keep them open, so she forced herself to stand up and went to Tobias. He'd backtracked around behind her to get to the viewing platform for the old Victoria Bridge abutment that had recently opened as a minor tourist attraction. He was using his smartphone torch to browse the timeline of historical information and accompanying photographs.

'I think this is the bridge my grandfather told me about. You know they weren't allowed to cross this bridge into the city at night, right? The military police would shoot them dead on the spot if they tried. No questions asked. A guy from my grandfather's company was murdered like that.' He looked up.

'I did know that.'

'Well, I'm not seeing anything about that on this timeline.'

She had no answer to that. It was a simple statement of fact, but she felt that peculiarly parochial sense of hurt pride when someone finds your home city to be lacking in some way.

'It's not exactly clear why your grandfather had such fond memories of his years here,' she said. 'Apart from a handful of decent white people and a club that played good jazz music.'

'I didn't really explain that, did I?'

'No, not really.'

'It's a pretty typical tale of forbidden love, actually,' said Tobias. 'A bit Romeo and Juliet, minus the misguided suicides.'

'She was white?'

'You guessed it. They met at the Carver Club. She was a volunteer. You know they had girls working there as volunteers, right? Some had Aboriginal heritage, but not all. She was a schoolteacher. They weren't supposed to date the customers, but I guess she ignored that rule.'

'They didn't marry, I'm assuming?'

'No, as accommodating as her parents were to old George – having him over for dinners and such – they weren't letting their daughter marry a black man. The way my granddad told it, they didn't so much object to him as what they foresaw as one hell of a hard life she'd be letting herself in for. Interracial marriages were also banned in Kentucky back then.'

'And your grandmother, what did she think of that story?'

'Oh, he only told me that part after she passed away.'

'When did he die?'

'Ten years ago. He was eighty-five. My grandmother died about six years before that.'

Olivia wanted details. It was a story that deserved more than just the bare facts, but Tobias didn't know any more than that, only that they wrote to each other for a few years after the war until she got married and stopped writing.

'Have you thought about trying to find your grandfather's lost love while you're here? Do you know her name?'

'Only her first name – Joy. And what good would finding her do? It's unlikely she's even still alive and who's to say her family would welcome a skeleton called George the black man tumbling out of their family closet?'

'You might be surprised. But I take your point.'

They headed down to the riverside promenade, past the Wheel of Brisbane and the Nepalese Pagoda, towards South Bank. It wasn't the most efficient route to Olivia's apartment, but she didn't mind, rowdy, squealing posses of drunken teenagers included.

The night was still warm and humid, but not uncomfortably

15

so. There was a salty tang in the air from the river, spiced with the scent of loose soil from the tropical gardens. She still felt queasy – the conviction that a good spew would make her feel better hadn't completely gone away – but it was more manageable now. Tobias offered to carry her bag.

'What the hell have you got in here?'

'Laptop, books, a stack of photocopies, a pair of heels I intended to wear tonight for the show but never did. General girl stuff, you know.'

'I'm happy to say I don't know. You girls make things tough for yourself with all the accoutrements you carry around.'

'I guess most of us accoutrement-carrying types are just used to it.'

They walked in silence for a time before Tobias spoke again.

'So this area – this is South Brisbane, right? – I'm gathering was a bit different during the war.'

'Well, yeah. There was a rollerskating rink up near where the bridge was, but apart from a few entertainment venues and hotels, it was mostly a collection of ramshackle warehouses, seedy boarding houses and brothels.'

'But look at it now, huh? A lush, tropical landscaped paradise with theatres and cosmopolitan restaurants and swanky hotels. It's like the past don't even exist here.'

'Maybe that's not such a bad thing.' Olivia sensed Tobias was disappointed there was so little trace of a past he could readily identify as belonging to his grandfather. Like going on a pilgrimage only to find the temple or the statue at the end had been replaced by a Macca's. 'Come here, I want to show you something,' she said. 'You haven't been to Brisbane until you see this.' She grabbed his hand and guided him up a set of concrete stairs off the promenade and into the parkland.

'So, it's a big pool?' he said when they reached the boardwalk.

'It looks like a Florida mega-resort.'

'Not just a pool. A beach. Man-made and in the middle of the city. Now that's something you don't see every day.' She led him around the back edge of the main lagoon closest to the river. The swimming areas were seductively lit by lamps and underwater lights. 'See the sand over there?' She pointed across the water. 'All trucked in. The lifeguard tower. The palm trees. The rocks. The water's heavily chlorinated, of course, to offset the pee of a thousand children, but it's a beach and you can swim in it.'

'Let's do it, then.'

'Now?'

'Why not?'

'Because it's after midnight and we'll get in trouble with security.'

Tobias shot her a look that said he was prepared to risk it and so should she. He was already removing his shoes, jeans and shirt.

'You coming?'

Ignoring the 'no diving' signs, he plunged in head first without a second glance, letting out a whoop when he resurfaced, shaking the water from his hair.

'Come on. The water's *sen-sa-tion-al*.'

Before common sense could make any ground, Olivia kicked off her sandals and yanked her dress off over her head. She took a running step up to the edge and pin-dropped into the deep end. The total embrace of the water, the swirl of warm and cool currents over her limbs and torso, was glorious. She pushed off from the wall, the fugue in her head dissolving as she glided like a minnow beneath the surface. She was smiling when she came up for air, almost laughing. When she turned to find Tobias, he swept his broad hand across the water to spray her in the face.

She squealed and returned fire. He then tried to dunk her by diving under and grabbing her by the waist. They were grinning at each other when they emerged, limbs entangled, to catch their breath.

Olivia, when she thought about it later, could only put it down to the moment itself as to why she'd put a hand on the back of his neck and drawn his lips towards hers. He took a small, surprised moment to respond. But what seemed like a spontaneous prelude to the inevitable was soon interrupted by the glare of a high-voltage torch swooping across the lagoon and a military-style instruction for them to vacate the water immediately.

~

Tie My Apron Strings, Would You?
– A review by Olivia Wells

As a new theatre company attempting to make its stamp on Brisbane's independent theatre scene, Retrorep TC's production of Gloria Graham's satirical play *Tie My Apron Strings, Would You?* was an inspired choice. Retrorep TC's revival – which recreates the play's 1950s suburban setting – opened at the Cremorne Theatre on Friday night and runs for three weeks.

The play was originally offered to the Brisbane Repertory Theatre (now La Boite) in 1954, but the company, under the directorship of Babette Stephens, had little interest in producing Australian plays at the time, preferring to stage fail-safe hits straight from Broadway or London's West End. Instead, it was produced by the flamboyant Brisbane producer Gary O'Donaldson and staged at the Theatre Royal in Elizabeth Street in 1955, a year after the original Cremorne Theatre, on what used to be Stanley Street, was destroyed by fire. Like many civic buildings in Brisbane, the American military forces commandeered the Theatre Royal in 1942. The Brisbane Arts Theatre staged the play again in the mid 1970s – the only Brisbane revival of Graham's searing social commentary until now.

Tie My Apron Strings, Would You? received a mixed reception by critics and audiences when it debuted. By then Graham was a poet and short story writer of some renown and, dismayed by what she saw as women's 'forced march back to the kitchen' after the war, wrote the play as a feminist critique, raising more than a few conservative eyebrows in the process. Sixty-five years later, the play may have lost some of its edge post second-wave feminism, but, like Ibsen's *A Doll's House*, we should remember the play was not only revolutionary for its time but that vigilance is required if we are to maintain, and further advance, our comparative liberation as women today. Graham died in 1975, but she would no doubt still be dismayed at the continuing gender pay gap that has reached a high of 18.8% since records began in 1994. Economic disadvantage – or enslavement, as Graham called it – is one of the central themes of the play as portrayed through the marriage of Irene Gilford, the play's protagonist, to husband Ronald.

Forced to resign from her teaching job when she marries shortly before the war, Irene joins the WAAAF in 1943 and rises to the rank of Sergeant, and when Ronald also returns to civilian life after serving in the RAAF, the two must pick up their marriage where they left off. The play begins eight years after the war. The couple have three children, but Irene feels increasingly suffocated and dissatisfied by marriage and motherhood. She dreams of escape and retreats into a world of both memory and fantasy featuring her American lover, Kenneth Wilding, a naval officer who died in the Battle of Guadalcanal. I won't give away the ending, but (spoiler alert) when Ronald discovers a keepsake cigarette case of Irene's – a gift from Kenneth that also contains his photograph – Irene reveals that she planned to divorce him after the war to marry Kenneth.

Like the classic American plays that emerged in the postwar era, *Tie My Apron Strings, Would You?*, while still firmly anchored in the satirical, takes most of its cues from realism. It was Graham's use of dream-like memory sequences that depict Irene's ultimately doomed affair with a US Navy officer during the war that primarily marked the work as revolutionary in the Australian theatrical scene at the time. For reasons that can't be entirely explained by form and substance, however, the play did not become a classic in the way Ray Lawler's *Summer of the Seventeenth Doll* did – the play that is credited with bringing naturalism to the Australian stage.

Clio Manning gives a standout performance as Irene Gilford. She brings to the character the sort of emotional fragility and sense of teetering on the edge one would expect of an actress playing Blanche DuBois. The role marks Manning's return to the Brisbane stage after a ten-year hiatus in Los Angeles. The role of Irene was originally played by Brisbane stage stalwart Gwendolyn Ecklund in what was her acting debut. The decision to cast Ecklund, untrained and a complete unknown, generated much to-do in the social pages at the time. By most accounts it was a solid start to her career, with one reviewer noting that she brought 'a much-needed sympathetic touch to the role of Irene'.

Christopher Larkin plays Ronald Gilford and gives a layered performance that captures the character's boorishness, as well as those aspects that mark him as a wounded and sensitive man who, despite everything, is still in love with his wife. The rest of the cast, who all double-up on various roles, are also strong, in particular NIDA-trained Luke Noels, who plays Irene's lover, Kenneth Wilding, with all-American charm, confidence and, importantly, a convincing accent.

The set design by Natalie O'Neill is a real treat, but it threatens to overpower the action on stage at times. Her 1950s kitchen is a garish parody of the real thing with oversized, colourful appliances. 'Outside' the house is represented by an overgrowth of snaking green vines, bougainvillea and bromeliads set on a wooden frame demarcating it from the interior spaces. It also heightens the insularity of the domestic sphere and Irene's feelings of suffocation.

The play's *Mrs Dalloway*-esque themes, however, were not the first thing that caught the attention of director Andrew Billings. He was initially drawn to the play because his grandfather was a young American submariner sent to Australia in 1942, where he met his future wife. Billings didn't know a lot about the period until he started research for the play, but realised his grandparents' story, like Irene and Ronald's (albeit fictional), was just one of the many family histories now woven into the colourful tapestry of Brisbane's past.

Unlike a few recent theatrical ventures that have attempted to bring the war era to life on the Brisbane stage, *Tie My Apron Strings, Would You?* is far less focused on the 'feel-good' music that defined the war period. This isn't a musical, and there's no obligatory jitterbugging, Lindy Hopping or even a swing dance number to 'In the Mood'.

There is, however, a moving memory sequence of Irene slow dancing with her American lover to Bing Crosby's 'I'll Be Seeing You' – a directorial inclusion that perfectly captures the mood of the play.

Gloria Graham is probably best known for her poetry, including her classic prose poem, 'The Olive Tree'. Famous for its melancholic lyricism, the poem was published in 1943 in the then-infant literary journal *Meanjin* and tells the story of a river sprite who, after her voice is stolen by an eel, makes peace with the river and transforms into an olive tree. Graham went on to write several one-act plays, often performed by amateur theatre companies, as well as a number of essays and works of short fiction. Since her death, there has been speculation as to whether Graham wrote a full-length manuscript based on her family (her father was a prominent unionist) and friends in Brisbane during the war. Much of her writing in the latter half of her career reflected her involvement in Aboriginal causes, of which she was a passionate advocate.

Retrorep TC's timely restaging of *Tie My Apron Strings, Would You?* is the perfect introduction to Graham and her sadly, and bafflingly, neglected work. This is a pacey and moving production by a polished, energetic cast who bring Graham's sparkling, witty dialogue to life. Director Andrew Billings has done a fine job of showcasing the pathos of the play without letting it descend into sentimental melodrama. This is Brisbane theatre at its best.

- 2 -

The amusing name of 'The Lobster Pot' has been given to the Quick Service Grill Room on the George Street frontage. Designed as a popular rendezvous with meals at modest charges, it features ... Lennon's famous five-minute grills.

—Lennon's of Brisbane brochure, 1941

January 1943

Dolly Beckett was in need of some fresh air. Corporal Charles Feely was an energetic dancer and, beginning with 'In the Mood' – belted out with characteristic vigour by Billo Smith and the Trocodero Orchestra – they'd danced the last three numbers together beneath a prismatic whirl of violet and blue lights at the Trocadero Dansant. The strains of the 'Chattanooga Choo Choo' pursued them past the palm trees and vine-clad alcoves on the perimeter of the ballroom as they escaped into the honeyed summer night.

They turned right down Hope Street and kept walking until, at Charles's urging, they slipped like thieves around the side of a darkened warehouse. Dolly expected Charles to kiss her, and he did, but not before he cupped her face in his hands and drank it in as if she'd been blessed with the features of Hedy Lamarr. Under the early wane of the full moon she could have been anybody at all, and she responded in a way

Gwendolyn Beckett never had to the stiff, inelegant fumblings of her fiancé, Robert.

The rapid rise and fall of her chest and the coil of heat unfurling inside her were, she realised, what she'd hoped for the night before Robert's last departure north. But he had not even looked at her as he'd shunted up and down like a matchstick that wouldn't ignite, his chest hair rubbing like sandpaper against her bare breasts, coyly revealed only moments before. With each exhaustive thrust his eyelids had squeezed tighter together, until finally, thankfully, he grunted, with one last heave, to a stop. It made her think of a steam train pulling into Central Station – minus the whistle. Afterwards, when she'd turned on her side, aching with disappointment, he put his arm around her and thanked her for the best going-away gift a guy could ask for.

This, then, was the way it was supposed to be. In her vindication, neither guilt nor shame flicked at the edge of her conscience. Was this how Maisie's cousin had gotten herself into trouble? She let the thought flit into the darkness and sunk further into the immediate, urgent present that was Charles Feely and his lips on her neck.

Encouraged by the rumble in her throat that tickled his ear, Charles whispered for her to follow. They ran the rest of the way down Hope Street hand in hand, Dolly struggling to keep pace with Charles's athletic stride. He stopped to let her catch her breath, and covered her face in kisses as she gasped with laughter. She had never been to this part of town before. She should have been cautious, perhaps scared, as they approached a rowdy hotel on the corner. But they stayed on the opposite side of the street, unnoticed or ignored by the strays and loiterers in uniform and those hoping to benefit from their overstuffed wallets. Charles led her across Montague Road towards a flank of three arches:

one of many that formed the gap-toothed underbelly of the Grey Street Bridge.

'There's a spot by the river,' he said.

They walked parallel to the bridge for a bit before Charles veered into the surrounding scrub. Dolly gripped the sides of his broad back from behind and kept her eyes on the rutted dirt path as Charles forged a passage, cigarette lighter aloft, through the foliage. Several feet in she heard a disturbance in the nearby undergrowth and screamed before she could think, flinging herself against Charles.

'It's just a water rat. See, there it goes.' He pointed the lighter in the direction of the noise as the horrid creature scurried away. But she didn't want to look. 'Come here. Come here.' He wrapped her in a thick embrace and patted her hair until her breath slowed. 'We're almost there, I promise.'

'I don't think I want to stay here any longer.'

'Hey yeah, sure, I understand. But let's have a cigarette first. The place I want to take you is right through here.' He didn't give her a chance to respond, but guided her with a firm arm around her waist until they reached a Moreton Bay fig. Charles laid his jacket on the ground just out of reach of the tree's sinewy base. It reminded Dolly of an illustration she'd once seen of the Medusa's head in a book on Greek mythology. Beyond the scrub palms and ferns, mangroves bordered the river: a twisted cage cordoning off the ribbon of moonlight across the water.

The air was pungent with leaf decay and dank, coppery soil. The cold from the ground seeped through the coarse fabric of Charles's army jacket, and what began as a cool summer breeze coming off the river soon turned the mugginess to a damp chill. Dolly's thin blue cotton dress, selected that afternoon for the purpose of dancing in a crowded, overheated room, was no barrier to the cold that came up from the earth and pressed in around them. Charles lit her cigarette and she burrowed into his side.

She wanted him then, powerfully – his heat, his clean American smell, all of him – in her bed and bathed in the soft yellow light of the bedside lamp; not out here in the dark, with its loathsome vermin and creeping, insidious cold. She only had to say the words and they would go to her bedsit, she knew that. Even if she could bring herself to be that forward, she'd be out on her ear quicker than you could say 'Yankee harlot' if she were seen bringing him into the boarding house.

Dolly smoked in silence. She convinced herself she could reasonably avoid getting caught, but still couldn't voice the suggestion that he come home with her.

'You're freezing, aren't you? Come here, doll.' Charles tossed his cigarette butt away then pulled her in with both arms to rub her back with his meaty palms. 'You wanna get out of here?'

She nodded into his shoulder.

'That's a yes? Come on then. I'll get you a taxi.'

He helped her to her feet, but her legs were numb and unprepared to take her weight. She stumbled and fell into the buttress of roots fused to the tree trunk like the wax of a melted candle. It felt as though her leg had been struck by the blunt side of an axe. She squeezed the fleshy underside of her upper thigh in an effort to dam the pain, sucking in air as though it was being administered by a straw. She was mortified enough without Charles seeing her cry.

He knelt down to apologise and ask how bad she was hurt. When her breath had settled to a series of shallow but steady hisses, she answered him. 'I'm fine.'

'Here. Take my arm, honey. I won't drop you this time, I promise.'

She brushed aside his outstretched hand. 'Give me a moment.'

When the pain had eased to the beginnings of a bruise, and she could move without wincing, she grasped the thick-wedged root she'd landed on to lever herself up. Instead of the knotted texture of hard wood, however, she felt something thin and satiny, like a dry membrane – a recently occupied snakeskin was her first thought. Unable to get to her feet fast enough, she screamed and scurried away like a crab.

Charles reached over to pick up the item, even as she begged him not to touch it.

'Hey, hey, hey. It's okay, honey. Look, it's just a stocking. See? Some girl left her nylons here.' He snatched it up and dangled it like a mouse by its tail. 'Reckon some fella and his date got caught in the act and she forgot to put them back on, if you know what I mean. Its mate is probably around here somewhere.' He checked if it had pooled in one of the crevices between the roots of the tree, but didn't find the second one.

Despite her inexperience, Dolly did know what he meant and this spot, the one Charles had corralled her to, was clearly known for that purpose. She felt silly and naïve. But he'd been nothing but courteous and attentive, and he hadn't demanded anything. He hadn't even tried to kiss her since arriving here. She was suddenly exhausted – too tired to think or care whether his intentions were honourable. And, if she were honest, she'd been hoping they weren't. It was just the location; it wasn't right.

She held out an arm and Charles helped her to her feet.

'You want a single nylon, doll?' he said, handing the stocking to her.

New nylons, a pair of them, yes, she'd love nothing more. 'I think we should leave it here,' she said. 'Maybe she'll come back for it.' Dolly rolled the stocking into a ball. She walked around the tree, looking for the best place to stow it, and almost tripped again – this time over a woman's black pump.

In the lick of flame from Charles's lighter, they spotted its mate lying askew a body's length away. Dolly looked at Charles. He was silent and his face, eerily contoured in light and shadow, told her nothing. She took a step towards the second shoe.

'Best not to touch them, I reckon. I'm going to have a look by the river. Why don't you stay here?'

'I'd rather come with you.'

Closer to the riverbank the ground thickened to a putrid, pasty mud. Dolly could only wonder at the ruin to her own brown leather pumps she'd used up eight coupons to buy. Unconcerned by the state of his boots, Charles squelched his way through an opening in the mangroves to reach the water's edge.

Dolly hung back, unwilling to wade through more sludge. She wasn't wearing stockings and if her feet got caked in mud at least she could wash them. Shoes in hand, she scanned the ground for a rock to wipe the worst of the muck off.

She didn't see the woman's bare legs at first, not until she'd scraped the sole of one shoe. They were wedged among the mangroves like perverse pick-up sticks. Dolly's own limbs stiffened to wood as she pieced the rest of the image together: the sopping dress wound like a shroud around the woman's torso, the thick cobweb of hair obscuring her face. The body was laid across the black-fingered mangrove roots as though they were a bed of nails.

The scream, this time, stayed buried in her gut.

~

When Maisie followed her to the ladies' restroom the next morning, Dolly expected some kind of recrimination after leaving the dance without telling her. That wasn't Maisie's way, however, and Dolly felt bad for pre-empting an attack. She did look terrible though, as Maisie's reflected face pointed out with a fair lashing of concern. The purple-grey crescents beneath her eyes were meshed with fine red lines.

'I'm just tired. I barely slept last night and … Well, I'm finding it difficult to concentrate. I've already stuffed up two connections this morning.'

'Why don't you take the rest of the day off?' said Maisie. 'I'll tell them you're unwell, that you've got an upset stomach—'

'No, no, I can't do that. You know what they're like about any of us calling in sick. And, please, don't say I've got an upset stomach. People will gossip.'

'All right, I won't, but you should at least take a break. Just lie down for ten minutes. I'll make you a cup of tea.'

'Do you think—'

'It'll be fine. Leave it to me. Where did you go last night, anyway? I went looking for you but you'd disappeared.'

'We went for a walk, that's all. I needed some fresh air. Nothing untoward happened, if that's what you're asking.'

'I never thought that. I know you're straight as a die, and even if you weren't I certainly wouldn't judge you. They won't be here forever, you know, and as far as I'm concerned girls like us should make the most of the good times while they're here.'

Dolly settled into the small settee outside the ladies' room. Unless she went down to the sick bay there was nowhere else to rest. When Maisie returned with a cup of tea and half a buttered scone, she realised she'd been dozing, even though she'd been conscious of her thoughts tumbling over themselves. Among the jumble of fractured impressions, the girl's shoes and stockings recurred, again and again.

'Here you go. Drink that up and I'm sure you'll feel better soon. Anyway, I'd best get back to it.'

Dolly felt marginally better after having tea and, with no desire to incur further disapproval from the shift monitor or the other girls, she went back to her seat to once again tell the steady stream of callers she was 'putting them through'.

A telegram, addressed to *Miss Dolly Beckett*, had been placed at her station. Her first thought was Robert. She ripped it open. But it wasn't Robert; it was Charles.

Meet outside Lennon's at 6? They know. Are you okay? Charles.

She hid the telegram in her purse. *They know.* He'd done it, then. He'd told the police. She'd believed him when he said he wouldn't tell them she was there too, but felt no less uneasy about it.

The woman next to her pulled her headset off.

'Not bad news, I hope?'

Dolly shook her head and mumbled something about her father being ill. Not a complete lie, if she was ever called on it.

'You really don't look so good, honey.'

Charles was waiting as promised, garrison cap at a fetching angle, with – and here she shouldn't have been surprised – a box of Whitman's Samplers. The Yanks were generous to a fault: that's what Maisie and the other girls repeated ad nauseam with superior, knowing airs. Flowers, Charles said, wouldn't have been practical, but was she fond of any particular type? You know, for future reference? She told him she liked orchids ... and daisies. Should she have added there'd be no need for future reference?

'I thought we could get something here at the Lobster Pot. You hungry?'

Dolly was starving and piqued at the suggestion, and smell, of a quick-service grill. Apart from the scone Maisie had brought her, she hadn't been able to stomach anything all day.

The diner was already busy, mostly with Americans and their bottle-blonde, corsaged dates, but Charles managed to get them a semi-circular booth along the wall. They sat down and she regarded him properly for the first time.

He was so very blond – his hair made her think of pale corncobs – and broad, and his eyes, though deep-set, were creased at the corners with laughter lines. He had pockmarks on his cheeks and forehead, but was no less attractive for them, she thought. Perhaps because he was constantly smiling: a wide, unabashed grin that left permanent grooves around his mouth and showed off teeth that were as white and straight as fence posts.

She'd retouched her lipstick and mascara before leaving work, but in comparison to the glossy, peach-faced girls surrounding them, in their floral frocks and matching hair arrangements, she felt like a schoolmarm. They were as vibrant as a flower stall, making her think of a French Impressionist painting. It didn't pay to look too closely, though: a girl at the table opposite had a pronounced overbite and an elongated face; her friend, terrible acne that no amount of powder could pancake over. Nothing, however, could dampen their delight at being so enthusiastically courted. It was pleasant to observe and Dolly had no trouble understanding why they wouldn't give a fig what anyone thought.

The waitress arrived and they placed their orders. Charles urged her to get a steak, which felt decadent – when was the last time she'd had a T-bone? – but he said it would do her good. He'd noted how tired she looked. He asked for a burger 'with the works' and fries. Almost as good as the ones back home, he said, and by far the best in this here town.

When the waitress left, he scanned the room.

'So, it's all taken care of, doll. I reported what we found to the MPs and they said they'd look after it.' He spoke as though he were planning to rob the place.

'That's all?'

'Well, I had to show them where she, you know, where the body was …'

'So that's it? They didn't ask you what you were doing there at ten o'clock on a Monday night?'

'They asked, sure. And I told them – well, they suggested actually – was I with a young lady? But I didn't tell them your name, I swear, honey. They understood the situation just fine and said they didn't need to know your name. That my account of events would be quite adequate.'

'But they know you weren't alone. That someone, a woman, was there with you.'

'I'm sorry, doll. There wasn't any getting around that. If I said I was alone, that doesn't look real good, does it? They might figure I killed her.'

Her selfishness was abhorrent, she knew that, but Charles, if he judged her for it, didn't let on. Once the shock of discovering the body had worn off – seeing what a drowned cadaver looked like; the loose, wrinkled skin, plastered with grass and leaves and mud – she'd become obsessed with the girl herself. She had begged Charles not to touch it, *her*, but he had gingerly lifted the curtain of matted hair from her face and now Dolly couldn't see anything else. The girl's dark, wide-eyed stare, framed by her plucked, startled brows, and gaping, colourless lips were more vivid than a child's nightmare that sends them scurrying to their parents' bed.

Death. They all lived with it: brothers, uncles, sons, fathers, husbands, fiancés, sweethearts, friends. They all waited for it: knew someone, or someone who knew someone, was going to be unlucky soon enough. But they never saw it, never looked at the grotesque reality of it. Death was only ever about loss. The vacuum that formed once you were told someone had gone: KIA, died from wounds sustained in battle, malaria, dysentery. All of them at home – civilians, as they were called – were protected from death. She realised that now; they weren't expected to face its brutal, visceral ugliness, only the terminal absence it brought.

Who, then, was missing this poor girl? A mother, father, sister, or a boyfriend, perhaps? Somebody, surely, was wondering where she was. But it wasn't her job to find out; she may never know who the woman was, and the fact bothered her a great deal. She asked Charles if any of the MPs had said what they thought happened to her.

'Not really, no. I mean, they have to do a postmortem on the body and all of that before they can tell for sure.'

'Tell what for sure?'

'Well, you know, one of the guys, the MPs, said maybe it was suicide. With that stocking tied around her neck, maybe she'd tried to hang herself first.'

It never occurred to her that the girl could have killed herself. Instinctively, she knew the man was wrong, the suggestion preposterous, but she didn't say so to Charles.

'I'm sorry I left you last night. I should have stayed with you, but—'

'No, no. You did the right thing. You had to … go to the police, of course. And it … well … I can't bring male guests into the boarding house, so what could you have done?'

But it didn't feel right that Charles had gone to the American military police. Why hadn't he gone to the real police? And why hadn't the MPs, after Charles notified them, turned the matter over to the regular police? Exhausted, and on the verge of tears, the sort that wouldn't stop once they started, she let the whole sorry subject go. Charles reached an arm around her shoulder and kissed her on the side of the head.

'You want me to take you home after we've eaten?'

'Yes, please.' She was simply too tired to care anymore if the other residents saw her with a Yank.

When the taxi pulled up outside the boarding house, Dolly's street was quiet, even for eight o'clock. Or perhaps she only noticed it because Charles was with her. It wasn't unusual for a party to be going on, or a duped boyfriend to be airing his grievances to the unresponsive night. She lived far enough up Gladstone Road in Highgate Hill to be away from any real trouble, though the odd brawl spilled beyond the confines of Boundary Street in West End from time to time.

Charles asked the taxi driver to wait, then came around to open the door for her. They faced each other on the curb, the browned-out windowpanes a protective sepia veil from prying eyes. The tangy smell of frangipani and rotten mango hung in the air. The symphony of frog, cicada and gecko twitter seemed to amplify the longer they stood there.

'Will you be okay on your own, honey?'

Her silence answered for her. She was a coward. But it was impossible to ask him to stay. The still fresh image of the girl's face didn't frighten her, ghastly as it was, but she didn't want to be alone with the residual unease its imprint had left inside her skull.

'Why don't I come in? Just till you fall asleep … Or I can stay the night, if you want me to?'

A small nod was sufficient. She would take the risk of getting caught. For discretion, Charles went back to the taxi and asked the driver to drop him a few blocks away. It's the last window on the right towards the back of the building, she told him. At least six, maybe seven feet up, but he wasn't perturbed. The woman in the room next to Dolly's was deaf, but she asked him to be as quiet as he could anyway.

Once inside, she opened the window and then went to the kitchenette to put the kettle on. She had no idea if Charles drank tea – she heard the Yanks weren't big tea drinkers – but it gave her something to do. When she turned with the steaming kettle from the stove, she found him standing in the doorway. She reeled back, setting in motion a dollop of boiling water that came out the spout and splashed, thankfully, onto the floor.

'You scared me half to death! I didn't even hear you come in.'

'I'm sorry, doll. I didn't mean to scare you. But you told me to be quiet, so I was. I thought you'd be waiting for me at the window.'

His earnestness is what set her off. The fact that he was in her tiny bedsit at all, where he looked comically oversized, and that she had almost scalded herself. She laughed past the point of tears until her sides ached. He couldn't see what the joke was – no, she wasn't making fun of him, she promised – but he chuckled with her, at her, with his big, white, American mouth, enjoying her unrestrained mirth.

He kissed her then, not waiting for her laughter to subside. Grabbed her shoulders and held her against the doorframe so she couldn't bend over in another fit of hysterics. She was neither shocked nor affronted; whatever delirium had overtaken her before seamlessly ebbed into another permutation, and Charles became its grateful beneficiary.

He left the way he came, although Dolly had no idea how he managed it. He'd tried hard not to wake her – dressing soundlessly and skimming his lips on the crest of her cheekbone – so she pretended he hadn't. She sat on the desk beneath the window, folding her knees in to her chest. The dawn light was still tenuous, and she watched the changing palette of the sky, staying until the last blush of apricot gave way to a strip of lemon on the horizon and the palest of blues. There was already a heat haze rising from the edges of the day. Gradually, the silhouetted rooftops and palm tree fronds took on the functional textures and colours of another workday.

She'd slept heavily, but there hadn't been nearly enough of it. The blame was entirely hers. It wasn't Charles who'd woken with fervent need in the darkest part of the night, though he didn't require any encouragement once she reached for him.

There was still plenty of time for a proper bath before she had to catch her tram. She turned the hot tap on and shut the bathroom door to let the room fill with steam. The addition of a private bathroom, though pokey and mildewed, was the reason she'd been happy to pay more rent than she could really afford.

Yesterday's discarded clothes were spread across the floor. She retrieved her dress, which was by the door. Too crumpled to wear again, she threw it over a chair and picked up a letter that had been lying beneath it. She must have missed it when she came in last night. She suspected her landlady enjoyed slipping residents' mail under their doors; what better way of keeping tabs on everyone?

The letter was from Robert. The sight of his strangled, skinny handwriting left her feeling strung-out. Compressed. She would have to read it. She took the envelope into the bathroom. The bath was too hot. She ran cold water and spread it around with her toes until there was a warm current she could comfortably slide into.

Robert's letters were never long; he was too conscious of the censors. He'd posted it before leaving Townsville. They were heading north by ship the next day, by which she took to mean Port Moresby. He was in good health, although he felt a bit poorly after the two-day journey to Townsville in an overcrowded troop train. Of Townsville, he wrote, there was an absolute dearth of women, to the point where men were brawling over girls 'who looked like the back of a bus'. The bloody Yanks – sorry for swearing, darling – naturally made the situation a hundred times worse. He was yet to meet one he thought was a fair-dinkum bloke and not a hustler or swindler, or both. But didn't the girls go for them! Only for their money, of course. Plenty of guys worried about their wives and fiancées back home …

She dropped the letter over the side of the bath, knowing full well what was next. He, of course, had nothing to be concerned about. If a bloke couldn't trust his woman, then she wasn't worth the worry. Robert was of the school of thinking that the Yanks were doing them a favour by 'sorting out the sheilas for them'. Well, he'd sorted her wrong and she wasn't the least bit sorry. She closed her eyes and let the memory of the night before stream over her naked, buoyant body.

- 3 -

You won't have any trouble finding out that everyone in Australia is in the war all down the line. There aren't many cars on the street; taxis are hard to get; streetlights have been turned off to save power; and the Prime Minister recently announced that all nonessential industries would be shut down for the duration ... So life for the Australians isn't as free and easy as it was, but they're out to win the war and to hell with comforts.

—Instructions for American Servicemen in Australia, 1942

~~Olivia Wells is~~
~~Olivia Wells has been~~
Olivia Wells hated writing about herself in third person. The stipulated bio of no more than fifty words should have been the easy part of submitting a journal article she'd written based on a recent conference paper. The title had been difficult enough ('The Woman Who Loved Those Yanks: the facts and fictions of Maureen C. Meadows and her narration of that desire').

She minimised the file and opened the email she'd drafted a week earlier. She read over it again without changing a single word or punctuation mark. It didn't need further revision; it needed to be sent. Yet she still hesitated. To quit now would be professional suicide. That's the first thing her supervisor, Mandy, would say. Then: 'Why, when you've done so much work already?' Mandy would do her utmost to convince her it was worth battling on for.

It was her own fault. She'd gone into her research project thinking she'd uncover something new about Gloria Graham: an unpublished story, a few poems, the phantom manuscript, some previously unearthed correspondence, and from that she'd build her thesis. But all she'd done so far was rehash the work of other academics who'd paid some cursory attention to Graham's work in the 1990s, then added a few thoughts of her own. And was there really anything new to say about anything these days?

A glass of wine – if there was anything left of last night's six-dollar bottle – might convince her to press send. She got up from the coffee table and went to the kitchen. There was a third of the bottle left. She lifted a clean glass from the dish rack and took it, the bottle and her phone out to the balcony.

It was a clear night and warm, especially for late March. But she wasn't complaining; she endorsed Brisbane's propensity for summer weather well into May. It was one reason she'd never seriously considered leaving – that, and the view from her apartment. It was part of her morning ritual to sit on the balcony with her first coffee of the day and watch the river, a pliable serpent, slither round the university on the other side. She often did the same of an evening, but with a glass of wine.

During the Brisbane floods, she'd stayed out there for hours at a time, transfixed, never quite comprehending its sudden ferocity or the breadth of land it had consumed. The river was dark now with a loose skin of reflected residential light. The moon was bright, but well past its baby-faced prime for the month.

The chop of a low-flying helicopter fractured the stillness, a barely perceptible shudder at first, then to a crescendo that couldn't be ignored. It came into sight as an intermittent red light, with a second bluish spotlight shaving riverbanks. After a few swoops over the area, the helicopter continued its mission upstream.

Olivia opened a local news site on her phone, but whatever the drama it was yet to be a headline. A text message from her flatmate, Cheryl, arrived.

Invited a few peeps for drinks tonight. That okay?
Sam coming. Be there soon x.

After texting her reply — That's cool. Will need wine x — she went back inside to tidy the living room. Cheryl worked for Arts Queensland and she had invited Olivia to the opening of an exhibition of an artist who, also a professional rival and 'frenemy' of Sam's, had received a grant through one of their funding programs. It wasn't just because Sam would likely be at the exhibition that Olivia had not gone. She'd set aside the evening to work on a lecture she was to give later that week, though the likelihood of that happening was diminishing by the mouthful. She returned the cushion she'd been sitting on to Cheryl's leather lounge and placed Cheryl's glossy photography books back on the coffee table. Before closing her Mac, she checked her emails, more out of habit than anything else.

The name 'Trevor Stephens' hijacked her attention. Her compulsion was to slam the lid down: shut down what amounted to a haunting of her inbox. She waited until her heart stopped galloping to read what he had to say. It was short and to the point:

Hi Livvy,
It's your dad here. Your mum gave me your email. I thought this the best way to contact you. I'll be in Brisbane next week and would like to see you while I'm there, if you'd be agreeable to

that. I got some news recently about my birth mother I'd like to share with you. Let me know how you feel about meeting up.

Love, Trevor

After her mother's warning, none of it should have surprised her, but she still had to read it three times to absorb and make sense of it. *Love, Trevor?* It had the makings of something better left for tomorrow. In the morning, when she was fresh, caffeinated, and not in a state of low-level anxiety at the prospect of seeing her supposed boyfriend who had not rung once in two weeks.

On that score, she wasn't going to let anger get the better of her. She would not, under any circumstances, resort to appearing needy or even resentful, despite the shameful amount of mental energy she'd expended on him in the last fortnight. She took a deep breath and moved on to the other unopened email.

It was a Google Alert for 'Gloria Graham'. She'd set up the alert over a year ago with no expectation of it yielding anything. 'Gloria Graham' was old news, but every so often she would get pinged about a Gloria P. Graham, PhD, who headed a genetic counselling graduate program in Cincinnati. Olivia knew quite a bit about Gloria P. Graham. Not to be confused with Gloria Graham, the American artist (b. 1940), or the Hollywood actress, Gloria Grahame (b. 1923, d. 1981), best known for her work in film noir pictures. This time it was about *her* Gloria.

The link took her to a radio transcript that had recently been digitally archived – probably because of the renewed interest in Graham's work since the revival of *Apron Strings*. Olivia skimmed it, her buzz quickly flat-lining when she found only a single mention of Graham as the playwright. The rest of it – some insights into the actress Gwendolyn Ecklund who played the lead role in the original production – would have been useful for her review two weeks ago. She'd read it more carefully later. There might be some pertinent nugget she could toss into her thesis, but it was hardly the trove she needed to salvage the whole thing.

RADIO TRANSCRIPT

ABC BRISBANE
Segment: Arts Sunday with Anne Sully
19 October 1975

ANNE: My special guest on 'Sunday Arts' this afternoon is something of a Brisbane theatre institution. Over the course of twenty years she's worked for all the major theatre companies in plays such as *Private Lives, The Seagull, A Streetcar Named Desire* and *Macbeth*. She's currently starring in a new production of *Hamlet* as Queen Gertrude, Hamlet's traitorous mother. Or is she? We'll get to that in a moment, but first let me introduce today's guest. It is, as you may have guessed, Gwendolyn Ecklund. Good afternoon, Gwendolyn. It's a pleasure to have you in the studio with us.

GWEN: Thank you, Anne. It's lovely to be here. And, please, call me Gwen.

ANNE: First up, congratulations on *Hamlet*. You opened last night and the season, I've been told, is close to being sold out. That must be very gratifying. I have to ask, though: do you still get opening-night nerves?

GWEN: Thank you, yes. The buzz around this production has been quite something. Yes, I do get opening-night nerves. I think if I didn't it would be time to retire. The nerves remind me to never be blasé – either about the role or the job of being an actress. They keep me on my toes, so to speak.

ANNE: I'd like to talk about your career and how you got started in the theatre. I believe you were a bit of a late bloomer and didn't start acting until you were in your thirties. How was it that you came to the theatre at, let's say, a more mature age than most?

GWEN: Pure happenstance, actually. Or luck. My husband, Robert, and I were out celebrating our tenth wedding anniversary and I ran into an old friend. We worked together during the war. And as it happened her husband, Gary O'Donaldson, was staging a production of a new play by Gloria Graham – a Brisbane playwright, incidentally. I believe she died only recently. But, yes, the actress they'd originally cast had been offered a role in an Old Vic production of *The Merchant of Venice*. My old friend Maisie thought I'd be perfect for the role, and she worked on persuading her husband that, despite me never having spoken a line of dialogue before, he should cast me. I have no idea what she said to convince him, but I thank her for it. I was thirty-three at the time, and a mother of two, I should add. I will also say that discovering the theatre at that age is what saved me, and my marriage. You know, I was so green as an actress – I needed a lot of hand-holding through the whole process – but because I related so utterly to my character I think I was convincing despite my lack of craft.

ANNE: In what way?

GWEN: The play was set in the 1950s, and my character, Irene, was essentially a desperately unhappy housewife who couldn't see any way out of a lifetime of domestic servitude without any source of fulfilment other than raising children. The main point of difference between me and Irene was that she'd had a taste of a career she enjoyed before marriage, and therefore had a greater understanding of what losing that meant. I'd worked as a single woman, of course, as a telephone operator – first at the Brisbane Exchange, and then for a time at MacArthur's headquarters on Edward Street. But I never had any expectation of a career beyond that. I was firmly brought up to believe marriage and children, and those two things alone, were the endgame for any woman.

ANNE: It's interesting you mention marriage and children, because I wanted to ask how you managed raising two children and having a career in the theatre. It can't have been easy twenty years ago.

GWEN: No, it certainly wasn't. My marriage very nearly didn't survive. I can laugh about this now, but it certainly wasn't funny at the time. Robert, my husband – he died a couple of years ago – initially forbade me from taking the role of Irene in *Tie My Apron Strings, Would You?* I told him if he didn't let me do it, I'd divorce him. Well, divorce in those days, I'm sure I don't have to tell you, was not a respectable, middle-class thing to do, especially in this town, so you can guess who won that round. But, yes, it was always difficult. I didn't work all the time, though, so that helped, plus keeping theatre hours meant I was mostly at home when the children needed me, even if I was often tired.

ANNE: Seeing *Hamlet* in its entirety for the first time last night, I was surprised the role of Gertrude is a comparatively small one in the scheme of the play.

GWEN: Yes, she only has about seventy lines. Not many for what is a pivotal character.

ANNE: What is it about the role then that draws an actress like yourself to it?

GWEN: A couple of things, I suppose. Firstly, her ambiguity.

Shakespeare is rather circumspect about her motives. We never really know if she was innocently taken in by Claudius's scheming and has no knowledge that Claudius killed her husband, or whether she knew what he was up to all along. For an actress, that's quite a gift, because you can decide and it's a way of putting your stamp on the role.

ANNE: And your Gertrude? Innocent or guilty?

GWEN: Oh, innocent, of course! [Laughs]. But not totally naïve, either.

ANNE: What else about Gertrude attracted you to the role?

GWEN: Apart from the curtain scene with Hamlet, which is quite intense, for me it was Gertrude's monologue where she's describing Ophelia's death. Even on the page, I've always found it incredibly moving, so to get the chance to perform it is a career highlight.

ANNE: Well, you certainly do it justice. You could have heard a pin drop during that speech. I mean, it was visceral, the emotion in your voice, when you were describing how this poor girl drowned. You make it seem effortless – is that easy for you to do? Accessing that kind of emotion on stage, I mean? It's something you're known for as an actress, that's why I ask.

GWEN: I wouldn't say I find it easy, no. But I always aim for emotional authenticity when I'm portraying a character. And that, for me, means being prepared to mine my own experiences, particularly the darker stuff, to do that. And the thing with Shakespeare is that the imagery is so strong that you don't need to ... [pause]. I just mean to say, that all you have to do is speak the words. It's all right there in front of you—

ANNE: Yes, the language is very vivid. He paints pictures with words. When you say 'right there in front of you' though,

46

do you mean for the actor or the audience?

GWEN: Both, I suppose. But it's the actor who has to convey that image to the audience.

ANNE: You're saying, then, that the actor still has a job to do? Even Shakespeare can be dead as a doornail if it's not spoken or delivered with some skill?

GWEN: Yes, I guess that's probably a good way of putting it. [pause] But the thing is, in this instance, I did have a real experience – an image – to draw on.

ANNE: In what way?

GWEN: I've never spoken about this publicly before, or even much in private to be honest, but playing Gertrude has – how should I put it? – brought up a rather unpleasant memory. Of a young woman who died.

ANNE: You mean you saw a woman drown? How awful.

GWEN: Well, no. She was already ... When we found her ... It happened during the war. Down by the river in South Brisbane, not far from where the milk factory is now. I'd gone down there with this American fellow – the city was crawling with them back then, as we all know. We'd been dancing at the Trocadero and we left to go have a cigarette. He took me to a place 'nice girls' didn't go, if you follow me. I was apprehensive about being seen, more than anything. This was during the brownouts mind, so I don't know what I was worried about. It was quite dark, though there must have been a reasonable amount of moonlight because we could make things out. We didn't see anything at first until, well, I quite literally stumbled upon a nylon stocking – just the one though. It was 1943 and nylons were rare as hen's teeth by then, you've got to understand. We then found a pair of women's shoes, and that's when Charles got the idea to go down to the river to see, well,

47

to see if ... I followed him because I didn't want to be left alone, and that's when I saw her. This girl. This poor girl. She was lying in the mangroves, sopping wet with a nylon, a stocking, tied around her neck.

ANNE: You found the body of a young woman on the banks of the river? And she'd been murdered? That's extraordinary. And, I imagine, very upsetting.

GWEN: Yes, yes, it was. But what's more extraordinary is that I never heard another thing about it. Not a single mention of her death in the press, which even now I find astonishing. It was like it never happened. Yet, the image of that young woman, the way she was laid out across the mangroves, has never left me. Ever. It's as vivid today as it was thirty-odd years ago. I've never stopped wondering who she was. I also feel it's time I went public with what I saw. That poor girl deserved ... I mean, I don't even know her name.

ANNE: It is curious, as you say, there was nothing in the papers about a girl who was strangled, presumably, and then dumped by the river. Do you think it was deliberately covered up?

GWEN: Anne, I honestly couldn't say. It was after the Leonski murders in Melbourne, so perhaps, yes. That wasn't a high point in our relations with the US Armed Forces, as some of your listeners may recall.

ANNE: Yes, I was only a teenager at the time, but I remember my parents talking about the murders in hushed, scandalised tones. There was also a woman, if memory serves, who was murdered by a US soldier in a city laneway here in Brisbane. Do you remember that? I don't recall what year it was.

GWEN: It was 1944. I remember it well. It was a very brutal murder. She was beaten, kicked to death, her jaw broken in several places. Her face was completely battered. Doris Roberts, her name was. She was found in a laneway, as you say. Her killer was a US paratrooper. He hung for it – in New Guinea several months later.

ANNE: That must have had quite an impact on you.

GWEN: It did, because I thought at the time that perhaps Fernandez – the man who killed Doris – could have also murdered the young woman I found in the mangroves. He'd been a paratrooper for the US Army since 1942, so it wasn't implausible. After following the case in the papers, however, it seemed to me that Doris's murder – brutal and disturbing as it was – was an impulsive act. Fernandez became enraged after she demanded money after they'd had sex in the laneway. At least, that was his story. By all accounts, he wasn't too bright and the manner of Doris's death, well, it just didn't seem to fit with ... with this other girl's death.

ANNE: Unfortunately, we have run out of time, so we will have to leave it there on that rather grim note. But thank you so much for joining us on 'Arts Sunday'. And perhaps if any of our listeners know anything about Gwen's River Girl murder they could give us a call in the studio.

GWEN: Yes, please do. I've sometimes wondered if I imagined the whole thing.

ANNE: Well, it's been a pleasure having you here this afternoon and best of luck with the rest of the show.

GWEN: Thank you for having me. It was lovely to be here.

- 4 -

Since American troops first landed ... the Australians have gone out of their way to welcome them and make them feel at home ... Australian audiences, at theatres and concerts, honor our national anthem by rising when the Star Spangled Banner is played.

—Instructions for American Servicemen in Australia, 1942

September 1942

Without regret. Without regret.

The words ticked over like a skipping rope to a nonsense childhood chant. Alice took a step back from the fire and watched the filaments curl under orange-blue flames before flaking away to nothing. The smell – acrid, nose-wrinkling – took her back to the night Jack grabbed her plait and held the end over a candle. She was eight at the time; he maybe fifteen.

The whole thing was cremated in less than half an hour. Its pelts reduced to fine grey powder and scraps of charred satin, stiff and bowed at the edges. She doused the last of the fire with a bucket of river water. The ash was swept away in black rivulets that trickled into the surrounding dirt.

It was cold now the fire had sizzled out. The moon was almost full, but the clouds drifting across its face made the night feel heavy and suspenseful. Perhaps she had been rash.

Without regret: Alice repeated the mantra as she shivered the two blocks up Merthyr Street back to the hostel. She hoped Val might have gone out, but it was only Monday, not one of her regular nights for jitterbugging. When Alice arrived Val was sitting on her bed painting her toenails and smoking, both tasks likely to incur the ire of Mrs Ingle.

'Where have you been? You look like you've been stoking a boiler. Are we that hard up for male labour?'

'Nowhere. I went for a walk, that's all.'

'Why the war paint then?'

'I don't know what you're talking about.'

'Look in the mirror. They're making tea downstairs. You want some?'

Val was right. There was an obvious smear of soot along her jawline. She looked at her hands and went down the hall to the bathroom. As she lathered them with soap, Val appeared and propped a hip against the doorframe.

'A simple yes or no will suffice.' She crossed her arms.

'Yes or no what?'

'Tea. I asked if you wanted some.'

'No. I'm okay, thanks.'

'Suit yourself.'

'Actually, I meant yes. Yes, please.'

Val did that thing with her eyebrows: one up, one down. Alice felt like a scolded puppy. She wiped her hands on a towel and checked her dress. It looked okay but smelled of smoke. She took it off and put on Val's robe, which was hanging from a hook on the back of the door, and returned to the room. Laughter drifted up from the common room; there was probably a card game going on. Someone was trying to play 'The Star-Spangled Banner' on the piano, but couldn't get past the first four bars.

Val's footsteps sounded on the landing. She nudged open the door with her hip. 'Here you go.'

She handed Alice her cup and put her own on the desk. Val had a secret stash of sugar she kept in a biscuit tin in one of the side drawers. She topped it up from the kitchen when Mrs Ingle or the cook weren't there.

'So what gives then? You've been acting like a strange cat all week.'

Alice didn't understand Val much. You could hardly tell she'd been jilted by her fiancé only a few days ago. Maybe those photos she and Val took of each other wearing the fur coat, before she burned it, really did cheer Val up.

July 1942

Alice had been a waitress at Lennon's quick-service grill, 'The Lobster Pot', for almost three months when Laurie, the restaurant manager, tapped her on the shoulder. She was wiping down tables after a busy Friday lunch.

'Come with me,' he said.

She followed, heart in mouth, like a lump of bread too big to swallow.

'How are you finding the job so far?' His face was unreadable.

'It's going well. At least, I think so. I mean, I like it just fine.'

She could only think that it had gotten back to him about the milkshake she'd spilled all over that poor girl's dress. But that wasn't her fault. She was ready to explain about the two Yanks who were skylarking about, trying to impress their dates with some mock football manoeuvre, when one of them elbowed her from behind.

'Good, good. From all accounts you've been keeping your head down and getting on with the job.'

She waited for him to go on.

'So, things are about to change around here,' Laurie said. 'The big brass from the US military have been moving in and the biggest one of all will be calling Lennon's home very shortly. You do know who I'm talking about?'

Alice thought she knew and nodded. She'd overheard people whispering in the café about MacArthur having arrived in Brisbane. One woman even boasted that she'd seen him being driven down Queen Street.

Laurie waited until his announcement garnered the respect it was due. 'What that means is the Yanks want their own waitstaff to work in their private dining room. They've a few girls coming over from the officers' mess at Somerville House, but they've asked me to help do some more recruiting.' He paused, waiting again for the import of his words to register on Alice's face. 'I told them I had a couple of wholesome types in mind. Not too plain, though – it's important to have a nice smile. The tips will be even better than The Pot.'

Alice wasn't sure if he was asking her to fill the position.

'That sounds like a good idea,' she remarked.

'Do you want the job or not?'

She said yes, of course. It couldn't be any more tiring than here, and it might mean her hair and fingers didn't reek of stale grease at the end of every shift. It even sounded glamorous. Val would have to be impressed when she told her.

Alice caught the tram to the Valley junction. High in spirit and spurred on by the tips she'd earned that week, almost two quid, she didn't change trams to go down Brunswick Street but went instead to McWhirters. She didn't really intend to buy anything. She was expected to send any extra earnings back home to the farm and that's what she more or less did.

Even with the war on, there were still pretty things to buy if you had money: satin scanties and negligées, fancy powder compacts, tasselled perfume spritzers and lipsticks in ornate gold canisters, patent-leather shoes and purses, neat pin box hats, tailored blouses and frocks. Alice felt heady, feverish, at the sheer prospect of it all: to be able to look, smell, touch and, perhaps, buy. She'd learned to reason herself out of purchasing things she couldn't really afford – the summer dress with lace revers around the collar or the silver embossed brush-and-comb set – but this was the first time she had money in her purse without a more important cause assigned to it. She had yet to collect her wages for the last two weeks, her tips being enough to cover the twenty-five shillings for her lodgings, lunches and a few extras like going to the pictures. Her mother wouldn't expect a few pounds again until the end of the month.

She couldn't have fine things back home, anyway. They'd only get ruined, and she'd be chided for getting above herself. Her former employer, Mrs Stevenson, never thought twice about buying herself a new dress or cosmetics or knick-knacks, or anything else Alice had started to covet. Working as a housemaid had opened Alice's eyes to how different rich and poor people really were. When the Stevensons built an air-raid shelter in their backyard, it'd been Alice's job to store the good china and crystal inside it. If anyone had stowed their best crockery away for safekeeping at home, there'd be nothing left to eat off. It wasn't that they were dirt-poor, but every penny counted, and you didn't go buying stuff you didn't need.

She did need a new coat, though. Her mother couldn't possibly begrudge her that. The English boxy style was popular. She'd seen them advertised in the paper at McDonnell & East, but they were at least six pounds. McWhirters had a similar range. She took a full-length English-style wool coat off the rack in a 'W' – she'd never fitted into an 'SW' – and tried it on. It was fully lined with stitched revers and pockets. A good fit and she looked very smart, she thought. The sales girl also said as much. Alice turned to look at herself from behind in the mirror. It was a far cry from her pilling, grey-serge hand-me-down. Winter had been warmer than usual, the hottest recorded June in forty years, but it was bound to get cool soon and she'd be coming home late most evenings. She looked at the price: six pounds six and twenty-seven precious coupons.

'Have you seen our new range of fur coats? They only came in yesterday.'

Alice followed the sales girl to the rack. It gave her more time to decide whether to get the wine or the blue, or if she should buy the coat at all.

'Isn't this beautiful? It's fox.' The girl held it out for Alice to stroke.

It was creamier than silk. Alice wanted to run the buttery filaments against her face.

'Why don't you try it on? I'll hold the other one for you.'

It couldn't hurt, just trying it on. Mrs Stevenson owned a fur coat, of course. Probably mink, or rabbit, Alice wasn't sure. She'd touched it once while tidying Mrs Stevenson's room. It was lying over the chaise lounge. She'd hung it back in the closet, amazed that anything could be that soft. It was the same long, boxy style as the woollen one but with a yoked back.

She couldn't quite believe her own reflection. It was like running into a movie star on the street, if she didn't look too closely at her face. It never occurred to her that an item of clothing could change a person like that.

The coat was fifteen pounds. She'd never spent that much on a single item in her life. It was not even a consideration. She slid her palms down over the pelts and sighed.

'We have a lay-by service,' the girl said. 'You'd just need to leave a twenty per cent deposit. And the best part is it's still only twenty-seven coupons for a coat that will last many seasons. You don't want to fritter away coupons on something that's going to wear quickly or become shabby. A coupon wasted is a coupon lost.'

Alice had the kind of face – ordinary as grass, she always supposed, but likewise appreciated when needed – that reminded some older officers of their daughters back home: their Bettys, Marions and Helens in Missouri, Texas and Connecticut. By the end of her second week serving Yankee brass in the dining room, she had earned enough in tips to pay off the coat. She made the final payment on a rare clear, windless day; though the weather had been mild, it had also brought frequent light rain.

Val was on the nightshift at the factory all week. That didn't mean someone else wouldn't barge into their room, though. Alice locked the door to their small room before removing the coat from its box. Glossy and abundant, it showed up the shabbiness of the furniture and the cheapness of Alice's other belongings. She saw her cracked hand mirror, chipped accessories and worn patchwork quilt not as items of comfort and retreat but as extensions of herself: comely, naïve and make-do. The coat was as out of place at a Presbyterian and Methodist girls' hostel as the King of England on a tram.

Among her modest collection of dresses, mostly boxy cut frocks in checked fabrics, there were none that came close in terms of quality; it was comical to even pretend she could get away teaming the coat with anything she owned. Val's clothes took up more than her half of the slim wardrobe. Alice looked through them for the tailored, dark-red number with black piping around the sleeves and collar Val often wore out dancing.

Alice found it heaped with a pile of other clothes over the chair in front of the desk they both agreed was of better use as a dressing table. Loose powder and a stray puff, mascara brushes, lidless compacts and containers of rouge, and half-a-dozen worn-down lipsticks in different shades of red lay strewn across the makeshift vanity like fallen soldiers: a battlefield diorama with a feminine accent.

She was roughly the same height as Val, but the dress was tight across her shoulders and bust. She yanked it down so it sat better – only it then pinched her waist. She couldn't get the zipper done all the way up. It was still nicer than anything she owned. Val kept a picture of Vivien Leigh as Myra Lester in *Waterloo Bridge* stuck to the wall by the mirror.

Alice removed the pins from her hair and attempted to brush it and shape her eyebrows the same way as Miss Leigh. She then selected a lipstick she thought suited her skin tone. Even as she sweltered beneath the dozen or more fox hides, Alice didn't mind what she saw in Val's portable vanity mirror.

August 1942

Even as winter intensified, slipping well into August, Alice couldn't bring herself to wear the coat outside. On occasions when she had the room to herself, with Val either at the factory or out 'having her fun', as she put it, Alice would put on the coat and Val's red dress if it were lying around, and pretend to be Mrs Frances Stevenson: a gracious society hostess noted for her charity work and impeccable style. Frances organised fundraisers for the Comforts Fund and the Red Cross and was often pictured in the papers either helping put parcels together for the troops or attending charity balls and opening nights, always in her fabulous fur coat. Frances would issue morale-sustaining platitudes in clipped vowels and a careful emphasis on plosive and sibilant consonants, the way Alice's high school English teacher, Sister Marianne, would speak when reciting the work of English poets.

It took an Antarctic front, the kind that whips the wind up Brisbane's hilly streets like an icy lash, to finally compel Alice to wear the coat outdoors. She was rostered on for a special Sunday luncheon being held in honour of a visiting brigadier general. The other girls were still at church when Alice returned to the hostel from Sunday Mass. Val hated going to church; she'd be recovering from her Saturday night dancing marathon in bed if she had a choice. Still, Alice bundled the fur into a ball and gathered it up as though smuggling out a litter of kittens. At the end of the street, after checking behind her, she put it on, greedy for its warmth, then walked around the corner to the nearest tram stop.

The conductress was the first person to call her *ma'am* when she punched Alice's ticket. Alice still found it strange seeing a woman in the job. A gentleman, a banker or something similar by the way he was dressed, also addressed her as ma'am and even offered her his seat. Men were generally polite towards her, but she'd never been afforded this kind of treatment before. She thanked him as she imagined Frances would.

Of course, the Americans called anything in a skirt ma'am, so that wasn't to be counted.

Before taking the staff entrance, Alice bundled up the coat again in the alleyway behind the hotel. It wouldn't do to leave it in the staff locker room, so she took it to the ladies' cloakroom. Several patrons were there to check in their own fur coats. They were well-dressed young women for the most part, although she recognised one older lady: Mrs Wilson, a friend of Mrs Stevenson who would often make social calls. She would let her tea sit for half an hour after Alice poured it, then complain it wasn't hot enough. She once said to Mrs Stevenson, 'She's one you'd need to keep an eye on', when she thought Alice was out of earshot. Mrs Stevenson had replied, 'Oh no, she's a good little country girl. She wouldn't so much as take a penny from Aladdin's Cave.' Mrs Wilson said she 'wasn't referring to the silver'. That made Mrs Stevenson laugh. 'Oh goodness, no. Not Alice,' she'd said. Alice had looked at the portrait of John Stevenson Jnr mounted on the wall, as she did several times a day, and felt a queer jolt in her stomach.

Alice hid around the corner until Mrs Wilson was gone. Daphne, the cloakroom attendant, didn't question her story that the coat belonged to a Mrs Stevenson and Alice had offered to check it in for her. She merely raised one eyebrow into a mountain peak before jotting *Mrs Frances Stevenson* on a ticket stub.

'Did you hear about that usherette shot by a Yank at the Lyceum on Tuesday night?' Daphne asked, holding on to the stub. 'Only a hundred yards from here. Walked right into the dressing room with a gun. No one stopped him! Shot her twice – in the stomach and the leg, then shot himself in the head.'

Alice had heard the story. One of the girls at the hostel had read an account of the shooting in Wednesday's *Telegraph*.

'She must have been terrified', was all Alice could think to say. It did seem unbelievable that a Yank, and a corporal, could stroll right into a picture theatre and shoot someone.

'Terrified is right. Apparently he called the theatre beforehand to say he was coming to shoot her and her boyfriend. Been pestering her for months, is what the girl told police. She told him she wasn't interested. Some men just can't take no for an answer, can they? And she's no spring chicken either – thirty-three! How many old maids do you know could drive a man to suicide? It gives me hope, is what it does. But you wouldn't have to worry about that. How old are you?'

'Twenty, but I should really get going – my shift's starting.'

'Well, here you go then.' Daphne handed over the ticket stub with a flick of her wrist. 'And tell Mrs Stevenson not to lose it.'

Alice put the stub in her pocket and went straight to the kitchen.

It was a little after nine when she collected the coat. One of the evening waitresses had called in sick and Laurie asked Alice to stay on. Daphne, to Alice's dismay, was also doing a double shift.

'Mrs Stevenson ready to go then? Hasn't she been here a while? You'd think she was being paid, wouldn't you?' Daphne dangled the question.

Alice stared back with a faint smile. There was something about Daphne's intent she was supposed to understand. She stood there, fourteen again, feeling the whispers of the girls behind her on the school bus. Later, at home, she discovered the bloodstain that had spread like a dark bruise over the back of her skirt.

'Well, anyway, those Yank officers must think she's a fox, or why else would she be here so long? Speaking of, which one of them do you reckon bought her such a specimen of a coat?' Daphne continued speaking as she retrieved the fur from the closet area beside the counter. 'She's a real piece though, if you ask me, sending you to fetch it for her. Who does she think she is? The Queen of Sheba?'

'Oh, she's quite nice, really. She's just finishing up in the dining room and I offered to get it for her. Really.' Alice laid the coat over her arm and stroked it. 'Thank you. Have a good rest of the evening.'

'I will when I knock off,' Daphne wittered on. 'One of these days. You finished up, are you? You should go out dancing. Those Sunday night dances at City Hall are real popular. But of course you can only get in if you're an AWAS or a WAAAF, or have a date with a soldier or a sailor. Stinks if you ask me. Aren't the rest of us entitled to a good time now and then?'

'I think I just want to go home to bed.' Alice could have crumpled with exhaustion. She bid Daphne goodnight again and left before the woman found another topic to offer an opinion on, careful to go via the dining room, lest Daphne detect a hole in her story.

Out in the lane, the cold was immediate. It was almost pitch-black, save for some light from the half moon. She slipped the coat on and stood for a minute to let the warmth penetrate her skin. It was a cloudless night and the dry air was crisp as tissue paper. The odour of the lane – rotting garbage, stale urine and engine oil – was unpleasant but not overpowering, and still preferable to the smoke-filled dining room. She tilted her head to gaze at the strip of night sky that ran like a coded message between the roof edges of the buildings. She'd never been much good at picking out the constellations, with the exception of the Southern Cross, but Alice preferred making her own patterns with the stars.

Daphne was right about Sunday-night dances being popular; couples milled about on the corner of Adelaide and Albert streets outside City Hall. A line of people spilled out between the columns of the main entrance and down the wide stairs. It would be next to impossible to get a tram home later.

'Alice! Alice!'

Val was calling from the queue, hands cupped around her mouth. She said something to the beefy sailor beside her, then jogged down the stairs to join Alice on the kerb.

'I thought it was you. I didn't recognise you in that coat – blimey! Where the blazes did you get that from? You haven't charmed some Yankee officer off his feet at that fancy hotel of yours and not told me about it, have you? What's it made of?'

'Of course not. It's fox and I bought it myself. From my tips.'

'Have you been hiding it from me?'

'No, why would you think that? I only bought it yesterday. It's not too much, is it?'

Val shook her head and exhaled sharply.

'Well, I never. Little Alice Parker from Kingaroy bought herself a swanky fur coat fit for Vivien bloody Leigh. Do I think it's too much? Too much of *what*? Why don't I try it on and I'll tell you if it's too much? Here, hold this.'

Val's navy coat had holes in both armpits. She handed it over as soon as Alice, reluctantly, removed the fur.

'Look at that. It's a perfect fit.' Val buried her hands in the pockets and spun around. 'Could I borrow it sometime? I promise to look after it.'

'I suppose that would be all right.'

'Geez, I wish Manpower had put me in a job where I could earn a few tips to buy a coat like this. The only tip they give you in munitions is how to keep your hair out of a lathe. How many coupons did you need? Must have been a few.'

'A dozen or so.'

They stood for a moment in silence, a tacit acknowledgement of Alice's lie, before Val relinquished the coat.

'Well, I better get back. Rocko's waiting for me.' She turned to wave at him. 'He's from Little Rock in Arkansas,' she added in response to Alice's blank expression. 'He reckons he's going to teach me to jitterbug. I haven't told him I'm already an expert at it. I'm going to surprise him, but I'm not sure we'll even get in at this rate. It's absolutely chockas in there.'

~

The knock came before sunrise. It slipped into Alice's dream as a plot twist; the door opened and John Stevenson Jnr's school pin and cufflinks were in her hand. She couldn't open her mouth to defend herself and her eyelids felt nailed shut.

'Alice.' There was another rap on the door. 'Alice. Your mother is on the telephone.' Mrs Ingle's tone was sharp. The call had probably woken her. Marilla Parker had made it clear that the housemistress's offer of a bed for her daughter was only grudgingly accepted because the nearby Catholic girls' hostel was full. She agreed on the proviso that Alice be excused from attending compulsory Sunday church services at the local Methodist church to attend Mass.

'I'm coming.' Groggy with sleep, Alice threw on Val's robe, which was slung over the chair. Val didn't stir. Gauzy dawn light slipped beneath the edges of the curtains.

Alice felt faintly nauseated by the smell of cooked cabbage that permeated the downstairs hall. She took the receiver from Mrs Ingle.

'Hello? Mother?'

'Is that you, Alice? I can barely hear you. Can you speak up?'

'Sorry, is that better?' Alice curved her hand around the mouthpiece. 'I don't want to wake anyone.'

'Don't tell me you were still in bed. It's almost six, for heaven's sake.'

Alice didn't bother reminding her it was Saturday and breakfast wasn't served until seven. Marilla only rang off peak.

'Anyway, this is costing a pretty penny. I rang to tell you your brother's got leave. He arrives in Brisbane on Thursday morning. I wrote and told him you'd meet him at the station. I should have liked to be there myself, but there's simply no way we can spare the hands at the moment, let alone the petrol for a trip to Brisbane. Do you think you could manage that?'

Half-brother, Alice wanted to reply, but petulance was her mother's pet peeve. She agreed, as she must, knowing she was the last person Jack would want to welcome him at the station. Her mother, satisfied, then asked the usual perfunctory questions, expecting the usual perfunctory answers: Was she eating well? *Yes.* And was she, more importantly, 'keeping out of trouble'? *Of course.* Rumours, Mrs Parker said with a cagey undertone, had reached them of girls in Brisbane picking up Yanks in broad daylight on street corners. Underage girls, they'd heard, had been caught copulating with GIs in the city's parks. She didn't want to sound alarmist, but by all accounts the city had well and truly succumbed to temptation and sin. Make no mistake: the devil would be rubbing his hands with glee.

Alice was saved from the lecture about moths and flames and singed wings by the telephonist reminding them they had one minute left or her mother would be charged for another five. Mrs Parker rang off after extracting a promise from Alice 'to not forget Jack fought Germans in the desert for almost a year'.

Back upstairs, Alice inched open the bedroom door in a vain attempt to not make the hinges squeak.

'You don't have to be quiet. I'm awake.' Val twisted her neck to look at Alice. 'What time is it?'

'Just after six.'

'Christ.' She turned back to the wall. 'I haven't had a Saturday off in three weeks and I get woken up at sparrow's fart.' She waited a beat before yawning theatrically and rolling over.

Alice had gotten back into bed. She rubbed her frozen feet together and pulled the covers to her chin. She'd given up asking Val not to swear. It only made her do it more. It was a shame you couldn't confess other people's sins for them. Alice apologised for waking her.

'It's all right. I want to tell you something, anyway. I've got some exciting news. But you have to promise not to: Breathe. A. Word. Do you promise?'

'Yes, but—'

'There can't be any buts. You have to promise.'

'Okay, I promise, then.'

'Rocko,' Val said, with exaggerated emphasis on the last 'o', 'asked me to marry him and I said yes.' She waited for Alice's reaction as though she'd played a winning hand of cards. 'You're supposed to say "Congratulations" – look.' She held out her left hand to show Alice the thin gold band on her ring finger. 'Rocko says he'll get me a nicer one eventually. So, what do you think?'

'You only just met him. It seems ... a little quick, that's all. But if you love him, I guess—'

'I do. And he loves me. Anyway, we're getting married on Thursday at the registry office. His submarine leaves in less than a fortnight so we want to do it before then. He's already got permission from his commanding officer. I was wondering if you'd be my witness?'

Alice hadn't the temerity to say no. She just said that Thursday was the day she was supposed to meet Jack at the station. Her reservations were entirely to do with what Marilla would say. It was only the wages Alice earned that had stopped her mother hauling her back to Kingaroy. Marilla endorsed with fervour Archbishop Duhig's opposition to marriages between Australian women and American servicemen, and if she found out Alice had been party to a girl marrying a Yank after knowing him for all of two weeks, Alice could say goodbye to Brisbane.

'So, you go to the station and meet your brother in the morning, then come to the registry office in the afternoon. We don't mind getting married later in the day.'

'Half-brother.'

'Why don't you bring him along? Rocko says he's got a friend who'll be our other witness, but if he can't make it for some reason, then Jack could do it. And I know Thursdays are your rostered day off, so you'll be lying if you say you're working that day.'

From her bed, Val reached around on the floor and tossed her clothes aside until she found a packet of Chesterfields. General MacArthur's arrival at Lennon's had put paid to Alice's Thursdays off over a month ago, but she'd have to ask to work the evening shift instead anyway. She told Val she'd do it, and felt dread immediately rise like dough from the pit of her stomach. For the first time, she demanded Val open the window if she insisted on smoking in bed. Winter was almost over, but the early morning still chilled the room like a freshly stocked icebox. Alice lay on her back, staring at the creep of mould on the egg-and-dart cornices above.

'And don't forget you promised not to tell anyone. They'll kick me out of the hostel if they find out I'm a married woman and I'll have nowhere to live. At least until it's time for me to go on a ship to America.'

'I won't, I promise.'

'And another thing. Do you think I could borrow your fur coat to get married in?'

~

Thursday began with a light frost on the ground. The dew glistened as the sun rose reluctantly into the pale sky. It was colder than it'd been for most of winter. Blustery winds were forecast. Val, as was her plan, had feigned stomach pains the afternoon before so as to be taken seriously when she called in sick to the factory that morning. When Alice left at eight o'clock, Val was as skittish as a gecko.

Alice waited at Roma Street Station on the fringe of the crowd. She stood beside a brick pillar in a futile attempt to find a windbreak, as Val's navy coat did little to fend off the stinging winds that whistled down the platform. It did, however, make her less conspicuous. She hoped, dimly, that Jack wouldn't see her, or she him, and they could pretend they were sorry to have missed each other. To her surprise, he had sent her a telegram on Monday confirming his arrival, bar any delays, for around ten o'clock. He'd even signed off *love Jack*. She was annoyed with herself for thinking, even for a moment, that it meant anything.

Her mother had never seen it, or chose not to. Jack's father was a war hero: one of the fallen at Gallipoli. Alice's father hadn't volunteered; he'd stayed because there were no other able-bodied men to keep the farm going. His brother had died at Pozières. He also didn't believe Australia should have to sacrifice its young men for a war that wasn't their business, for a king who lived on the other side of the world. Rolly Parker had a few contrary opinions that Marilla took on like Donald Bradman at the crease.

It was closer to eleven when the crowded troop train, heralded by the smell of burning coal and grease, panted into the station. Diggers in scruffy uniforms hung out of the square wooden windows, whooping and waving, as the crowd – with some exceptions, including Alice – cheered them on over the hiss and screech of the braking engine.

Alice retreated as the eight-carriage train disgorged its load of rowdy men. She didn't like the way they moved in packs, shoving and shouting at each other.

She saw him first, down the other end of the platform; he'd been in the last carriage. Alice waited until he was about ten feet away before she stepped out from the pillar.

'Jack.' She held up a hand in a motionless wave.

'Alice. Well, here we are then. You gonna give me a hug like a good sister?' He put an arm around her shoulders and squeezed until she strained to draw breath. She could feel the hardness of his torso and the lean, python strength of his arm. He let her go and flicked her behind the ear. She ducked and moved out of his reach.

'Bloody hell, it's cold.' His army jacket was strapped to the front of his pack, but he made no attempt to put it on. 'So, what's the plan?'

'I don't have one.'

She hadn't thought beyond the moment of greeting him, only that she had to leave him at some point to be at the registry office no later than noon. Rocko could only be spared for a couple of hours in the middle of the day. Val had pleaded with Alice to get there as soon as she could.

The entrance to the hostel, which was a converted Victorian mansion on Spring Street, overflowed with boisterous soldiers checking in for their Brisbane furlough. Alice waited outside while Jack claimed a bunk in one of the dormitories and offloaded his pack. The nasty August wind kept her huddled against a wall and wishing for her fur coat.

Across the road, Albert Park was largely deserted. Ferocious gusts howled along the tree-lined walkways, flexing palm fronds and lobbing hard pods from the fig trees like hand grenades. The most sensible place to keep out of the wind was the air-raid shelter. Yet she was still surprised to see a couple, walking hand in hand up Wickham Terrace, turn left onto Spring Street and straight into the concrete bunker. He was a skinny, pimply GI and she was even younger than Alice; a mere schoolgirl, by her reckoning, who squealed as she tried to keep her skirt down and her blonde hair out of her face as it flapped loose from its pins.

Marilla would regard the girl's shameless delight and her high-spirited laugh as evidence of a defective moral character intent on leading men astray. Alice didn't doubt her mother's views on such things – Marilla's certainty in her own opinions were too foundational to Alice's sense of self – and though the girl was obviously fast, Alice found it hard to see anything vicious or conniving in her behaviour. Perhaps the girl was just naïve, but Alice, by her own admission, was far more so. She assumed what the girl was doing in the air-raid shelter was sinful, but had no idea of what it might be.

She didn't mention the girl and her GI to Jack when he came back out. Neither of them had yet brought up the topic of 'the Yanks', but his sense of grievance about them was palpable. He introduced her to his mate, Ken 'Kanga' Stewart.

'Pleased to meet you, Alice,' Kanga said. To Jack he added, 'She looks like a fair dinkum sort to me, mate.'

A look she didn't understand passed between them.

'She might be dumb as cattle, but at least she's not a floozy. Got enough sense to stay away from the Yanks. And if I find out she don't, I'll knock it into her.' Jack smiled at Alice, his tone light, meant for Kanga as good-natured brotherly teasing.

'The receptionist said there's a tearoom beneath City Hall run by the Red Cross. You want to head there? I'm starving. Alice can come too,' Kanga said.

Alice looked at her watch. It was just after eleven.

'You got somewhere else to be, Miss High and Mighty?' said Jack.

'Well, no. I can come for a little while. I'm just meant to be meeting a friend. For lunch, that's all, and I said I'd meet her at twelve. And I should go by Lennon's to check when I'm rostered on next week.' The first lie would have been enough, even if it made Jack angry.

'I haven't been here an hour and you've already got somewhere better to be.'

'It's not like that. We made plans last week before I knew you were coming ...'

'You should have bloody cancelled.' He didn't add 'you stupid moll', but she heard it anyway.

70

'Would your friend mind if we joined you? That'd be beaut, wouldn't it, Jacko? Lunch with a couple of pretty sheilas to kick off our first day of leave.'

Alice looked at the scuffmarks on her shoes, so sick to her stomach she could have cried. Ordinarily she'd have liked Kanga; he seemed nice. His blond hair was wispy on top, but he had high, ruddy cheeks and a ready smile, and there was kindness in his eyes. For Jack, he seemed an unlikely friend.

'That's got the makings of a solution to me. Kanga's a smart guy, isn't it he, Alice?'

'I suppose so.'

'So where are we going then? I could eat a draught horse.'

'The Lobster Pot.' Barely audible, it was the first place she thought of. It was on the way to the registry office, at least.

They went to Lennon's first so Alice could pretend to check her roster. Jack and Kanga waited in the vestibule; cross-armed sentries by the Grecian column near the telephone switch. The head porter, Alice couldn't fail to notice, looked wary. She avoided eye contact with him and hoped he had enough nous not to ask Jack to leave.

'I'll only be a minute,' she said, loud enough for the porter to hear, and affected a brisk walk across the foyer to a discreet passageway near the main dining hall. The roster was pinned to a corkboard outside the spring-loaded door that opened onto the kitchen. She had been given next Monday off, a pleasant surprise, but was on for the rest of the week.

Jack and Kanga had not moved when she returned, and the porter, thankfully, was engaged in loading a woman's suitcases onto a trolley. She was the kind of woman Alice sometimes waited on in the Americans' private dining hall. Her straw-coloured hair had been coloured and styled into an elaborate

71

updo in a salon. Her lips were as plump and red as tomatoes, her long, white mink coat so glossy it appeared to shimmer. She opened her satin purse with a matching gloved hand and gave the porter an American dollar bill. Alice – and Jack and Kanga, she sensed – watched her glide across the vestibule towards the Wintergarden lounge to be met by an American colonel, who kissed her proffered polished cheekbone before putting his arm around her shoulder.

The realisation winded her; the blow almost physical. Then, shame that seared through her like a grass fire. The looks on the street, the curious, sometimes sneering stares when she'd walked down Queen Street wearing her beautiful fur coat – she had never really understood. Jealousy, she'd weakly put it down to. But it was clear now: through Jack's and Kanga's eyes, she saw herself like they did that woman. She wanted to be sick.

'Let's go,' she said the moment they could hear her. Heading for the stairs, Alice didn't wait for an answer. She didn't look back to check if they'd followed.

Once on the footpath, however, she hesitated. The Lobster Pot formed part of the hotel frontage onto George Street. If she sent Jack and Kanga in to get a table, she could tell them she planned to meet her friend outside, then duck across the road and find Val. As plans go, it was terrible, but there was little option beside the truth, which was even less of an option now.

Alice pivoted to face them, but lost her courage when she saw Jack's expression. His arms were still locked at right angles. She'd always been most fearful of his silences. Kanga, in deference to Jack's mood it seemed, wasn't talking either. His eyes were cast down, hands thrust in his pockets as he rocked back and forth on his heels.

Alice had witnessed only one brawl, outside the Ascot Theatre at New Farm. A threesome of Aussie soldiers took on two

Yanks, both of whom had dates. She didn't hear what one of the Yanks said to the Aussies, but it was enough to get him rammed into a brick wall. The intent to harm, the anger and viciousness fuelling their punches and kicks, frightened her more than the violence itself. Jack would need little excuse; his mood, always a precursor to his worst rages, guaranteed he'd find a reason to hit someone.

Val called to her from across the road: a single, warbled, desperate *Alice!* There was no sign of Rocko. The wind rushed at her, skewing the fur coat and her hair sideways. She shielded her face with an arm. Without waiting for Alice to respond, she dashed onto the road.

Alice buried her face in her hands and gritted her teeth. She heard Kanga say, '*Fuck.*'

From Jack, it was a low muttered 'Je-sus-fuck-ing-Christ': every syllable hammered with contempt.

The horn flared long and hard, the driver of the Ford Anglia staying on it well after he swerved to avoid Val. He yelled from his window: 'Why don't you watch where you're bloody going, you stupid flamin' tart.' A few passers-by shook their heads with pointed expressions at Val, who came direct to Alice, her face showing no comprehension of the near miss she'd had.

'Are you all right? That was, that was … so close, Val.'

Val didn't speak straight away. Tears rimmed her lower eyelids. Alice could see the effort she was putting in not to cry.

'He couldn't make it.' Her voice was small, her eyes fixed on the buttons of her own navy coat.

Alice didn't know what to say.

'You okay, love? You had us all real scared there for a moment.'

Val glanced at Kanga and nodded. She expressed no curiosity as to who he was.

'How about we go inside and grab a table?' said Kanga. 'Get

you a glass of water. You'll be right as rain after that.' With a hand on her back, Kanga guided her through the double doors to The Lobster Pot.

Alice went to follow, but was stopped by the grip of Jack's hand on the back of her neck. His fingers and thumb dug in like a clamp.

'So, your friend's a Yankee tart who can be bought for the price of a cheap fur coat.'

When she didn't answer, he seized her chin and jerked it towards him. Her mouth was dry and she couldn't hold his sweltering gaze. He pushed her head away with his fingers flat to her cheek.

'Lying bitch.'

'Hey, mister, you can't a treat a lady like that.'

Within seconds, the GI was thrown against the wall with a fist trained to his head.

- 5 -

*Six servicemen were shot, one fatally, a civilian was wounded by
a bullet, and two other soldiers were injured when servicemen
rioted at the corner of Creek and Adelaide Street last night
… The shooting occurred when soldiers rushed military police
carrying riot guns while they were on duty outside a canteen.*

—*The Courier-Mail* (27 November 1942)

'*Mirrored Psyche*. Heidi Yardley is the artist,' Cheryl said in
response to an enquiry about her latest acquisition. The painting,
mounted above the TV, was of a woman kneeling in a clingy
white gown against a charcoal background, and in place of a
head she had an arrangement of pale-pink roses, lilac orchids
and purple snapdragons sprouting from the neck of her shirt.
Cheryl, who graduated the same year as Sam with a degree in
visual arts, had a knack for spotting talent whose work would
appreciate before they died.

Olivia initially found the flower-headed woman creepy when
Cheryl brought her home a month ago, but the painting had since
grown on her. Cheryl could make anything, including herself,
into an event. Tonight she was wearing a wrap dress in a large,
red-floral print on navy (Melbourne bought) that made no secret
of her bountiful body that rivalled an Ecuadorian mountain range
for curves. Assisted by chocolate-fountain hair and eyes, she

had that Nigella Lawson thing that regularly reduced men into whimpering saps. Olivia could turn heads – she was arguably, as an ex-boyfriend once cringingly described her, more 'exotic' and certainly more lithe – but Cheryl had powers Olivia could only grudgingly admire from the sidelines.

Along with Sam, Cheryl had arrived with two other friends, Zach and Caitlin, and another guy, Matt, whom Olivia hadn't met before.

'There could be some others coming as well,' Cheryl said breezily.

Sam was the last to enter the apartment. Olivia had waited for him to greet her among the general melee in the living room: a 'Hey, babe', a perfunctory kiss, but she may as well have been a piece of furniture to be stepped around. He walked past her to the kitchen to put a six-pack of XXXX Gold in the fridge. She felt the sting lodge in her throat like a burr and began moving extra chairs from the dining table to squeeze onto the balcony. Cheryl hustled everyone onto the small concrete terrace where they conducted impromptu gatherings.

'You guys hear about the body found by the river earlier at St Lucia? It was on Twitter,' said Zach, who'd taken one of the comfortable outdoor chairs.

'Oh yeah? There was a helicopter flying over about an hour or so ago,' said Olivia. 'I guess they found what they were looking for. Do they know what happened?'

'Only that it's "not suspicious",' Zach said, air quoting the police euphemism.

'That's really sad,' said Caitlin. Positioned between Cheryl and Zach, she sat hunch-shouldered, with her hands wedged beneath her thighs, as though apologising for occupying any space at all. There was a general murmured agreement.

'How was the opening? Decent crowd?' Olivia asked.

She stole a glance at Sam across the table, hoping he might acknowledge her presence with an answer, but he was busy rolling a cigarette from the tobacco pouch on his lap. Next to him was Matt, the stranger who was yet to say a word.

'Not bad for a Tuesday night,' said Cheryl, reaching for the bottle of red on the table. 'I think Ben even sold a couple of pieces.'

'He's just good at convincing idiots with money they're buying "real" art,' Sam chimed in without looking up.

'You're still working on that part, aren't you, Sammy?'

Only Zach, Sam's best friend since their disaffected school days on Brisbane's southside, could have got away with that swipe.

'Actually, Liv, you would have liked this one piece Ben did,' Cheryl ventured. 'What was it called again?' She waved her fingers round like a whirligig. 'Anyway, he painted this huge snakes and ladders game board as a backdrop and then collaged in different Brisbane landmarks – City Hall, Customs House, Lennon's, Cloudland and so on – in a kind of loose map of the city during the war.'

'*Coil and Toil*,' said Caitlin.

'That was it – thank you.'

'Double, double, toil and trouble,' said Olivia.

'The name is a reference to the river and everyone being industrious during the war,' Cheryl said with a note of annoyance. 'He did it for a Brisbane-themed exhibition he was part of last year.'

'Just call Ben the Ken Done of Brisbane,' said Sam, exhaling a mouthful of smoke over his shoulder and tossing the pouch to Zach.

Caitlin looked down at her knees, which were still firmly clamped together.

'You know it wasn't actually called "Cloudland" until after

the war. And it wasn't used as a dance hall, either. The US military used it to accommodate troops,' said Olivia.

Cheryl gave Olivia the look she deserved. 'Yes, I remember you pointed out the same historical inaccuracy in that play you took us to last year.'

'*Brisbane*,' Sam scoffed. 'It was called fucking *Brisbane*, for fuck's sake. Talk about wearing your provincialism on your maroon sleeve. Would the STC put on a play called *Sydney*?'

'What was it about?' asked Caitlin.

'It was about Brisbane during World War II. Written by a local playwright.'

Olivia had enjoyed it. To Sam, she said, 'What do you think David Williamson's *Emerald City* was about? Sydney. It was a metaphor for Sydney and it premiered at the STC.'

'Never heard of it,' said Sam.

'All right, you two,' interjected Cheryl. 'Anyway, Liv, I think you would have appreciated the piece. More than some, at least. What did you call it, Sam?'

'*Piss and Weak*.'

'Did it sell?' asked Olivia.

'I don't think so. It's a bold piece, colour- and theme-wise, so its appeal is limited. I'd like to see the State Gallery purchase it.'

Sam emitted a braying noise. It wasn't unusual for him to be combative, but his tone tonight had an edge beyond campy bickering. The paper tiger was filing his teeth. It had taken almost three years of missing cues and misreading signs, and she still didn't always see how she'd set things in motion, but she'd done something to upset him. Surely not Tobias? Olivia couldn't see how Sam would know.

She got up to refill her glass inside. The conversation was heading into well-traversed territory: Brisbane's apathy towards the arts (which Olivia didn't entirely agree with), the dire state of arts funding (for which Cheryl would somehow be held personally responsible), and who deserved what meagre handouts there were, and who didn't (a subject Sam was particularly fond of). The importance of art itself, the reasons for creating art in the first place, were never tabled.

Olivia didn't have it in her tonight. As she stepped inside, what began as the burn of held-back tears behind her eyes spread through her like heated oil, slick with humiliation. She snatched up her phone, which also contained a credit card, and left. It was unlikely anyone noticed; she didn't huff on the way out or slam the door. She could have been collecting the mail. Out on the street, even well clear of the apartment block and its boxy yellow eyes, she held on to the warm, liquid emotion slopping about inside her.

She looked at her phone and thought, *Fuck it*. She rang Tobias, her heart somewhere up around her larynx. After the night of their ignominious frog-march from the South Bank pool, they'd met up once for coffee in the city. At her suggestion, they'd also gone to the MacArthur Museum on Edward Street. Tobias got a kick out of imagining what his grandfather would say about him strutting around MacArthur's faithfully maintained office in which the General had commanded the entire Pacific Theatre of war. Olivia even took a sneaky picture for him – 'Instagram fodder' – posing behind MacArthur's desk with his sunglasses on, pretending to smoke a pen from her bag.

It was Olivia who'd backed out of any further rendezvous, knowing her conscience wasn't quite up to it.

Tobias picked up as she was about to disconnect the call.

'Well, hello there.'

The Lychee Lounge in West End was only a ten-minute walk away and the bar was a local favourite for those whose income bracket accommodated their cocktail prices. As per Tobias's instructions, Olivia found them in the cosy Opium Lounge, tucked away at the back. The alcove, with its four-sided, red velvet-upholstered lounge and plump cushions, was a well-heeled bohemian's delight and usually impossible to snag on a weekend.

'Glad you could join us,' Tobias said. 'You remember Clio?'

'Of course. How are you?'

'Totally shithouse, actually, but it's lovely to see you again.' She wasn't slurring, but her voice and gestures were loose, easy. Charming. She got up and greeted Olivia with an air kiss and an embrace over the cluster of hexagonal drink tables in the middle. The half-drunk glass of white wine in front of her was still frosted with condensation.

'Clio's girlfriend,' Tobias explained, 'decided she's not moving to Brisbane after all.'

'I'm so sorry. That's really shitty. I should leave you two alone.'

Clio threw out a hand as if to shoo away a fly. 'Don't be silly. Sit down, join us,' she said. 'It's not like I didn't know it was coming. She doesn't want to uproot her life in LA. Can't really blame her, though I am.' She slumped sideways across one of the seats before adding, 'I just wish she'd told me before I left. Instead she waited like – what? – six months or something?'

'Long distance doesn't work, babe. You know that,' said Tobias.

Clio crimped her mouth in resigned agreement. 'Anyway,' she said, 'let's talk about something else. Poor Tobias has been listening to me moan about it all night.'

'It's my round. You want another?'

'Fuck it, why not. One more can't hurt.'

'Olivia?'

'A red? Any kind.'

'Sorry,' said Clio after he was gone. 'I'm sure you weren't expecting this. I don't know what I'd do if Tobias wasn't here. He speaks highly of you, you know.'

'Oh. Well, he's ... I think he's great, too. I mean, I don't know him as well as you do, obviously.'

'Well, he likes you. That's all I'm going to say.' Clio flicked her eyes in his direction as he swaggered towards the bar. 'He said you were doing a PhD on Gloria Graham. That's so impressive.'

'It's not. Believe me. I'm questioning why I even started it.'

'But that's normal, isn't it? Not that I'd know, but a few people have told me it's normal to feel that way about doing a PhD.'

'Maybe.'

'Speaking of Gloria Graham, did you know it was my idea to put on *Apron Strings*?'

'No, I didn't. Andrew, your director, just said ... Well, he kind of took credit for it without really saying so, if that makes sense.' Had she assumed it was Andrew's idea because he was the director? The conversation was a bit of a blur, blame it on the opening-night champagne, but she would have recalled if he'd given Clio credit for the idea. Surely.

'So where did you get the idea to do the play?' she asked. 'No one seems to have any idea who Gloria Graham is these days.'

'Gloria Graham was a friend of my grandmother's sister, actually. They even lived together for a while. She died of lung cancer or, maybe, breast cancer? – you probably know – and June, my great-aunt, nursed her in her final years, or so I've been told.' Clio picked up her glass and drained what was left in one mouthful. 'I never met her, though. She died like maybe a decade before I was born. But that's how I knew of her.'

'Right. That's ... *Wow.*'

Olivia had come across a mention of a June Atkinson as

Graham's 'companion' in her later years in a volume on (a lot of obscure) Australian literary figures, but the short biography had not given any more information than that.

'But, to answer your question, I was going to this Australians in Film event in LA and I had about half an hour to kill, so I went into the Samuel French shop and, bam, just like that, found a copy of *Tie My Apron Strings, Would You?*. I was just like No Fucking Way. This is like' – she shrugged – 'meant to be.'

'And the rest is history,' Olivia added.

'Exactly.' Clio readjusted herself so she could stretch her legs out on the seat.

Olivia had a scramble of questions in her head. She stared at Clio with a desire to – what? Crawl over and take a hold of her smooth, freckled, indolent shoulders? Shake answers out of her? Clio looked back and offered a docile, resigned smile.

'So what else do you know about Gloria Graham? Like anything. At all.'

'Nothing you wouldn't already know, I'm sure.'

'But I mean what did your great-aunt June used to say about her?'

'I wish I could tell you but, honestly, I was a kid. I don't remember anything that specific—'

'Here we go, ladies.' Tobias distributed the two wines and the beer he'd safely cradled back from the bar to the lounge.

'Gracias,' Clio said to him as she reached for the white. To Olivia, she said in the tone of an afterthought, 'I have some old letters somewhere. Most of my shit's been in storage for the last ten years, so I couldn't really tell you what's there, but I'm pretty certain I still have the box I'm thinking of.'

'Are you serious? That would be … Oh my god.'

'Don't get too excited. Might not be anything there that's interesting to you.'

Olivia's instincts as a researcher told her she should heed Clio's advice. At best, her experienced self scolded, whatever Clio had would be the equivalent of half-a-dozen pieces of a thousand-word jigsaw. Yet the prospect of being the first to examine what could be primary documents pertaining, even loosely, to Gloria Graham, made her feel like Howard Carter must have when he first peered into Tutankhamun's tomb.

Olivia's phone was vibrating, and she excused herself to go outside. It was Cheryl and she should have answered. Instead she let it ring out, then composed a text message.

Sorry to walk out like that. I'm okay. Couldn't deal with Sam any longer. Talk soon x.

As long as ur ok. Don't know what Sam's problem is. He's been a fair douche canoe all night x

Back inside, Clio and Tobias had moved on to discussing Shakespeare.

'I'm trying to talk Tobias into playing Othello,' said Clio. 'Andrew and I want to do it for our next Retrorep TC production. What do you think? Wouldn't he make a great Othello?'

'Don't ask her that. She's never seen me act.' He turned to Olivia. 'I'm trying to tell Clio that I probably won't be around that long. My contract, and my visa, expire at the end of October.'

'We'll see,' said Clio with a conspiratorial look aimed at Olivia. 'Anyway, Tobias here has had enough of me for one evening. Says he needs his beauty sleep, so I wondered if you want to come back to my apartment and I'll try and find that box for you?'

After finishing their drinks, they went outside to wait for the Uber Clio had ordered. While Clio hung off the Boundary

Street kerb checking number plates, Tobias put his arm around Olivia's shoulder.

'You okay? I'm sorry we didn't get to talk.'

'No, that's okay. It was good to see you and meeting Clio here was quite serendipitous, as it turns out.'

'Good. I'm glad you two got on. I'll call you tomorrow, hey. If you're … you know … don't have a problem with that.'

'No. As in, yes, that'd be … nice.'

She caught the scent of sandalwood on his skin as he leaned in to kiss her goodbye on the cheek. She could breathe that in all night, given the chance.

'You coming?' Clio was standing behind the open door of their Uber. 'Hop in.'

While Olivia climbed inside, Clio threw her arms around Tobias and said goodbye. Pulling the seatbelt across, Olivia felt her phone vibrate on her lap. She buckled herself in and flipped it over. Sam. She let it go to message bank.

- 6 -

If they are still in effect, you might get annoyed at the 'blue laws' which make Australian cities pretty dull places on Sundays. For all their breeziness, the Australians don't go in for a lot of drinking or woo-pitching in public ... So maybe the bars, the movies, and the dance halls won't be open on Sundays, but there are a lot of places in America where that's true too. There's no use beefing about it – it's their country.

—Instructions for American Servicemen in Australia, 1942

September 1942

Business at the Queensland Book Depot was booming. QBD was, after all, Brisbane's premier supplier of books, stationery, fountain pens and Bibles: the best remedies for bored and homesick American servicemen. That many of the store's new titles had been available for some months in the United States was not, in June Atkinson's opinion, good for the store's, or Australia's, reputation. But she viewed it as an opportunity to introduce the visitors to Australian literature and perhaps educate them about their host country. She was judicious about her targets, though: you'd be hard pressed to interest a GI who'd barely started shaving in Xavier Herbert's *Capricornia*. Or the works of Christina Stead, to which June was particularly partial. But an officer, say, acquainted with Hawthorn, Whitman and

Poe, who wanted to expand his world via books, was likely to be receptive to her thoughtful suggestions.

'Mrs Atkinson, I need to step out for a half hour or so. Do you think you can manage on your own?'

'I'm sure I can hold down the fort just fine, Mr Maclean.'

Mr Maclean had been reluctant to give June a job when two of his sales clerks joined up a month out from Christmas the year before. He made it clear he didn't approve of married women working when he hired her, but it seemed to June he didn't have much choice. Paying her two-thirds of a man's wage no doubt softened the blow.

For June's part, she was glad to have work that occupied her time and made some use of her mind since Peter had been shipped off with the Eighth Division to Malaya. They were crying out for women to fill jobs left by men in canning and textile industries, not to mention munitions, which at least paid well, but she couldn't see herself working in a factory. The Department was even offering temporary teaching to married women, but she'd be damned if she'd help them out with their labour crisis after they forced her to quit the job she loved when she married Peter.

There was more resistance handing women positions left vacant by thinking men. Not that a bookstore clerk was taxing in that regard, but Mr Maclean was more Victorian than most when it came to what women could do. So far, she'd found the job satisfactory, even fulfilling at times, and the moment it wasn't she could go and work for the Americans. When it came down to it, though, she'd much rather sell books than type requisitions all day. That was a job for bright young things.

The lunch rush had subsided and, as there were only a few customers browsing the aisles, June took the opportunity to tidy the shelves. It was a temperate, glossy-looking afternoon:

the first preview of spring. Men rolled up their shirtsleeves and people lingered outdoors, dawdling back to work after eating their sandwiches on park benches in the sun. June was stirred by the mood of her university years: the easy warmth of a spring afternoon spent lying with friends on a thick green lawn scattered with frangipani petals in the Botanic Gardens while they pretended to study or read poetry. They'd been reciting Tennyson's 'The Lady of Shalott' – and inserting obscene verses of their own devising – when Peter, then a stuttering history major in her English literature class, shyly asked if he could join their group.

The tinkle of the doorbell drew her back to the present. An American serviceman – a sergeant of some description, if she had her insignia right – headed to the military history section where she was putting Napoleon and Nelson back in their places.

'May I help you?'

'Yes. I'm after some Australian poetry. Have you any recommendations?'

'Yes, of course. The poetry volumes are this way.' June spoke over her shoulder as she walked down the aisle. 'Were you wanting something contemporary, or perhaps something more classic? The works of Henry Lawson and Banjo Paterson are very popular.'

'Contemporary, thanks. I'm familiar with the bush poets already.'

She was taken aback he'd even heard of Lawson and Paterson. She wanted to ask what he thought about their work, but his manner, in stark contrast to most of his compatriots, did not invite friendly chitchat. Only his uniform and his accent – decidedly northern; Boston? New York? – marked him as a Yank. He had neither smiled to show off a gleaming set of teeth nor called her 'honey', an oversight she was tempted to tease him about but feared getting a cold, unimpressed stare for her trouble.

'So, this shelf here is all Australian poets. My picks would be Kenneth Slessor and Dorothea MacKellar, and perhaps, Mary Gilmore. But I'll leave you to look for yourself and, well, take your time browsing.'

'Thank you.' He gave her a curt nod and took a volume off the shelf before she'd even walked away.

Mrs Stevenson was waiting at the cash register. Mr Maclean would have chided June for not attending to the lady the second she trundled through the door. Frankly, June found his obsequiousness to wealth embarrassing. She refused to be any more pleasant to the woman than she was with every other customer.

'Are you enjoying your day, Mrs Stevenson? The weather looks lovely out.'

'Quite so. Would you mind showing me your best fountain pens?'

June unlocked the cabinet behind her and brought out their three most expensive Sheaffer pens and the Montblanc. Mrs Stevenson wouldn't bother with the cheaper Parkers. June responded to her questions about their design and the merits of vacuum versus lever-filled.

'I'd probably go for the Eversharp Skyline, myself. Would you like to see one? We've only just got them in.'

June was sure Mr Maclean had acquired them through the black market. They were popular with a certain kind of American – high-ranking officers, usually – and they'd sold out of their original stock in a matter of weeks. She went to retrieve one from the office, aware of the Yank in the poetry section. She glanced in his direction on her return. He was reading, his expression a study of concentration one might expect of a field surgeon.

'We've supplied a number of these to General MacArthur's office.'

'Well, if they're good enough for the General ... I'll take two, thanks. And my usual letter paper, please.'

June pulled out a compendium of Mrs Stevenson's preferred Clairefontaine notepaper and envelopes and rang up her purchases. Right on cue, Mrs Stevenson told June how her son John, a flying officer with the RAAF in London, as if June needed reminding, appreciated receiving letters from home on quality paper. Nice for some, June always wished she could reply. She'd never once known Mrs Stevenson to purchase a book when she came in.

She bade the woman a nice day and remained behind the counter to regard the American at an unobtrusive distance. He was serious to the point of arrogance, she decided. He would have made a better Russian with his brooding countenance and straight black hair, a lock of which hung over his brow like a parenthesis.

He eventually came over with a copy of Slessor's *Five Bells: XX Poems.*

'Did you know he's a war correspondent?' he said, placing the slim volume beside the register.

'I can't say I did, no.'

'I've read some of his reportage. He's very good. Could I get one of those Eversharps you sold before?'

'Yes, of course. Just a minute.' She retrieved another one from the office and placed it on the counter. 'Do you need ink?'

'No, thanks. You'd think the US Armed Forces would keep MacArthur well supplied with all his stationery needs. Pens have a tendency to go missing, though, don't they?'

He looked her straight in the eye. She couldn't tell if what she saw on his face was a twitch of a smile or not. He wished her a perfunctory good day as June handed over his items in a paper bag. He was the first American she'd encountered for whom civility appeared to be a chore. Though maybe she'd just become accustomed to unsolicited compliments by book-buying Americans. Not that she took their flattery seriously – she was a married thirty-two-year-old former schoolteacher, after all – but words, oft repeated, like 'honey' and 'gorgeous' didn't bounce off her like rubber either. She'd never bought into the notion that a woman's worth was tied to her youth and attractiveness, and had spent much of her life trying to prove otherwise, but she had learned to accept a compliment about her looks, many sizable grains of salt notwithstanding. And she didn't mind it, not one pinch.

It could have been the expectancy imbued in the spring evening, but June had no heart to return to her empty flat after she locked up the bookshop. Adelaide Street swarmed with workers leaving the city and those staying behind for the six o'clock swill. She thought about seeing a picture at the Regent – a few customers had recommended *The Maltese Falcon* – but decided to try to catch Rhia at the university, see if she wanted to get a drink or dinner.

A brisk detour via Albert Street and down Queen had her boarding the one-man 47 outside MacArthur's headquarters in under five minutes. She slid onto a spare bench seat, only to be wedged between two beefy Yanks; in her green and white floral dress, she felt like a slice of cucumber in a sandwich as they shuttled down Edward Street towards the gardens. One of them, if she were ten years younger, would have no doubt asked her already if she'd like to go for an ice cream somewhere. There were some advantages to not being the freshest bloom in the bunch.

Despite the overstuffed trams, June liked the bustle of wartime Brisbane. Even the sporadic brawling between Yanks and diggers didn't put her off. It was the endless complaining about the inconvenience of it all she found tiresome. The energy of the place was fetching; there was a hum to the city that had never existed before. It's what she'd loved about Sydney when they'd gone for their honeymoon just after war broke out. Peter had insisted on visiting and commentating on every historical site the city had to offer, and at the time she'd joked how she was glad they hadn't gone to London after all as their honeymoon would have been one long, continuous lecture.

She hadn't received a single letter from him since Singapore fell. The impersonal listing as 'missing' in the paper – *Cpl. Atkinson, P. J (Inf.) New Farm* – had left her feeling as brittle and discarded as a stub of chalk. Despite this silence, she wouldn't be drawn into filling the void with her imagination. It did no good to think of the worst that could happen to the man she considered the other half of herself. In private moments, when she thought of him despite herself, a vice would take hold of her throat and clench so hard she could barely draw breath. The only remedy was to keep occupied.

June alighted with the sandwiching Yanks as the tram clanged to a stop at the bottom of Alice Street. Her watch, always a few minutes slow by the end of the day, showed it was nearing five-thirty. Cutting through the gardens to the university was the best option if she was to catch Rhia.

Out of breath as she reached the gates at the southern end of the gardens, June chided herself for thinking Rhia would still be there. But when the sandstone building came into view, she couldn't miss her dark-haired friend. She was standing on the impossibly green lawn, head cocked, rummaging through her handbag, an unlit cigarette poised between her lips. June called out to her as though she might vanish.

'Well, fancy be. Look what the cat dragged in.' Cigarette removed, Rhia held out her arms and gathered June into a long hug. 'What are you doing here?'

'I came to see you. Are you busy? Of course you're busy. I should have telephoned, but it was a spur of the moment thing. I just couldn't face it tonight. The flat, I mean.'

'Oh, June. I'm never too busy to see you. Are you hungry? I know it's early, but I'm starving. But let's get a drink at the Bellevue first. We should hurry, though.'

Lennon's may have been the fashionable place to be seen with its sleek modern design, but June infinitely preferred the three-storeyed Bellevue with the intricate lacework of cast-iron balustrades that ran the gamut of its long balconies. The corrugated awning would soon be littered with velvety lilac bells when the jacarandas came into bloom. One advantage of being banished to the ladies' lounge, Rhia observed, was at least they stood a chance of being served before the taps were shut off at six.

'I'm getting a G&T. You want the same?' Rhia offered.

'Perfect. Mind if I freshen up first?'

Rhia had claimed the olive velvet chesterfield by the window when June returned. There were four drinks on the low table in front of her.

'Putting your smarts to good use, I see.' She took one of the sweating glasses and joined Rhia on the settee. Before she'd even taken a sip of her drink, June felt her tension crumble away. All thanks to Rhia, her dearest friend, who would call a spade a bloody shovel if need be.

'Heard anything about Peter? Or shouldn't I ask?'

'Nothing. The newspaper said next of kin would be furnished with a telegram as soon as there was any more information, but I'm still waiting for mine.'

'I'm sorry, darling. That must be awful.' Rhia gently squeezed June's arm. 'Look, I'm going to a party tonight. A gathering, really – writers and bookish types. Why don't you come along? It'll be a hoot.'

'I don't know. I haven't mixed with that crowd in years.'

'All the more reason to come. It's at the Christesens' house in Dutton Park – do you know Clem and Nina?'

June shook her head.

'Well, that doesn't matter. They won't mind if I bring a friend. Clem started a new literary journal called *Meanjin Papers*. Just what this cultural wasteland needs, if you ask me.'

The gin had gone to June's head in a pleasant way and Rhia's company was a tonic in itself. June asked how her parents were going. She liked Gordon Graham; his reputation as a fierce union leader belied a gregarious, generous man with a mischievous sense of humour. He was the only man she knew who believed women working in war industries should receive the same wage as a man, an opinion that put him at odds with his fellow unionists.

'Dad's well. Plenty to keep him busy as you could imagine. His latest fight is with the munitions industry. Mum's completely occupied with volunteer work. The comforts fund, of course, but her latest thing is camouflage nets. She's officially joined – and I think this is right – the Queensland Voluntary Net Camouflage Makers' Association. They're aiming for ten thousand nets by October, barring any more twine shortages. She's been working on me to join. I think I'd end up wanting to string myself up.'

'Your mother makes me feel terribly guilty.'

June knew she should do some sort of volunteer work. She'd tried knitting socks when that trend started, but she detested knitting and hadn't finished a whole pair. Even her sister served meals and mended buttons at the American Red Cross canteen in her spare time.

'You and me both. I'm thinking of offering my services as a volunteer driver for the Yanks. The problem is fitting it around a full-time job. I also need time to write.'

June asked her how the university job was going. Rhia said it was fine. She'd recently moved to the Examinations Section, which was repetitive and dull, but there were stretches when there was little to do and she could get on with her own writing then.

'What are you writing at the moment?'

'Oh, a few poems. Always dabbling in those, as you know. And a couple of short stories. Clem's asked me to submit something for his next edition.'

'What are they about?'

'Women and, well, freedom, I guess. Don't you think things have changed since the Yanks arrived? I mean, it's not just the Yanks, of course – although they've certainly been helpful in their own way.' Rhia sighed and turned her head to look out the taped-up window. 'Sexual liberation is one thing, but it's more about how women are now able to earn a living in ways they never could before. It's quite a remarkable time we're living in.' She stopped to light another cigarette. When she was done, she sat back against the sofa and laid her arm out along the back ridge, idly fingering the velvet upholstery. 'I want to capture that, the excitement of being a woman on the cusp of … Well, something big, I hope. Anyway, it's just a jumble of thoughts at the moment. Tell me what's going on with you. How's that sister of yours? She still working for the Americans at Somerville House?'

'Yes, but they sent her to work in the postal section as her typing wasn't much good. Did I tell you she's got a Yankee boyfriend? A serious one, at least to her way of thinking – Frank from Kansas. He's with the 81st out at Eagle Farm. Aircraft mechanic.'

'No, you definitely did not mention that. How serious? And why *be* serious when there's so many to choose from and more fun to be had by being unserious?'

'Mum and Dad would agree with you there. Mum's worried she's going to go and marry him because Edith is susceptible, in her opinion, to anything that's "all the rage".' June exchanged her empty glass for the second drink. 'She's wishing now she'd done what their neighbour Mrs Barrett down the road did. She took her five daughters to live in Warwick back in April to get them out of Yanks' way.'

'It's like Mrs Bennett, but in reverse.'

'More a ploy to prevent a case of the Mr Wickhams times five.'

'But *Kansas*? Does Edith know what she's getting herself in for? She'll be wishing for a pair of ruby slippers to get out of there. That's the problem with the young – they only think in terms of love and romance and happily-ever-afters. At our age, you realise love doesn't have to be a fairytale. It can even be a sweet, temporary interlude. On which note, I've been thinking of taking a Yank as a lover myself.'

'You've met someone?'

'Not yet.' Rhia winked before draining the rest of her second gin.

'You're as incorrigible as ever.'

'I am, aren't I? I'm also starving. Shall we go grab a bite at some grotty tearoom? I know just the place on Albert Street. There's even a brothel across the road for entertainment. You should see the queue. We can take bets on the turnover time.'

~

The woman who answered the door greeted Rhia with an extended embrace. She kissed June on the cheek and introduced herself as Nina. She had a soft, broad face with a high forehead and a dimpled chin. Her light-brown hair was parted in the middle and smoothed into a bun above the nape of her neck. It was not a fashionable hairdo, but she exuded an elegance that seemed at odds with the modest weatherboard house. On the way over, Rhia mentioned Nina's parents had emigrated from Russia when she was thirteen. June felt a certain kinship with the woman knowing she'd been a senior mistress at St Aidan's Girls School.

Bookshelves, stacked almost to the roof, lined the entry hall, but the living room was decoratively sparse. A framed photograph of Anna Pavlova hung on one wall. June was surprised to discover a number of Americans among those mingling in the room. It was soon apparent they were all poets or writers who'd been drafted into the armed forces and, yearning for some kind of literary hub while in a far-flung land, had found their way to the Christesens. Harry, whom Nina introduced as a self-taught poet from Baltimore, offered to get Rhia and June a drink, and returned with two glasses of whiskey.

Rhia fell easily into conversation with the good-looking soldier-poet and the two were soon having a spirited discussion about Modernism and Rhia's chief bugbear: the conservatism of Brisbane's artistic sensibilities (when it had any) and its populace in general. June, although not uninterested, had little to contribute, and claiming her feet were sore from standing all day soon gravitated to a vacant spot on the sofa.

Sitting down, she realised how tired she was. She imagined closing her eyes and the soft relief that would steal over her if she dared. The living area took on the quality of a drawing room play: pleasantly aware of the chatter and laughter in a subdued way, it was as though an invisible wall set her apart from the action. Rhia's throaty laughter chased by her usual three-tiered cough, struck like a school bell at varying intervals, keeping her tethered to the present.

'Time that is moved by little fidget wheels / Is not my time.'

June refocused her eyes, conscious now that she'd drifted off for a moment or two. She recognised the man, but looked at him as though he'd spoken to her in Japanese.

'"Five Bells" – from the book of Mr Slessor's poems you sold me this afternoon. You looked as though you were somewhere else. That midpoint between time and place where only memory exists.' He crouched in front of her and waited, it seemed, for her to confirm his hypothesis.

He was right, of course, but she had been unaware of it until he pointed it out. Peter had been right there in the room with her. They were laughing at something their cat Eliot did as a kitten, but she couldn't remember what.

'Sorry, I must have dozed off.'

'I shouldn't have woken you, then. My apologies.'

'No, I'm glad you did. I might have started snoring or drooling and then what would you think of me?'

His lips curved slightly on one side. She glanced at her lap; there was no reason for him to think anything of her at all.

'I think you'd rather be at home in bed than at this gathering of Brisbane's literati, plus or minus a few Yankee strays.'

Put like that, she had to agree. The sudden onset of tiredness was so heavy it smothered everything like a wet blanket. Harry's whiskey was partly to blame.

'I'll borrow the jeep and drive you home. Where do you live?' he asked.

'New Farm, but there's no need for you to do that. There's a tram that runs that way from here.'

'Don't be ridiculous. I'll grab the keys from Harry. I don't think he's ready to go anywhere yet. He and your friend went out to smoke on the back porch.'

June should have refused, but the offer of a free ride home blew any haze of doubt that lingered over what Rhia often called 'the dying embers of propriety'. She rose to go and say goodbye to Rhia, dimly registering that he – for she didn't even know his name – must have been cognisant of her presence for some time.

The engine ground to life. Like a starlet's eyelids, the hooded brownout covers cast the gaze of the headlights down so they could see only a few feet ahead. The jeep pulled away from the kerb more smoothly than June expected.

'I haven't told you my name,' he said when they reached the end of the street.

'And I haven't told you mine.'

'You're June. Your friend told me.'

'And you are?'

'Karl. Karl Salzberg.'

'Nice to meet you, Karl. And thank you again for the ride home. I appreciate it. I can now say I've ridden in a US army jeep.'

'You may not think much of jeep travel by the time we arrive. Here …' He reached around behind the seat to grab something. 'Put my blouse on. It's going to get cold.'

She thanked him and wrestled her arms into what she figured out was his army jacket, suppressing the bubble of amusement in her throat at the word *blouse*. The sleeves hung like wide-mouth eels over the ends of her hands, but she was soon grateful for the protection it offered when the air whipped through the doorless seating cavern and walloped the canvas roof. Loosened from its chignon, June's hair flayed the side of her face; she put up a sheathed hand to keep the ends from flicking into her eyes.

'It can be quite invigorating on a warm day, if you wear sunglasses and a headscarf.'

'I'm sure it is.' She wanted to add: Like Isadora Duncan? Her appraisal of him in the bookshop as arrogant no longer seemed right, but there was still something about his manner that made him less than easy to be with. It wasn't rudeness – she could hardly accuse him of that since he'd offered to drive her home – but there was no telling what he was going to say next. Perhaps it was just because he didn't follow predictable patterns of pleasantry. She tried to read his expression, but it was too dark to see anything other than his murky silhouette.

The motor was excessively loud, but June didn't think that was the only reason he was quiet. The forceful dose of fresh air had revived her enough to want to talk and there were things she was curious to know. Where was he from? What did he write? She assumed he was a writer of some kind. But she had lost her nerve in the bluster. He was also focused on the road and the hazard of being able to see so little ahead.

She reached for her purse as they approached the tollbooth at Kangaroo Point. He brushed her hand away as she tried to give him sixpence and said something she didn't catch. Then he turned his head in her direction and raised his voice.

'I believe this bridge opened in 1940. Is there a story behind that?'

His tone indicated he knew very well he'd employed a silly pun. She also thought she detected a touch of smugness, or perhaps just disbelief, that the city had built a bridge over a major river crossing only two years ago: another glaring example of Brisbane's provincialism.

'It's named after John Story, a public servant who advocated for the bridge's construction. As far as stories go, I think that's about as interesting as it gets.' She didn't add she'd been at the opening of the bridge with her husband. Peter, with his belief that history is merely a series of collective moments, had wanted to be there to witness that one. June wished Karl could see it as it used to look at night: the flipped reflection of the lit-up city rippling across the canvas of the river.

She thought she saw him nod. They didn't talk again until they approached the New Farm end of Brunswick Street. Peter had never thought much of her navigation skills and she did not want to give this stranger the same impression. It mattered somehow that he should think her competent.

'My street will be coming up on the right ... This one. My flat is on the corner over there.' She pointed to a laneway on the opposite side of the road. 'You can just let me out here, though.'

Karl veered slightly to the left to do a U-turn instead. As they swung around, the front left corner of the jeep clipped the front wheel of a bicycle. Karl jerked on the brakes as rider and bike fell with a sickening clatter to the ground. A uniformed man scrambled out from beneath the bicycle and kicked it towards the jeep. Once on his feet, he fled down the road.

Karl leaped out of the jeep and gave the man chase for a dozen or so strides, but the GI had enough of a start to get away. Karl stood with his hands on his hips for a few moments before he turned and stalked back towards the stricken bicycle. He came around the front to where June was still seated.

'Are you all right?' He leaned in and touched her shoulder. 'Sorry about that. He appeared out of nowhere.'

'It wasn't your fault. I'm okay. Just a little shaken. At least he wasn't injured, I suppose.' Her heart rate had subsided, but the initial tremor of fright still echoed inside her.

'No. He probably deserved to be, running off like that ... I better find out who this belongs to. You don't know who owns one around here, do you?'

'My neighbour in the flat above me does. If it's a Malvern Star, it's probably his. He often leaves it inside the fence round by the side of the building.'

June waited on the path with the bike while Karl parked

outside her flat. She was surprised the commotion had not brought anyone out of the flats or a neighbouring house. Karl took the bike and wheeled it behind her through the wooden gate, the bell rattling in injured protest. She was about to instruct him where to put it when she heard a hoarse 'thank you' from beneath the tangle of bougainvillea that had overtaken the fence. A young woman was slouched against the brick fence pillar, her knees tucked to her chest.

June knelt down and placed her fingers on the girl's elbow.

'Did he hurt you?'

The girl did something with her head that was neither a nod nor a shake. Her face trembled as she looked at June before she dropped her head to her knees.

'Shit,' said Karl. 'I let the mongrel get away.'

~

June drew the curtains back from the window that faced the laneway. The morning sun had moved on, taking with it the heat that had blazed directly into the living room, which was still stuffy. She opened the window right up to try and catch the breeze tickling the vine leaves on the latticework fence outside. She then plumped the sofa cushions again, shooing Eliot away so she could brush his fur from the seat cover. There was no reason the place should be spotless. Karl had already been inside the flat the night of 'the incident'. He was only coming by to return Mr Bellincioni's repaired bicycle; there was no need for him to see her.

She couldn't claim she was tidying for Gladys's sake, either; her mother-in-law had written to say she'd decided to stay in Toowoomba at her sister's farm for at least a couple more weeks as there was, in her words, 'more use for her there'. June could imagine Gladys hoisting up her sleeves and marching out to the milking shed to learn the art of squeezing a cow's udder. When Peter had proposed his mother move in after he enlisted, June could see it was a reasonable suggestion; it was a better option than getting a boarder and, for the most part, she enjoyed Gladys's company. She could certainly be counted on to share a sherry of an evening. But June also liked having the place to herself when she needed solitude.

She had considered the girl's story often during the intervening week. June had no problem believing Valerie had been grabbed from behind and dragged into the yard. The overgrowth of crotons, trees and bougainvillea was probably why the attacker chose her garden. But he must have checked no one was in her flat first, for surely she would have heard any movement had she been home. Of what he did to her once he'd pulled her behind the fence, Valerie wouldn't say. She'd answered most of their questions with a nod, a shake, or both. He'd stuffed her mouth with what sounded like a tie – that was about as much as they'd been able to extract from her.

She was the colour of watery milk when they had brought her inside, her eyes dull and flat. June was shocked by how cold and damp she felt. They put her on the sofa and wrapped her in a blanket. Eliot had curled up beside her, which she seemed to draw some comfort from, even stroking him under the chin. Some colour returned to her face after June gave her tea laced with the last of her fortnight's sugar ration.

June had thought her pretty in that way most young women are when the awkward vestiges of adolescence have left their face, but their cheeks still retain some plumpness, and their eyes aren't dimmed with too much knowing. Her brown eyes were round and smallish, but her dark hair and brows set them off to some effect – one, June imagined, many a GI would be taken by. Her red linen dress, a smartly cut number with a shirt collar and buttons to the waist, finished with black piping on the sleeves and pockets, suited her complexion. She was a tiny little thing.

As to the bicycle, it must have been right by the gate, as the soldier had leaped on it as soon as he heard the jeep turning into the street. But June had never known Mr Bellincioni to leave it there, something he confirmed himself when he returned from an overnight trip the next day. For what appeared to be an opportunistic attack by a deviant GI, June found certain details difficult to reconcile.

June heard the jeep pull up out front and went over to the window. She couldn't see very well through the latticework fence, but she could discern Karl removing the bicycle from where it had been affixed to the back of the vehicle. He wheeled it in through the front gate and headed down the side of the building where Mr Bellincioni usually left it propped against the fence facing onto the main road. She stepped back, hoping he hadn't spotted her. She expected him to take the stairs to Mr Bellincioni's apartment, but instead he returned to the jeep to look for something. His khaki figure then passed behind the latticework as he returned via the front gate.

By the time he rang her doorbell, she'd worked herself into an inexplicable panic. When she opened the door, Eliot shot out like his tail had caught fire, and Karl scuffled sideways in a bad imitation of Fred Astaire to dodge the grey tabby.

'I was hoping for a friendlier reception. Here, I brought you these. I believe that's what my countrymen do when they visit the home of a lady here.' He handed over a large box of chocolates and two pairs of nylons. 'I take it you can use those. Us doughboys supplying nylons to Australia's womenfolk has become quite the tradition, I've gathered.'

'I've heard that, too, but these are the first I've received.' She wondered if she should accept them. It was such a personal gift, but a much-needed one. 'Thank you, that's very generous of you, but I can't imagine why you would think it necessary to get me anything at all.'

'For the inconvenience I caused you the other night—'

'That was hardly your fault.'

'Regardless, I am ashamed by the actions of what I hesitate to call a fellow American. A guest in your country and he attempts to rape a woman then steal a man's property.'

'It's not the best public relations exercise, is it?'

He cast his eyes sideways and sighed. 'No, it's not. Your friend upstairs says he doesn't want to report the bike being stolen. He's happy that it's been repaired. I promised him brand-new tyres and a chain. Truth is, even if they caught the fellow the MPs wouldn't give him much more than a slap on the wrist.'

'Property theft is one thing, but he attempted to rape a girl.'

'Yes, but since she doesn't want to file a report there's nothing we can do there.'

Valerie had managed to be vocal about them not calling the police. She was convinced they'd say it was her fault. Though exactly why she thought that was a mystery. Because she'd been walking by herself at night? What woman didn't these days? There wasn't a lot of choice, especially for those working nightshifts at factories, as Valerie herself had been. June had wanted to shake her. Had she not heard about the Leonski murders?

'I've started asking around. Checked with a few military hospitals to see if anyone's been treated for grazes or even a broken arm. No luck, I'm afraid. He'll try it again, I've no doubt.'

'All the more reason Valerie should report what happened.'

'Anyway, I should let your neighbour know I've returned his bicycle. He said he'd be home today.'

With a tight smile, a grimace really, Karl tipped his hat at her in what she gathered was a goodbye and left. Leaving the door open, she turned on her heel and tossed the box of chocolates and nylons on the sofa. The careful tidiness of the room embarrassed her now, as though she'd turned up at a picnic in an evening gown. She went out to the garden, ostensibly to look for Eliot. He was sunning himself on the rusted wrought-iron two-seater in the sunken corner of the yard. She thought about joining him with a book, but the seat was covered in fine-powdered dirt. Dried leaves were caught like marooned boats between the slats, while bougainvilleas encroached through the curlicues of the backrest in outbursts of magenta. Like all of Brisbane, it desperately needed a fresh coat of paint.

She wiped away some of the grime and perched on the edge of the seat to stroke the cat. He was as good as fully grown now. Peter had meant well bringing him home in the week after her miscarriage. In her mood, she'd been revisiting *The Wasteland*. Peter thought Mr Mistoffelees a more apt name, but June wanted to call him Eliot. He was really Peter's cat, although she'd come to love the animal with a fierce devotion since he'd left.

The breeze ruffled the edges of the leaves overhead, moving them like shadow puppets across her face. There was a faint scent of eucalyptus in the air. She was usually restless on Sundays while the city fell under a narcotic spell. It was a rare pleasure to succumb to the drift and stillness of the warm afternoon, to feel time spool out in ribbons around her.

'He is rather a nice cat. Do you mind if I join you?' Karl's posture was less assured than she'd come to expect.

'Of course not.' June scooped up Eliot and laid him across her lap. She felt a blush come up in her cheeks.

'Your neighbour's quite the amateur landscape artist. He showed me some of his paintings. The one of the Glass House

Mountains is particularly good. I'd like to see them while I'm here.'

'They're only about an hour's drive away. On a nice day it'd be quite invigorating in that jeep of yours.'

'Yes, I can imagine ...'

This time June couldn't mistake the slow creep of a smile on his face.

'I recommend taking a picnic. There're some lovely spots in the national park.'

'Well, it's a beautiful country.' Karl paused to take off his hat and smooth his hair down. The same errant lock dislodged from his crown and fell across his brow. He ran the cat's tail through his fingers. 'Would you come with me?'

Mr Bellincioni's bicycle bell rang out before June could respond. Eliot sprang from her lap as her neighbour called through the latticework fence: 'Thought I'd take her for a spin and see if she's as good as you say, Karl.' He dinged the bell again and cycled off down the street.

'*But I hear nothing, nothing ... only bells, / Five bells, the bumpkin calculus of Time.*'

'Slessor?'

He turned his face to hers.

'Indeed. It's a very fine poem. So, what do you say?'

- 7 -

There isn't any need for a lot of do's and don't's for Americans in Australia. Common sense and good will go a long way there … As a matter of fact, the Australians, especially the girls, are a bit amazed at the politeness of American soldiers.

—Instructions for American Servicemen in Australia, 1942

From the outside, the electric-blue fibro duplex was not much to look at, but it was perched at the upper end of a steep crescent drive in the bushy suburb of Bardon.

'The view from the balcony is pretty special. Not that you'll be able to see anything now,' Clio said as she unlocked her front door. It opened onto a living area with polished floorboards. Facing opposite were floor-to-ceiling windows and a glass-paned door to the balcony. The kitchen was to the left, partitioned off by a quaint 1950s servery with yellow cupboard doors. Musk-flavoured incense lingered in the room.

Clio switched on the Art Nouveau lamp – reproduction, Olivia guessed – on the side table beside the door. In the golden light, Olivia could see Clio's interior design wasn't simply a reflection of her personality but a material extension of it, constructed out of books, ornaments, lamps, cushions, throw rugs, DVDs, posters and photographs. Forced to label it as a style, Olivia would have said it was cluttered chic with a bohemian accent. She'd never had the knack for it herself: the ability to arrange things, many things, arty things, in a way that looked thrown together but wasn't. It only ever looked like mess.

'Would you like a tea? I'm having one. I need to sober up. I've got peppermint, chamomile and spiced apple, Earl Grey, green tea ...'

'That'd be lovely. Peppermint sounds good.'

Clio threw her bag on the servery bench (gold asterisk-flecked laminate) and went to turn the kettle on.

The bookcase was usually the first thing Olivia browsed in anyone's house, but it was the posters of various theatre productions around the room that drew her in for initial inspection: Shakespeare's *The Taming of the Shrew* and *As You Like It*; Noel Coward's *Private Lives*; Louis Nowra's *The Jungle*; *Camino Real* and *Cat on a Hot Tin Roof* by Tennessee Williams; and a Perth production of a David Williamson play Olivia had never heard of. Some were university productions, she noticed, others from independent theatre companies based in Brisbane and Los Angeles. She dutifully found Clio's name on the cast list for each one. The publicity poster for *Tie My Apron Strings, Would You?* was last in line, near the door to the balcony. Olivia still wasn't convinced a giant hot-pink electric mixing bowl really captured Graham's intent for the work.

'Turn the tree on, if you like,' Clio called from the kitchen.

Olivia presumed she meant the pink cherry blossom beneath the poster. It stood on a wooden crate covered with a square of green velvet beside the lounge.

She toured the rest of the living room, studying the montage of postcards, promotional cards for exhibitions, plays and films stuck to the walls. A print of Millais's *Ophelia* hung above the art deco credenza – polished walnut, smooth edges, to-die-for – which was desecrated with a similar kitschy array:

Vargas pin-up girl drink coasters, a bobble-headed Shakespeare figurine, scented candles, packs of tarot cards. Olivia picked up an unframed photograph of Clio smiling broadly as another woman kissed her on the cheek. They were holding margaritas and sitting in a pool against a backdrop of hazy arid mountains and a couple of long, skinny desert palms. On the back, someone had written: *Clio and Maddie, Palm Springs 2013* with a love heart. Olivia quickly put it down, feeling she'd pried where she shouldn't.

The sepia photograph of a wartime wedding party was a safer option for closer inspection. It had been mounted on stiff tawny-brown cardboard. The bride wore a simple white dress with a knee-length veil and a practised high-cheeked smile. She was clutching a bouquet of lilies. Everyone else was in uniform: the groom and his best man were both American servicemen, while the bride's attendant was in a WAAAF uniform. *March 25th 1944* was neatly printed on the back.

'Is this a picture of your grandparents?' Olivia asked.

'The one on the sideboard?' Clio moved to where Olivia could see her and propped herself against the circular edge of the servery. 'Well, yes. But there's a story behind that picture.'

'Really?'

'We need wine if I'm going to tell that story. Hang on.' Clio brought out the pot of peppermint tea with two mismatched mugs and placed them on the coffee table: a battered, colonial-style thing that was like none of the other furniture. Cheryl would be appalled. She then went back to the kitchen to fetch two wine glasses and a half-empty bottle of red. 'Shall we?' she said, holding the bottle aloft. 'Have to wait for the tea to cool, anyway.'

'Sure. So, your grandfather was a GI?'

'Yes, but I only found out about ten years ago. It was a big secret, you see. One of those hush-hush, family-shame things.'

Roosting on the edge of the amber lounge, Clio poured the remainder of a merlot evenly between two glasses.

Olivia settled on the other lounge. 'Why on earth not? I mean, they were married. What was there to hide? Was your grandmother pregnant?'

'No, though my dad was born exactly nine months later ... No, it was because, well, I'll tell you how I found out first. It's a good story, so bear with. It was just before I graduated from uni and I was living with Nan in her house in Rosalie. It meant I didn't have to pay rent while I was studying and someone could keep an eye on her, make sure she took her medications, that kind of thing. Looking back, it's easy to see *now* she was in the early stages of dementia, but none of us, my parents, my aunt and uncle – well, it was gradual.'

Clio paused to take off her sandals, throwing them towards the alcove that led to the bathroom. 'It started off small, like she didn't know where she'd left her slippers, or she'd leave a tap running. She knew who everyone was though, so ...' Clio shrugged. 'But she always had this thing with talcum powder. Like, ever since I can remember, Nan has smelt of jasmine-scented talc. As a kid, whenever we went to my grandparents', I'd go into the bathroom and pretend I was a figure skater because the tiles would be covered in this slippery film. Then I came home one day after rehearsals to find Nan sneezing and coughing, like uncontrollably, with this ghostly white aura around her head. She was prone to respiratory infections as it was and I start panicking, thinking we've got to get her to a doctor. So as I'm calling my dad, I go into the bathroom to look for her spare asthma puffer and, I kid you not, the bathroom was *covered* in talcum powder. It was like a snowstorm had blown through. And I was like, *What the fuck?*'

Clio stopped talking to take a sip of wine. She adjusted the cushion behind her back and tucked her feet up under her bum. 'Anyway, as I'm waiting for Dad to arrive, Nan, in between coughing fits, starts saying stuff like, "Frank's coming. Frank will be here soon." And I'm like, "Who's Frank, Nan? Frank's not coming, Doug's coming. Your son, Doug. We're going to take you to the hospital." But she was adamant this guy Frank was on his way over and that we had to have a White Christmas for him. Then she started calling me June, her sister, and asking me to turn the wireless on because she wanted to listen to Bing Crosby's "I'm Dreaming of a White Christmas". The whole thing was completely surreal. It was like she was somewhere else entirely. About sixty years in the past.'

'So, Frank – he's the groom in the picture?'

'Yep, that's Frank. My biological grandfather. Shit, that's my phone ringing. I better get it – it's probably my mum. I rang her earlier and told her to ring me back even if it's late.' Unfolding like a crumpled flamingo, Clio got up to rummage through her bag. 'Have a look at those books,' she said to Olivia, waving a hand towards the top of the bookcase. 'Check out the inscriptions – you might find them interesting.' She went into her bedroom to take the call. 'Hi Mum … yeah, I'm okay …'

Olivia heard Clio tell her mother she had a friend over so not to worry. She tried not to listen in, feeling she'd already intruded into Clio's life in a way that breached some kind of etiquette in terms of how fast two people were supposed to get to know each other. She liked Clio a lot, but was wary, distrustful, of friendships that ignited too quickly. Her best friendships, like the one she'd cultivated with Cheryl, had always been a slow burn from acquaintance to long-term friend.

Olivia got up, reluctant because she was comfortable, to peruse the bookcase. The middle shelves were mostly dedicated to plays and screenplays. She scanned the spines along the top shelf – a not-too-shabby collection of classic Australian novels – before picking off a few for closer inspection: Ruth Park's *Poor Man's Orange*, *Come in Spinner* by Dymphna Cusack and Florence James, Thea Astley's *A Descant for Gossips*, Christina Stead's *The Man Who Loved Children*. None of them bore an inscription. Xavier Herbert's *Capricornia* and his lesser-known work, *Soldiers' Women*, were at the end of the row.

'You don't see too many copies of this these days,' she said aloud, prising the latter from its stiff-backed neighbours. It was an early paperback edition. The cover depicted a young naked woman, a girl really, with a soldier's jacket draped around her shoulders. She was crouched on the floor beside a soldier's kit and helmet, surrounded by bottles of booze. Her expression was somewhere between come hither and Linda Blair from *The Exorcist*. Olivia turned the book over to read the blurb: *Under the shadow of war, young girls surrendered their innocence and wives betrayed their homes.* She snorted.

As instructed, she looked to see if there was an inscription: *Junest, this is truly the most awful piece of 'literature' I've ever had the displeasure of reading. To you, my dearest friend, I bequeath the laughs and outrage. Rhia xx.*

With dizzy disbelief, Olivia put it together. *Rhia. Gloria.* She actually wanted to squeal for the first time in her adult life. It wasn't the discovery of an unpublished manuscript, but it was a rare glimpse into Graham's personality, an intimate and unfiltered one. Rumour had it she burned most of her private correspondence before she died. Olivia showed Clio the inscription.

'I think that's Gloria Graham.'

Clio smiled, indulgently pleased.

'Are these—' Olivia swept her hand in an arc to indicate the books on the top shelf. 'How did you *get* them?'

'They belonged to my Great-Aunt June. She didn't have

children of her own so I was like a proxy grandchild. Nan had a pile of her books and the things in that box I'm going to find for you. We discovered it after Nan died when we were cleaning out the house, as you do. June was a big reader. Always had a book with her – that's how I remember her, anyway. Have a look at this.' Clio ran her right pointer finger along the slim spines of poetry volumes until she found *The Wasteland*. 'Her husband gave her this one. Look,' she said, holding open the cover for Olivia to read: *To my dearest wife, no moment with you has been wasted. Love always, Peter (Nov. 1940).*

'Corny, isn't it?' said Clio. 'But sweet. I never met him. He was a POW for most of the war. Dad said his health was always pretty poor. He was basically an invalid for the last ten years of his life. June nursed him until he died sometime in the sixties.'

'That's sad.'

'I know, right. He was a history teacher before the war.' Clio slipped *The Wasteland* back in place and took out the volume next to it. 'And I have to show you this.' She handed Olivia a copy of Kenneth Slessor's *Five Bells*. 'Read *that*,' she said, opening the cover and tapping the poem inscribed on the first page with emphasis.

It was addressed to 'J':

Our Time
Marched by the clangs of war
The final chime brings
Home casualties
Into the past, we go
My heart shell echoing
It's the sound of sorrow
That hollow of departure
My love
   Always, K.S. 1945

'Wow. But who's K.S.? It can't be Kenneth Slessor, surely?'

'No, no. His name was Karl, I'm pretty sure … Okay, I really have to find that box for you.' Clio grabbed a chair from a small outdoor table that had been repurposed as an indoor dining setting. She took it over to the linen cupboard between the bathroom and the bedroom. 'I think Karl was a US serviceman stationed here during the war.' She was standing on the chair in front of the open cupboard. 'And grand old Aunt June had a war dalliance with him. I only knew her as an old lady, obviously, but even so, I would never have picked that about her. She was always just so, I don't know, not prim and proper, but – what's the word I'm after? Genteel, a bit posh, maybe? You know, like butter wouldn't melt.'

Olivia watched as Clio rearranged stacks of shoeboxes, board games, magazines and other general cupboard contents in her quest to find the box. The bat wings of her watermelon-pink top were outstretched in full flight. She had the kind of legs that seemed made for skinny jeans. A look Clio probably took entirely for granted, or at least pretended to. As a dutiful feminist, Olivia knew she was supposed to be above assessing another woman's body in such a way, but it came from a place of wistful admiration.

'Found it. It's behind this thing.'

Clio yanked the crumpled air mattress off the top shelf and let it fall to the floor. The box behind it once contained Bowen Mangoes, going by the orange and green lid. Olivia took it from Clio so she could climb down from the chair.

'Just put it over there.' Clio pointed to a spot on the Persian rug beside the coffee table. After dusting herself off, she got down on her knees and seesawed the lid off. 'Right, let's see if it's in here.'

Buried in the nest of theatre programs, play and concert tickets, newspaper clippings about shows, postcards, movie pamphlets, birthday cards, and even used wrapping paper – what Olivia would suggest amounted to a slight hoarding problem – was the actual tin box Clio had been looking for. It was a 1950s MacRobertson's confectionery box, painted pale peach with a pink and a yellow hibiscus on the lid. Olivia imagined the box was something a serious collector would be interested in, an accidental objet d'art care of its distinct aesthetic and its sheer ability to barrel through the decades intact, bar a few dints and a spot of rust.

'This is it,' said Clio. 'Now, I can't promise anything. But ...' She flattened her hand purposefully on the lid. 'This was where I found that photo of my grandparents. I didn't finish telling you how we found out about Frank, did I? Did you want to hear the rest?' Clio placed the tin on the coffee table and picked up the cup of tea Olivia had just poured.

'Of course.'

'Hmmm,' Clio said, swallowing a mouthful of tea. 'Well, after the talc incident, Dad didn't know who this Frank was either. He knew Albert, his father, wasn't his biological father, but not much else. After Nan died about six months later, we started the task of cleaning out the house. It was Mum, actually, who found all her old papers. And that's how we discovered, or confirmed really, that Dad's father was a Yank named Frank from Douglas County, Kansas.'

'What did you find?'

'There were a couple of letters. The first was from a guy, a friend of Frank's in the 81st Squadron in New Guinea, informing Nan that Frank had died in a workshop accident. From that letter we gathered Frank was most likely an aircraft mechanic. The 81st transferred to Port Moresby in 1944 from Brisbane, which makes sense. They'd been based at Eagle Farm before that, pretty much from the time the Americans arrived in Brisbane. Dad did some research, which is why I know all this. Believe me, I'm not some weird history freak. Well, unless, it's about Shakespeare.'

Olivia smiled. There was no point taking offence. 'And the other letter?'

'An official one from the US Armed Forces saying Nan's marriage to Frank had been declared "Null and Void". Yep, exactly,' Clio said in response to Olivia's expression of disbelief. 'They said he hadn't received the proper permissions from his commanding officer. That may be true, but Dad thinks that it was really because they didn't want to be financially responsible for her, or give her US citizenship. She was pregnant with my dad when that letter came, too.'

'Wow. Yeah, that's … And she kept it all a secret after that?'

'Yep, we think it was a stigma thing. Embarrassment. Shame. Plus my adoptive grandfather was … Not a prick, exactly, but he was aloof. Reserved. Cantankerous in his old age. He was a friend of Nan's cousin. The cousin, David his name was, died in New Guinea too. My grandfather visited the family when he returned to give back the cousin's watch and stuff. There was a sense that he'd done my grandmother a huge favour by marrying her. It wasn't a happy marriage. But, anyway, enough about that. You're probably dying to know what's in that box!'

'Not at all, I find this stuff fascinating.'

'Well, anyways, I'm going to stop talking and let you have a look at what's in there' – she pointed with a dramatic flick of her wrist at the box – 'while I go take a shower. It's been a really long, emotional day. Is that okay with you?'

'Of course. We could have done this some other time.'

'Don't be silly. I'm glad you're here. I'd be wallowing in my own misery otherwise. Thank you. I mean that.'

Olivia waited until she heard the bathroom door close. The tin lid was jammed at an odd angle, making it difficult to open. The hinge mechanism needed adjusting. After prising it off, and breaking a nail in the process, she put her nose to its contents, taking in a bouquet of must and vanilla from decaying paper. The box contained mostly letters and the odd telegram. There were other bits of ephemera that had obviously been kept as mementos: an ID card, tickets, ration coupons, faded photographs, yellowed newspaper clippings.

On top was June's Certificate of Service and Discharge, which had been folded in two. June was evidently the woman in the WAAAF uniform in the wedding party. According to the certificate, she had enlisted in December 1942 and was discharged on compassionate grounds in July 1945. Beneath that was a postcard addressed to Mrs June Atkinson at a New Farm address dated as received on 1 December 1942. Olivia turned it over. It was essentially a form letter where Peter, the sender, had filled in the blanks or crossed out the statements that weren't relevant.

IMPERIAL JAPANESE ARMY

I am interned at N° 4 P.O.W. CAMP THAILAND
My health is excellent.
~~I am ill in hospital.~~
I am working for pay.
~~I am not working.~~
Please see that ... MUM ... is taken care of.

My love to you Peter

Olivia carefully laid it aside and removed a black-and-white sketch wrapped in tissue paper, now crisp with age. It depicted the figure of a woman, some distance away from the artist, in a grassy clearing propped on her elbows with her legs stretched along the ground. Her head was turned towards the mountain in the background, distinguished by its crook-necked peak as one of the Glass House Mountains. *Mt Coonowrin, Sept. 1942* had been written in neat block letters on the bottom right of the picture. On the back, in the same neat cursive as the poem inscribed in *Five Bells*, it simply said: *For June, a memory worth preserving, Karl.*

Olivia removed all the letters to see if any were addressed in the same hand. She soon discerned, by the cursive flourish of the capital letters in 'Sergeant J.M. Atkinson', they were all from June's father, Hugh Morton, addressed variously to a hostel in Sydney, Warrnambool Airbase in Victoria, and then later to another one in Townsville.

She read a couple of them, gleaning a few insights into the Morton family during the war years, before Clio emerged wearing a kimono-style dressing-gown in a bright floral print, towel-drying her hair. There was a pleasant waft of coconut about her.

'Anything interesting?'

'Yes, but nothing relating to Gloria Graham so far. I found out your grandmother worked as a volunteer for the American Red Cross.'

'Yeah, she witnessed the Battle of Brisbane, you know. From a bathroom window in the Red Cross building. I don't think it's there anymore, the building.'

'Did she really?'

'I don't know for sure. It's just something I remember Dad saying.'

Clio threw the towel over the back of the chair she'd been standing on earlier, then tousled her Edie Sedgwick hair with her fingers. Olivia didn't resent Clio for her blasé attitude to her family history, or even the fact she had one, but it made her feel something, like a slight skin irritation that would go away if you didn't think about it.

'Did you want to stay the night? The air mattress is already out,' Clio added with a wry inflection. 'Clearly that's a sign.'

Olivia checked the time on her phone. It was after midnight. She was tired, and an Uber fare home would be around thirty bucks.

'Are you sure?'

'Of course. I'd say just hop into bed with me, but I'm terrible to sleep with, apparently. And I have to have the fan going full bore all night. Used to drive Maddie insane. Probably another reason she broke up with me.'

It was pitch-black when Olivia woke and it took a disoriented few moments to remember where she was. She'd fallen asleep without any trouble, too tired to care where she put her head, but hadn't slept well. The mattress was underinflated and the sagging pillow of air between her and the ground had turned cold. She'd been half conscious of her dreams, vivid fragments of past and present that featured everyone at Cheryl's soiree to Tobias and Clio to Clio's dead relatives. A symptom of an over-stimulated mind and probably too much wine, going by the clenching ache across the back of her skull. She half slid, half rolled off the air mattress to go to the bathroom and get a glass of water. She searched her bag for some ibuprofen, found two left in the blister pack and downed them both.

It was only 3.30 am. Phone light leading the way, she took the pillow and blanket over to the blue couch. The phone battery was low; she should have asked Clio if she had a spare charger. The thought brought back the strand of her dream in which June's lover, Karl, in uniform, had asked to borrow Olivia's pen to sign a volume of his poetry after a reading at Avid Reader bookstore in West End. He'd inscribed it: *To Olivia, Ding Dong!* But she couldn't make out his signature: only the 'Karl' part and the 'S' of his surname – the rest an indecipherable scrawl. She had the sense she did know it, though: the ghost of a fact shape shifting the more she tried to recall it.

She opened the browser on her phone and typed 'Karl + American Poet + World War II' into the search bar, then added 'shell echoes' for good measure. The first hit was a Wikipedia entry on Karl Salzberg: an American poet, essayist and journalist born 10 October 1913 and died 12 May 1997. She scrolled down to the longer biography, duly noting, among other things – such as, he was born into a large Jewish family from Brooklyn and married twice – that he served in the Pacific Theatre during the war and wrote a volume of poetry while he was there called *Shell Echoes and Other Poems* that later won the Pulitzer Prize for Poetry.

Well. Olivia felt as smugly self-satisfied as Sherlock Holmes. There was no chance of sleeping now. She couldn't wait to tell Clio. She switched on the cherry-tree lamp, wincing until her eyes adjusted to the intense pink glow. She pulled out the next letter, a fat one, to June from her father; Mr Morton had an enjoyably sly sense of humour, she was discovering. Two letters had in fact been jammed inside the thin envelope. She unfolded the one written on unfamiliar notepaper. The handwriting, though, she gleefully recognised.

~

Dear Junest,

Sorry for the sluggish reply, things have just been terribly hectic. I've officially started 'driving the Yanks around' and am probably enjoying the metaphor of that more than the actual job. Though it's not so bad as far as war work goes (imagine me with the Land Army out in the fields with a plough?) and being a night owl I cope better than most with the overnight shifts. But I'll tell you more about it in a moment.

Congratulations, first up, on making Sergeant. It's heartening to see common sense and diligence are given their due reward in the services. How are you finding the actual work? I imagine much of it is rather dull. I don't wonder at all that you'd miss pompous old Maclean, but do you miss the bookshop?

Have you had any more of those bizarre postcards from ~~the Japanese Imperial Army~~ Peter? Such a way with words and from the culture that brought us the haiku! I know how much he preys on your mind, darling, so I hope you are taking some comfort knowing he's alive, at least. Don't lose hope.

And what's the latest on Edith's romance with young Frank the Yank? They got engaged at Christmas was the last you told me, after he'd been involved in some altercation in a public bar which put a dampener on things (I long for the details on that!). I'm gathering they haven't set a date? But he's a nice enough fellow, isn't he? You said he was well mannered and had made an effort with your mother and father. Despite that, I do understand your lack of enthusiasm for the match. Edith is, as you say, inclined to fill her head with romantic notions about a lot of things, but I don't think you should rule out the possibility that she genuinely loves Frank, even if she does think there's a yellow-brick shortcut between Kansas and Hollywood Boulevard. And if it turns out to be the biggest mistake of her life, she can always come back home. My guess is there'll be a few war

brides who'll end up with their tail between their legs when all this is
over. Mum told me recently she'd heard about a girl who'd married an
American, then found out afterwards he had a wife and daughter back
home in Michigan. I'm not suggesting Frank is already married (he's
from Kansas, surely that's some guarantee of wholesomeness), but I
can't help thinking Edith hasn't put a great deal of thought into what
'marrying a Yank' and moving to 'Douglas County, Kansas' actually
means. But I'm preaching to the choir, aren't I? There's probably not
much you and your parents haven't tried to dissuade her.

Speaking of Yanks, I've kept in touch with Harry a little. He sent
me some of his poems to look at. He's keen for my opinion of them.
Which means, of course, he's keen for me to say how wonderful they
are. Luckily, he is rather good, but I wouldn't have fancied him in the
first place if he wasn't. He's in Sydney at the moment. I don't ask
questions and he doesn't ask them of me. It's really not like that, but I
expect we'll see each other if he's in Brisbane again. How's Karl? The
last I heard from you was that he'd gone 'up north' to report on the
campaign in Gew Nuinea (did that one pass the censor's snip?).

So, then, the driving job. There were very few hoops to jump
through to get it. The hardest part was turning up at the office in
Adelaide Street and joining the Women's National Emergency
Legion. Yes, you read correctly – I've tossed my principles aside and
joined an acronym. I'm officially a WNEL now, whatever you want
to make of that. Then it was just a matter of producing my driver's
licence and doing a driving test for the Americans. There was an
induction lecture where we learned the finer points of map reading and
the difference between a knoll and col (which is the lowest point on a
mountain ridge between two peaks, in case you're wondering). The
condescension of the whole thing almost killed me. The uniform is the
biggest letdown – an ill-fitting khaki shirt and drill skirt that combine
just so to resemble a burlap sack sealed off at the neck with a brown
tie, and stockings as thick and droopy as an elephant's hide. American

wives can sleep easy. I won't be setting hearts, or any other body parts,
aflame in this get-up. Definitely not the distinguished navy blues
you're doing justice to in the WAAAF.

All that aside, there is something I wish to tell you which is
quite extraordinary. I've been mulling over it for two weeks now and
I feel I must tell someone. I should add that I also took an oath of
secrecy — though I'd argue that's more about not disclosing where we go,
rather than sharing something that might have been said along the way
by indiscreet officers: ('Keep mum, she's not so dumb!')

I can hear you telling me to get on with it, so here goes: The other
week I was privy to an interesting and, I have to say, rather disturbing
conversation between a certain brigadier general and the provost marshal
whose name I won't mention but rhymes with 'prawn'. Anyway, I
was driving the pair out west to inspect a new building the Yanks are
looking to requisition when the BG asked the PM if they'd made any
'progress' (the BG's inverted commas, not mine) on what he called 'the
River Girl case'?

What 'River Girl' case? You might well ask. Well, I can assure
you there's been exactly zilch about a girl being murdered by the river
in The Courier-Mail or The Telegraph. What I gleaned from the
conversation is that her body was found in the mangroves somewhere
by the river in South Brisbane. The BG asked if there was any way
it 'could be passed off as a botched abortion'. That would keep it out
of the papers, apparently, because girls died all the time that way, 'but
you didn't read about it'. He then asked if she'd been pregnant, as that
'would make the suicide hypothesis easier to sell'.

The PM said — and I remember this bit clearly — 'It'd be easier to
sell if she clearly hadn't been manually strangled. The stocking around
her neck was just for show. The bastard crushed her windpipe like a
peanut shell.' The BG then asked, with that being the case, did the
PM think they had 'another Leonski on their hands'. It wasn't out
of the question, but they did have a suspect — a coloured soldier — and

were planning to make an arrest soon. He was apparently known to the girl and also happened to be in the area that night. All purely circumstantial, even by the PM's own admission. There are witnesses, he said, who can place the soldier at a nearby hotel. The soldier, so the PM put forth, also suffers from that affliction known as being of a poor character. This based on his involvement in a violent brawl a month or so earlier with some of his paler though no less punch-ready compatriots. If that's your criteria then over half the men in the Allied forces stationed in Brisbane are of a poor character.

The BG then said (slightly paraphrased): 'I don't care who you arrest, but there is no way in hell we can have the Australian public knowing a Negro killed a woman. Can you imagine the goddamn shitstorm if that happens? Arrest him, convict him, hang him, and I'll make sure the press is kept under control.'

Suffice to say the girl's muddy death has been covered up at the wish and command of the highest echelons of the US military because the publicity would be catastrophic as far as US military relations with the Australian public goes. These men must have thought I was deaf, or, because I'm a woman, dumb as a mule.

Of the poor girl herself, they said very little. They didn't even mention her name, though I gathered she was from around the area.

I was reminded of that young woman you said was attacked outside your apartment last year. The two incidents are unlikely to be related, but on the one hand we have a rapist that got away scot-free, and on the other a coloured man accused of rape and murder on grounds you wouldn't build a dog kennel on, all of which smells suspiciously of a turd called convenience. In the face of what is a gross miscarriage of justice, I guess I'm just feeling helpless to do anything about it. Given that – and at the risk of sounding like a deranged Miss Marple – I wondered if you might tell me what you remember about the girl you found in your yard that night? You noticed marks around her neck, didn't you? I seem to remember you said her name started with a 'V' and she worked in the munitions factory at Rocklea – is that correct?

Anyway, I've probably said enough here to get myself court-martialled, so I'm going to sign off, post this in the morning and hope for the best.

Keep well and much love,
Rhia xx

P.S. Harry arrived in town last night (a very nice surprise) and I asked him to deliver this in person when he heads back to Sydney. No point risking interference if it can be avoided.

– 8 –

Amid the clatter and roar of countless machines hundreds of Queensland women are to-day doing a vital war job in a huge munitions factory … Few had worried their heads about the complexities of machinery before they entered a Queensland factory …

—*The Courier-Mail* (13 July 1942)

September 1942

Val dropped her cigarette butt in the dirt and stamped it out with a twist of her ankle before trekking up the brick stairwell to the ladies' change room. Fay Abernethy came around the corner on her way down.

'Heave-ho, Watts. Shift starts in five. Get your overalls on.' Her tone was light. She could have been joking, but Val, like all the girls, knew the forewoman always meant business. She never yelled. 'How's the stomach this morning? Better, I trust.'

Val nodded. 'Much better.' There was no way of telling if Fay knew she'd been faking. Rumour had it Fay played poker in her spare time and once relieved an American colonel of a hundred pounds.

'Lickety-split then.'

From the second-floor landing, Val could see Fay striding off in the direction of the main workshop, oblivious, it seemed, to the morning chill. She was the tallest woman Val had ever met – eight inches taller than herself, at least. She wondered if Fay would have preferred to be a man. She certainly walked like one, and no one had ever seen her wear a dress or even a skirt.

Val pushed open the change-room door. Everyone else was at the machinery shop. She removed her overalls from her locker – as much as she hated the baggy, shapeless things, they were comfortable, and warm. The early spring cold snap had come from nowhere. A gust of wind set off a thunderous rattle of sheet iron above her head. She put her shitty old coat on over her overalls. It was so snug she could barely keep her arms straight. A real treat to the eye, she was. At least Rocko couldn't see her dressed this way.

The correction took only a second, and the hitch of her breath: Rocko would never see her again, at all. *Fool, fool, fool, fool.* She saw herself, as someone else would, standing dumbly expectant, dolled up in Alice's fur coat, outside the registry office on George Street. Watching the messenger boy on a bicycle hand her a letter: 'Are you Valerie Watts?' Why compound her humiliation with a lie? He could have just not turned up, no furphies about shipping out early to give the Japs the slip: *Ssshhh! Top secret! Loose lips sink ships!* and all that nonsense. She would have got the message – emphatic as a foghorn. Just another stupid girl hoodwinked by a big, fat, lying, stinking Yank. She wasn't the first and she wouldn't be the last.

The floorboards were already vibrating when she entered the shed. Val sometimes felt she was the only one who didn't consider industriousness its own reward. If they weren't paid as much as a man for doing the same job, why prove you were as efficient? Fay clocked Val's arrival with a twitch of her eyebrows and a jerk of her thumb in the direction of the far back corner.

Val headed down the centre aisle between two rows of lathes and hoppers. The machinery and its operators appeared as little more than dull blobs in the gauzy light that filtered through the dusty ceiling windows. With its high roof and polished floor, Val often pictured the shed as a dance hall with herself at the thrumming centre.

'Where've you been? Ya six minutes late.' Vera flicked her head at the clock. 'Abernathy will dock every one of 'em from your lunch break.'

Val shrugged as she pulled down the safety catch on the lathe next to Vera. She was spared answering by the shrill grind of a welder firing up in the section behind them. The smell of smouldering metal stunk up the workshop like a drunk's fart. The sort her father had made a specialty of.

'We dancing tonight?' Vera mouthed over a second blistering screech.

'Do Yanks prefer blondes?' Val yelled back. She coughed as acrid air hit her throat. Her eyes were watering. Bloody right she planned on dancing – till her feet fell off and yesterday's scorching humiliation was pulverised into the floor.

Vera gave her a gloved thumbs-up.

On a Sunday night, Val had only to step inside the City Hall auditorium before she was hustled onto the dance floor, such was her reputation for cutting a rug. She could triple and drop step, turn, pretzel and swivel kick faster than any girl in the room, but it was her fearlessness that made her the most sought after. A capable partner knew they could swing her higher and wider than even the best girls were prepared to go, and she never baulked at an impromptu shoulder flip or a pull-through.

And while beginners mastered the basic *da-da-dasida* rhythm of jitterbugging, and the more advanced executed eggbeaters and barrel rolls, Val, propelled by an adept partner, would do overhead side splits and tumble dives. The gasps of admiration were one thing, if she noticed them at all. Her body, its flow and movement, would yield entirely to the music, fusing with its beats and rhythms until she couldn't distinguish where the music ended and she and her partner began. The exhilaration was in the effortlessness.

Her first time, back in May, inside the vast circular concert hall – modelled on the Pantheon in Rome, with fluted Corinthian pilasters, a high rounded balcony and a domed ceiling – had flamed a whole-body desire to have her own moment of significance. She just needed the right partner. He appeared, from nowhere it seemed to Val, as the lights dimmed and the US Army band lifted their trombones and trumpets, dipped their saxophones, and the drummer kicked off with the opening bars of Benny Goodman's 'Sing, Sing, Sing'. As they coasted into Woody Herman's 'The Golden Wedding', a crowd had gathered to watch them. To Val, he was simply Jimmy the GI. She wasn't even sure what he did. They won the jitterbug contest that first night, but by some unspoken agreement they never saw each other outside of the dance floor.

It was Vera who suggested they skip their regular Friday night at the Troc for the 'Special Patriotic Dance' at City Hall. With proceeds going to the Comforts Fund, Vera reasoned, it was as good as doing volunteer work. Val's patriotism had little to do with it: she simply wanted to win whatever was up for grabs for the best female dancer. It was a different sort of crowd to Sunday night – more subdued, older, with more women in uniform than not.

They'd only been there an hour before Vera disappeared. Jimmy, Val conceded, was probably at the Troc. The Merry Makers Band had launched into the fourth ballad in a row and Val was bored, though at least she wasn't stuck with some digger who moved like a table. The Australian captain leading her around in a slow foxtrot to 'Moonlight Serenade' was surprisingly capable. He was well into his thirties and his eyes were half closed; that he was from Melbourne was the most he'd volunteered about himself. An unintentional sigh escaped Val's lips, though she couldn't have even said why.

'What's the matter, sweetheart? Missing your fella?'

'Hmmm.'

'Up north, is he?'

'Townsville. With the air force,' she added.

'Well, I bet he's missing you, too. He's a lucky guy to have such a sweet little thing waiting for him at home.'

Val gave him the smile he expected. As 'Moonlight Serenade' drifted into its final melancholy bars, she excused herself, saying she needed to look for her friend. It wasn't too late to get a tram over to the Troc if they left now. She squirmed through the press of bodies around the refreshment table. For the price of admission, she at least wanted a cup of lemonade. She gulped it down. It was cool and tangy, but not as sweet as she normally liked. She went back for more anyway. As her cup was refilled, she felt a tap on her shoulder from behind. She turned to see Jimmy, catching a whiff of his cologne: the same kind as Rocko's. It threatened to undo her for a moment, make her forget why she was here tonight.

'I went looking all over town for you,' he said with a grin. 'You trying to avoid me?'

'Of course not. You think any of these blokes can burn up a floor like you?'

'Well, let's show 'em how it's done. I just had a word with the band. I hope you're in the mood.' He lifted the lemonade from her hand, took a swig, then slammed it on the table. 'Ready?'

He was like something out of a corny movie. She laughed, her feet prickling with readiness as the familiar saxophone arpeggio kicked off everyone's favourite opening refrain. She'd been waiting all day for this. Jimmy took her hand and pulled her into the pulsing centre of the room.

'Don't eat them all. I want to keep some for later.' Val slapped the back of Vera's hand. The box of chocolates sat between them on the steps outside City Hall. Val wrapped her cardigan tight around her middle. No longer warm from dancing, the chilled night had ceased to be pleasant relief.

'Aw, c'mon. Just one more?'

'Oh, all right then. But that's it. Where's this bloody Yank of yours with the beer he promised? I'm freezing. We'll get piles if we sit here much longer.'

'He's coming. He said he'd be straight back,' said Vera.

'Five more minutes. Otherwise I'll miss my tram.'

'Stop worrying about the bloody tram. Bill will put us in a taxi if it comes to that.'

The crowd from the dance had mostly dissipated, though a few stray uniforms and lip-locked couples were propped against the palm trees spaced along the frontage. Those seeking more privacy had drifted down Adelaide Street to find a shop entrance or alleyway. Val got up to stretch her legs and get some blood flowing to her toes. There was a particular manoeuvre, a quick piece of reverse footwork with a twist and a flick kick, that she hadn't quite mastered, and she marked through it on the landing, trying to pinpoint where she'd gone wrong. She'd wanted to ask Jimmy to show her, but he'd left before she got the chance. Probably with some girl who thought he'd make a good trophy.

'You can stop showing off now,' Vera called. 'No one's watching you.'

'Shush. I'm trying to figure something out. And get out of my chocolates.'

'Then show me some moves so I can win a fancy-schmancy box of chocolates.'

'Come up here, then. What do you want to learn?'

Vera stood up, licking her fingers. She tried to speak but her teeth were stuck with caramel. She grabbed Val's arm instead and pointed with all the subtlety of an air-raid siren to a group of three Aussie soldiers who had appeared from behind a phone box further up and were now walking down Albert Street.

'Him. That's the bloke. The one I told you about. He kept staring at you when you were dancing. The short one was there, too. You know him?'

It was too dark to make anything of their faces, but the stocky one was the man who'd steered her inside the diner yesterday. His efforts to comfort her had been well meaning, but clumsy. She also recognised the tall one, Alice's brother. Had an impression of him as scrappy and sharp-chinned – good-looking, if you liked that kind of thing – though she'd paid him little notice. Val hadn't seen the fight he'd started outside the diner, and Alice wouldn't say what set him off. He seemed to need little excuse. Val knew the type well enough.

She pulled Vera further beneath the awning and turned her back to the men.

'It's Alice's brother. My roommate. You met her once at the pictures, remember?'

'Oh yeah. Possum-face girl.'

'Don't be like that. She's all right.'

'When are you going to quit that place? Imagine if we got an apartment near the Troc. No one like my old man or your housemistress telling us what to do and what time we have to be home.'

'And who's going to rent a place out to two single girls like us?'

The conversation was an old one. Val would move out of the hostel in a heartbeat if it were an option. But it wasn't, at least not while she was paying to keep a roof over and a mattress under her father, as well.

Before Val could gauge whether the men had passed the stairs, a taxi pulled up outside the City Hall entrance. Vera scurried down to meet its passenger, who was talking to the driver through the window.

'We're here! You got the beer?' Vera threw her arms around the GI, one of those hardy, farm-bred sorts, and planted a kiss on his cheek. He put a hand on her bottom and squeezed it.

By then, Jack, Kanga – Val remembered his name now – and the other guy were almost at the intersection of Albert and Adelaide streets. They'd stopped to view the scene at the taxi. The GI was gesturing for Vera to hop in, and Vera waved at Val to come and join them.

'Come on,' she yelled. 'Bill says there's a party going on at a house in Hamilton.'

~

The night, hushed and moonless, was thick and dark as a tar pit when Val and the rest of the late shift scraped down the dirt drive to the factory gate. Val could barely see her own hand in front of her face. She hurried to the Compo Road gate, attuned to the distant rattle of the tram sparking its way to the end of the Salisbury line. Work overtime for a few minutes, or natter too much in the change room, and there goes the last tram into the city.

She sat at the back of the Dreadnought next to a window, letting her head collapse against the seat. There was nothing to see through the black that had settled in heavy folds over the outer suburbs. Those who spoke kept their voices hushed in deference to the late hour and the general weariness around them.

The week since her wedding-that-wasn't had slipped by with so little notice Val was sure it had been longer. For Rocko himself, her sorrow had to be of little substance; she had barely known him. But on the spongy grass in the shadowed tangles of a Moreton Bay fig in New Farm Park, she'd been as certain of the rightness of him, of the two of them together, as the air she breathed. Their names would still be there, carved in a love heart by Rocko's hand into the base of the tree. At the time she'd expected nothing; had wanted only to be with him then and there. Only girls like Alice were fooled when a man pulled a French letter from his pocket for the first time. Val didn't have Vera's appetite for uniforms of all sizes, stripes and colours – it's a wonder the postman didn't get a look-in – but she would have accepted it as two people merely taking what pleasure they could in a world that had seized control of their lives and was holding their futures to ransom. So why ask her to marry him if he hadn't believed, if only fleetingly, that something bigger than themselves had brought them together? Why had she said yes? Because she thought it meant something? The answer made her a fool.

A resolve of sorts mustered inside her, steadily clacking over like the wheels on the tram. She would get on with it; make the most of what the war had to offer. Be more like Vera. Besides, things were changing for women. Some people, if you listened to a few of the older women at the factory, truly believed that. Maybe she could open her own dance school after the war. She owed no one anything, though she should probably go see her father. Make sure he was eating and occasionally bathing. It had been three months.

She changed trams in the city, catching the last one to New Farm for the evening, and alighted at the corner of Brunswick and Sydney to walk the few blocks home. There was a small side street she usually took that led to the back entrance of the hostel. It meant climbing over the fence as the gate was usually locked, but it was quicker than going all the way around to the front.

Crossing over to the other side, she caught a draught of cigarette smoke. A GI was leaning against the latticework fence outside the apartment block on the corner. A strange spot if he was hoping for a pick-up. Back down towards Brunswick, on the side that bordered New Farm Park, was the place to try his luck. Val expected him to say something – a 'How's it going, honey?' or some other line they threw out to any woman who might bite – and she prepared a smile on approach, ready to give him a polite, friendly rebuff. When he didn't speak, the smile withered on her lips. His silence, so unlike any Yank, had the slap of a reproach.

She walked past, eyes fixed to the footpath, halting her breath to prevent the mingle of air between them. His weathered boots, she noticed, were crossed, one foot over the other. She felt his gaze sear down the length of her spine like a welding iron. She heard him stomp out his cigarette, knowing it wasn't coincidental even before a hand clamped over her mouth, before an arm seized and then squeezed her torso like a heavy snake. Next was the squeaking of a gate, the dragging of her feet over concrete, the thud of her back hitting dirt. All the air punched from her lungs. He stuffed her mouth with something. Her teeth clamped and slid against folds of fabric as his hand wrapped around her throat, pinning her to the ground. Sour, boozy breath and gamy body odour flooded her nostrils in her desperate siphon for oxygen. Bile flushed her throat and it was then that she knew, the awareness so brief she almost missed it: he didn't smell like a Yank.

~

October 1942

Val, along with five other women including Vera, had been sent to inspect a mountain of bullets stockpiled in an outer warehouse. Every single one needed 'a little twist' to make sure there were no loose caps. Otherwise they might explode in some poor digger's rifle. A fine crop of blisters had bloomed along Val's forefinger and right thumb. But for the rhythm and monotony of the task, she was grateful. The continuous, easy movement kept her hands from shaking, and her mind still enough to curb the barbed edges off her panic. Blunt the terror that clawed at her throat and chest every night, leaving her cold and sweating, the sheets damp and pungent. She hadn't slept properly in weeks. How she got through each day, she didn't know, she couldn't remember most of them. They'd simply accumulated like the .303 bullets passing through her fingers from one pile to another. *MQ VII 1942*. She had no idea what made a Mark VII different to a VI or a V – that's just what they were – but the etching felt personal. If she lived to be a hundred, she'd remember it as the headstamp on a period of her life she'd do anything to forget.

She plucked another from the pile. The wretched things were lighter than they looked – designed, she supposed, to travel as far and as accurately as possible – but she felt their weight in an entirely different way. The weight of intent: what it was meant for once she tested the cap and placed it in a different pile, so it could be taken away, then given to a soldier to put in his rifle. She didn't think she was stupid – she understood why her job and manufacturing bullets were necessary (though that didn't stop her from hating it) – yet, she must be missing something because it seemed too straightforward. It was a simple series of steps, really, between it being in her hand, then one day, soon, possibly blowing someone's chest or head apart. Somebody, yes, a Jap – the enemy – but still a person, a person who was alive now, but soon wouldn't be. It was so obviously and intentionally brutal, and final.

Yet, it couldn't help *her*. The thin, metal cylinder with the pointy end – 'they're called spitzers, girls' – that was potentially, hopefully, on its way to maim or kill an enemy soldier was impotent, regrettably and distressingly so, in her own fingers. She pressed the pointed end of it into her palm, wishing it hurt more, and hoping it would quell the relentless nausea that was roiling up again like sediment in a rain-swollen river.

She tossed the bullet onto the 'done' pile. Her fellow twisters screeched at her to 'Be careful!' as she fled out onto the verandah. It was no good though; she never actually threw up. The urge to be sick seemed more overwhelming each time, but there was no such relief. It just stayed there, bilious and green in the cauldron of her stomach. She took hold of the wooden railing and bent over at the waist, letting her head fall towards her knees. It was only ever a temporary reprieve.

She would not cry; she would not cry. She hated herself for crying. It was all she ever did.

A warm hand caressed the base of her spine. 'Val. It's me. Are you all right?' Vera asked. 'Do you need some water?'

Val shook her head without looking up.

'You know what you gotta do. I'll help you, yeah. It's really not as bad as it sounds. My cousin swears it worked a treat for—'

'Vera, you get your tush back inside that warehouse. And you, Miss Watts, go down and wait for me in the office.' Fay had a talent for appearing from nowhere, though how she managed it, for she was hardly a garden sprite, no one knew.

The office was in a brick dwelling adjacent to the change rooms. The only other time Val had been inside was to fill out paperwork the day she arrived at the factory. She stood there now, waiting for Fay, in a room that had all the charisma of a bank clerk. Not much larger than a cupboard it contained a desk, filing cabinets, and stack after stack of paper. A slash of afternoon light from a high-up window cut across the room, showing up the suspended dust in the stuffy air. Pinned to the wall was an aerial map of the factory site. The camouflage of the fake road and tennis court over the top of the main machinery shop slightly more convincing from the air than at ground level.

Fay entered the room, closing the door behind her. 'So what is it, Watts? Boy trouble? Yank trouble?'

She didn't want to give Abernathy the pips, but the words she needed didn't exist, at least not in any form that explained anything. Could she say it felt like something had blasted apart inside her? Like a little faggot of cordite sticks exploding inside a .303, she was unrepairable.

'Is this a guessing game?'

Val looked up briefly, catching something in the forewoman's eyes that wasn't an admonishment. A 'no' tried to push its way through the lock in her throat.

'Are you pregnant?' Fay asked with an emphasis on each syllable. 'Is that it? I can't help you unless you tell me.'

Val moved her head enough to give Fay an answer. A crop of tears, unable to cling to her chin any longer, plopped one at a time onto the floor. She hadn't even felt them roll down her face.

'Okay. That explains a few things.' Fay put her hands on her hips. 'You sure?'

The best she could manage was a shrug, but of the abject truth of it, Val could no longer deny.

'Have you told anyone else?'

'Vera,' she said. The name came out like the creak of a rusty door hinge.

'A deep well of home-remedy knowledge, I'm sure. And what exactly did she suggest? A Coke bottle?'

Val jerked her chin up. The trick, Vera had said, was to 'shake it really hard and get it up there as quick as you can'.

'I hope you know that's nothing more than an old wives' tale. Same goes for lying in a bath of scalding water while drinking a pint of gin.'

She hadn't tried either, but only because the hostel didn't afford the kind of privacy needed for desperate measures. But things could go wrong even if you went 'somewhere'. Everyone knew about the girl who was dumped under a mango tree.

Fay stood over the desk and wrote something on a sheet of notepaper. She tore it off the pad and handed it to Val. 'My address. Finish the shift – I don't want any gossip – go home, pack a few things in a bag, pyjamas, a toothbrush, then come straight over. Your father died last week, didn't he?'

'Yes.'

'Good. You got an aunt or uncle you can say you're visiting?'

'An aunt, somewhere. I only met her once.'

'That will do. I'm giving you two days leave to see her. Sort out your father's estate.'

'He didn't—'

'It doesn't matter. I'll see you tonight. There's a tram that stops at the corner of Annerley and Park roads.' Fay moved to usher Val out of the room. 'You'll need money,' she added before opening the door. 'Thirty-five pounds. Can you manage that?'

'I … Well, yes, but not all of it right now.' She didn't have that much. But she had her father's watch plus the ten quid she'd found stuffed in a sock under his mattress. She could only assume he'd won it betting on something then forgotten it was there.

'Bring what you can and I'll loan you the rest.'

Val nodded. She'd sell the watch as soon as she could get to a pawnbroker. It was the only thing of value he'd owned. She knew the story better than her own mother. It had belonged to his mate, Thommo, who collided with a grenade somewhere in the Somme. His right arm was blown off with such force it landed in the trench he'd just crawled out of. Her father later buried the arm and kept the watch. He'd never sold it, which said everything about what it had meant to him. Val had no such qualms. It was her father, after all, who would say with irksome predictability, his voice thick with liquor and the remnant brogue of his Scottish ancestry: 'It's an ill wind that blows no good, petal.'

Val looked at Fay as she passed her at the door, a myriad of questions posed in her eyes.

'Not here,' said Fay.

Something eased around her neck and jaw as she walked back to the warehouse. There was a loosening in her face, one that would let go a torrent of tears if she didn't contain them. If she became the girl under the mango tree, then so be it.

- 9 -

A direct private entrance from George Street leads to the Private Bar, whose modern serpentine counters faced with dark green marble provide a cool contrasting note to the creamy tan Wombeyan marble of the walls.

—Lennon's of Brisbane Brochure, 1941

Clio had dropped Olivia home in her '95 yellow Corolla. Olivia, she'd declared, was a *genius* for working out who 'KS' was. She'd been happy for Olivia to take the tin and its contents and 'just return it whenever'. Clio hadn't read the letter from Gloria Graham to June about a girl being strangled and dumped by the river, confessing she hadn't read *all* the letters; she cited the callowness of youth for her lack of interest. Olivia was grateful for Clio's callow youth as that meant she was probably the first one to set eyes on the potentially game-changing letter since its intended recipient. Olivia didn't know what it all meant in terms of her thesis yet and would have to sit down and think about it, but thank goddess she hadn't sent that email about quitting to her supervisor, Mandy.

To consider the letter when her faculties weren't wholly operational was futile. She went out to the balcony without any goal in mind except to take stock of the day outside. Its temperate, twittering cheerfulness felt like an assault. Her jaw was tight and her eyeballs actually ached. There was no evidence of last night's revelry; Cheryl would have taken care of that. She dropped into a rattan chair and closed her eyes, letting the sun massage her face. Her synapses screamed for coffee, but that would only deter sleep, which was the only thing she had planned for the next few hours.

It was only an impression; a phrase she'd skimmed over: *River Girl*. She got up so fast she hit a knee on the table. She limped inside and fired up her Mac, bringing it over to the dining table. The radio transcript was still open in her browser.

She read it all the way through, the implications simmering low in her spine. The silence around the young woman's death was staggering: she was murdered, there was a nylon stocking tied around her neck, her body was found dumped in the mangroves by the river, yet it had not been sensationalised as front-page news. Even by the censorship standards of the time, this seemed heavy-handed. She wondered what else was kept from the good citizens of Brisbane during the war years 'for their own good'.

Wanting to check for herself, Olivia opened the National Library's Trove website to search their digitised newspapers. She needed some dates to search first. The transcript mentioned 1943, but that was all. She grabbed the tin box from the other end of the table and retrieved the letter: it was dated 11 February 1943. The best she could find for anything more specific was Gloria's mention of 'mulling over it for two weeks'. That put the conversation Gloria overheard around 28 January, though the girl must have been killed at least a few days before that. The only other useful element from the radio transcript was that it couldn't have been a Sunday night as the Trocadero would have been closed, as well as Eklund's mention of 'a reasonable amount of moonlight'.

Olivia did an online search for a 1943 calendar that included the cycles of the moon. The full moon had been on 21 January: a Thursday. But what was 'a reasonable amount of moonlight'? The moon would still have been practically full on the Saturday night and by Monday waning gibbous. Monday 25 January it was, then.

She searched *The Courier-Mail* and *The Telegraph* in the week leading up to that date, then each day for the two weeks after. There was a small article on the Monday itself about an 'allied serviceman' who had drowned in the Gardens Reach of the Brisbane River the night before. Some Australian soldiers had seen him giving cigarettes to monkeys earlier in the evening. A boy spotted him removing his shirt before wading through the mud into the water. Olivia remembered reading somewhere that the Botanic Gardens once had a zoo, which explained the monkeys, but thought it safe to conclude the event was unrelated.

It occurred to her that Graham hadn't mentioned *Truth* – the Sunday-only scandal rag of the time – in her letter. Olivia searched the 31 January edition. It reported news of a brawl in a Sydney hotel; the dealings of an Australian soldier 'with middle-east experience' who'd been involved in a whiskey racket; and an inquest into a woman who'd been declared 'insane' after drowning her two babies. There was also a story about a forty-three-year-old woman who was due to stand trial over the death of Laura Margaret Mowat: 'a 27-year-old woman, postal clerk at Brisbane G.P.O., who, in an attempt to shield her reputation, had allegedly submitted to an illegal operation.' If convicted, the forty-three-year-old faced a life sentence with hard labour.

Olivia checked the two weeks after that and, failing to find anything, the edition from the week before. All contained similar articles spotlighting the salacious, the awful and the infuriating. Of the latter was the story of a 'young Springhill mother' whose husband shut her in a room, caught her by the throat and threatened to murder her, then 'submit to his attentions against her will'. She also detailed other 'remarkable allegations' of spousal abuse, including how she came to have two black eyes, but the magistrate chose to believe her soldier husband, AMF Sergeant Clarence Young. Olivia's nostrils flared drawing a splintery breath of injustice for Mrs Mary Young.

Old newspapers were their own breed of rabbit hole. Olivia would have to take Gloria's and Gwendolyn's word for it: there was no mention of the young woman's murder in the press. She could probably access old Queensland police records, though, and unlike Gwendolyn she had the internet to tell her where to start with that.

She wondered, on that note, if Gloria ever got anywhere with chasing up 'V' who worked at the munitions factory. 'V' names for women, Olivia conceded, were common back then: Vera, Vivian, Violet, Virginia, Valerie. *The two Vee-Dees* – where had she heard that? Olivia said it out loud a few times until it came to her: the war brides documentary she'd watched at the State Library last month. The same one, she presumed, the play's director Andrew's grandmother had been involved in. Olivia was sure there was a woman in it who worked in munitions, but whether she was one of the 'Vee-Dees', she couldn't recall. Andrew had only told her during her interview with him for her theatre review that his grandmother married a US submariner; he never mentioned anything about her working in munitions, and Olivia hadn't even thought to ask her name. She hoped there was a DVD copy available somewhere so she didn't have to go back to the State Library and watch it on tedious VHS. Google did her one better: 'queensland war brides documentary' brought up a YouTube link to *When Love Came to Town: Queensland War*

Brides and Their GIs. It had been uploaded to the platform in two parts by Gillian Stretton in 2013.

The video began with some introductory information about World War II; the Americans' entry into the war after Pearl Harbor in December 1941; the steady build-up of American troops in Brisbane from Christmas 1941; General MacArthur moving his headquarters to Brisbane in July 1942; and the ensuing 'war brides' phenomenon that saw an estimated ten to twelve thousand Australian women marry American servicemen, with about seven thousand taking place in Queensland alone.

Olivia scanned forward until she saw 'Valerie Billings' at the bottom of the screen identifying the woman being interviewed. So that was Andrew's grandmother. She backtracked a few seconds and pressed play. The same voice-over introduced Valerie as a former dancer who met Arthur 'Rocko' Billings, a US submariner from Arkansas, at a picture theatre. The interviewer, off camera, asked Valerie how she met her husband.

Well, I remember that night clearly because it was the same night that a girl, an usherette, was shot at the theatre by her American boyfriend. He then shot himself in the head. I think he died in the hospital, but the girl survived. That all happened after we left, but we were very shocked to hear about it in the papers the next day. But, yes, I was at the Lyceum with my girlfriend Vera. She worked at the factory with me. Everyone called us the two Vees. Some wit dubbed us the two Vee-Dees after word got out Vera had the clap and narrowly missed a stint in the lock hospital. You can't imagine it now, but that's what they did – locked girls up for carrying VD. Never the men, mind. Perhaps I shouldn't have said that? I'm sure you don't want to know about that kind of thing.

So that's where the two Vee-Dees came from. Olivia got the impression the interviewer had some difficulty keeping Valerie on track. She prompted Valerie to go on by asking her if she remembered the moment she met Arthur.

Oh yes. Arthur was at the theatre to see a different picture – was it a western? I think it might have been. He was with a friend and they both had dates. The movie must have finished because we were in the foyer and, well, I mustn't have been watching where I was going because I walked smack bang into the back of him. I said something colourful, I'm sure – it was like walking into a slab of concrete. He turned around, but instead of apologising I said, 'What are you, a brick shithouse?' Excuse my French. And you know he didn't get mad, not one bit. He just laughed and said, 'Well, whaddya know, it's shoe girl.' I had no idea what he was talking about, so I'm looking down at my feet trying to work out what was wrong with my shoes. He made some joke then about me being out to get him because when I'd been dancing a few months earlier one of my tap shoes came flying off my foot and went into the audience. It hit him, apparently. Then he asked if he could have my phone number. I remember his date looking very indignant.

Olivia scanned forward again past footage of two other interviewees until it came back to Valerie. She was talking about doing dance classes as a child, her mother dying when she was only five, and then how she was selected to become a ballet girl at seventeen for the Cremorne theatre before the war. She and a few other women left the Cremorne over a pay dispute, which was a mistake in Valerie's words because she 'was very promptly sent by Manpower to work at the munitions factory'. There was the confirmation Valerie worked at the Rocklea Munitions Factory. The interviewer steered Valerie back to Arthur and whether he called Valerie after their encounter at the picture theatre.

*Well, no, funny you should ask, I didn't give him my number. I
was living in a girls' hostel in New Farm, you see – it was run by
the Methodists, or was it the Presbyterians? It could have been both.
But they were very strict about that kind of thing. The hostel was for
country girls who'd come to the city to work mainly, but not all of us
were. I often trod a fine line with the housemistress. Anyway, I told
Arthur I worked at the munitions factory and, if he really wanted
to, he could find me. And that's what he did. The very next day he
was waiting outside the factory gates when I finished. We went to a
milk bar in the city and had ice-cream sodas. Funny the things you
remember, isn't it?*

Olivia paused the video. How many girls' hostels run by
the Methodists and/or Presbyterians could there have been in
New Farm? Google didn't take long to tell her the hostel had
to be Archibald House, which operated as a Presbyterian and
Methodist girls' hostel from the 1930s well into the 1970s. June
had also lived in New Farm, going by the address on that bizarre
POW postcard from her husband. Olivia found the postcard
from among June's letters and looked up the address on Google
Maps. The apartment building no longer existed, or the exact
address, but it would have been about a block and a half away
from Archibald House. Enlarging the map, she could see the
back entrance to Archibald House was at the end of what had to
be June's street, which finished in a dead end.

Olivia went back to the video. Valerie talked about going
rollerskating at the Blue Moon skating rink with Arthur and
to a services dance at City Hall. The footage then cut away to
panned images of City Hall, the US Army band and pictures
of couples jitterbugging and the like. The voice-over informed
the viewer that Sunday-night dances at City Hall commenced
in May 1942 and were very popular, but only started after the

state government and local council were forced into allowing them because there was nothing else for young people to do in Brisbane on Sundays. The footage cut back to Valerie talking about her first dance with Arthur:

Well, that's the funny thing! I didn't dance with him first that night. There was this fellow I used to dance with a bit – Jimmy – oh, he was fantastic, the best actually, and he must have seen me come in. He was short, too, only an inch or so taller than me, but he could move like nobody's business. I remember he had this cleft chin with a round face and dimples. He wasn't particularly handsome, but he was never short of female attention. It was never like that between us, though. But, yes, when I arrived with Arthur, Jimmy was over in a shot and said, 'Sorry, fella, but this one's mine.' So we hit the floor and ... well, I guess Arthur must have realised then he wouldn't be teaching me anything about jitterbugging. He was a good sport, though. That's what I liked about him. He never got riled up about anything.

Olivia fast forwarded through the next fifteen minutes of footage before Valerie appeared again. She was talking about Arthur proposing to her only two weeks after they met. The interviewer asked her about the six-month waiting period the US Navy imposed on its men wishing to marry Australian women and the stipulation that only men of a certain rank – above a petty officer – were allowed to marry.

Oh, I don't remember anything about that. Maybe those rules came in later. I do remember he had to get permission from his commanding officer. But the fact is we didn't end up getting married straightaway anyway. We were supposed to meet at the registry office on George Street and he never turned up! I was devastated, I don't mind telling you! We'd all heard the rumours about girls who'd been led astray or engaged under false pretences. Often to men who already had wives back home in America. I thought I'd fallen for the same trick and felt like a right fool. He sent a note via a messenger boy that his submarine was shipping out two days earlier than planned, but I didn't buy it.

We met up again well over a year later. To be honest, I'd forgotten all about Arthur. My father died not long after he left me standing at the registry office and, well, you know … I had a bit of a rough time of it around then, actually. But Arthur, well, what happened was I ran into one of the girls who'd also left the Cremorne. This must have been, gosh … 1944? Anyway, she told me about a revue show they were putting together with some American entertainers at the Theatre Royal. 'Khaki and Lace' it was called. They needed a few more dancers, so she asked if I was interested. It was a volunteer thing, but I jumped at it. Anyway, during one of the shows, just before the curtain went up again after intermission, the MC came on stage and said there's a man in the audience who'd like to ask one of our dancers something. I was still in the dressing room at this stage, so one of the stagehands came to fetch me and the MC ushered me onto the stage. So I'm standing there, with only one toe shoe done up, and the MC says, 'Have we got the right girl, sailor?' And from somewhere in the auditorium, a man – you couldn't see the audience because of the stage lights – shouts back, 'That's her!' Then he runs down out of the audience and onto the stage, and that's when I realised it was Arthur …

Someone was knocking on the door – in the testy, indignant way favoured by irate neighbours. Olivia stopped the video and got up to answer it.

'Sam?'

His face was like stone.

'Can I come in?'

'Um, yeah, I guess so.'

'I left my wallet here last night.'

'Okay, well, I haven't seen it, sorry. I only got—' Olivia stopped, sensing a DIY hole she didn't want to make any deeper.

Sam brushed past her into the living room. 'Cheryl said she put it on the bookcase.' He moved his head as if following a pinball until he spotted it on a pile of art books, topped by a glossy doorstopper on Australian surrealism with Albert Tucker's *Victory Girls* on the cover. Sam snatched up the wallet and shoved it in his back pocket. When he turned around, Olivia caught such a blaze of hatred from him that she took a step back as if he'd punched her in the solar plexus.

She couldn't help herself: 'What the fuck is going on with you?'

His face, his expression, bloomed with contempt.

'Why don't you tell me? You're the one who ran out last night. Just upped and left. Meet up with your black lover boy, did you?'

Olivia felt instantly sick. She was reminded, in an out-of-body way, of that question, 'When did you stop beating your wife?', which gets trotted out to show the problem of a logical fallacy.

'I … I met up with a friend. A girlfriend, Clio, and stayed at her place.'

'Then why didn't you answer when I called?'

'I … well, I was with someone. Clio.' Self-preservation prevented her from asking how he could possibly know about Tobias. They stared at each other for a minor eternity before Sam pulled his iPhone out and began scrolling for something.

'Care to explain this?'

He thrust the phone so close to her face she had to tilt back to view it. The photo was grainy and poorly lit, but was as clear as it needed to be. She couldn't remember the moment itself; didn't think she'd been that drunk. It was from the night of the play. They were standing at the bar in the Fox Hotel. Tobias was leaning in to tell her something, his hand was on her waist; she was touching him on the arm and throwing her head back with laughter – her hair, thanks to the humidity that night, was an unbridled, woolly bouffant. If the image were better lit it would have made a good stock photo for 'flirting couple'.

'Who took that?'

'A friend.'

'Which friend?'

'Doesn't matter.'

'Yes, it does. That's like, well it's—' She wanted to say it was an invasion of her privacy. It probably wasn't though, legally speaking, as much as it felt like a rib-piercing violation. 'I want to know who took it.'

'Zach did, all right. You were so caught up with Kanye you didn't even know he was there, did you? He and Matt were out having a few beers – you remember Matt from last night – and he was quite surprised to see you there slutting it up on the dance floor.'

'He looks nothing like Kanye. And we were just talking. What's wrong with that?' Zach, Matt, Caitlin: they must all have known about this last night at the apartment.

'Zach saw you walking up the road with him afterwards.'

'Nothing happened! You're making it out to be something it's not. And you were supposed to come with me that night to the play, but you didn't. You had better things to do, remember? Like you always do.' She could hear her voice going up an octave into her shrill register – *You sound like a banshee*, Sam once told her post-fight – but, pumping with high-octane humiliation, she didn't care.

'Oh, so I don't pay you enough attention, that's it? What are you? A preschooler? More like a fucking whore.'

She absorbed his words like a sucker punch, feeling the acid burn of them in her throat. Her ribs glowed hot beneath her skin. If she apologised, backed down, admitted she'd made a mistake, then maybe she could beat their relationship into its former shape. It was her fault for expecting more than he wanted to give. If she called more than twice in one week, expressed a desire to see him more than a few times a fortnight, he would paint her as needy, too demanding, not independent enough. And she'd played along for three years, congratulating herself on how cool she was with it. She'd never once suggested marriage, children, or even moving in together – she didn't even want those things – yet she still expected too much from him. Tobias, maybe, was a lapse in judgement, but she didn't feel sorry for any of it, not even for the moment in the South Bank pool.

The silence was now a presence of its own. The adrenaline that had flooded her lymphatic system only seconds ago was already draining like sump oil, leaving her spent and hollow.

'You're such an arsehole.' She said it more to herself than him, as a summative comment on their entire relationship. If not exactly revelatory, there was clarity to the statement that forced her to see what she'd allowed herself to normalise, and accept. Like when he never turned up the morning she was due to have a termination and she went to the clinic in Greenslopes by herself. She'd forgiven him because, of course, he hadn't actually meant not to come. He intended to be there; he'd just 'had a late one' the night before and had overslept. Cheryl had been the one not to speak to him for weeks after that; Olivia had lasted all of three days, mollified because he had been half-a-dozen-roses sorry.

He continued to glare, his mouth tight with derision. There was naked animosity in the narrowness of his eyes. It surprised her on one level that he cared this much that she'd cheated on him (not that she had).

'And I'm not sorry.'

He closed in and gripped her by the throat with his right hand, marching her backwards until she was up against the wall by the TV. He brought his face in to hers, pinning her against the wall with his other hand flat against her sternum.

'You're not fucking sorry? You make a fucking fool of me and you're not fucking sorry?'

The part of her watching it all – detached, unbelieving, appalled at the bad theatrics – wanted to laugh. Not that she dared. She'd humiliated him; that's what this was all about. Another man had encroached on what he deemed to be his property, and she'd opened the gates, welcoming the interloper, compounding his shame with witnesses.

She grabbed his forearm and tried to wrench him off.

'Let-go-of-me.'

Her voice was compressed and flat. The pressure on her windpipe was desperately uncomfortable – she had to fight against her gag reflex – but she could still breathe. His fingers and thumb dug painfully into the sides of her neck. But by the set of his eyes, she could see he was keeping himself in check. The simmer setting he'd been on for two weeks, not quite boiling over. He'd only been physical in a fight once, slamming her down on a table and smacking her across the face. What had provoked him that time? She couldn't remember. His contrition the next day had deflated her outrage and it became an apparition neither of them mentioned again.

She said it a second time, slowly.

'Let. Go. Of. Me.'

And to her surprise he did. But he wasn't finished: she took in his left fist, a flash of movement in her peripheral vision, and ducked to miss the punch intended for her head. He hit the edge of Cheryl's *Mirrored Psyche* painting instead, which fell off the hook, the canvas catching and tearing on the corner of the TV on its way to the floor.

Cheryl would be apoplectic.

- 10 -

Christmas lights will twinkle after all this year. On the bank of the river, in the Botanic Gardens reach, coloured lights from a 50ft. Christmas tree will give their friendly message from America to Australia ... the American Red Cross Service Club will light the tree for Allied Servicemen ... Army bands will play Christmas music, and in the light of coloured lanterns troops will sing Christmas carols.

—*The Courier-Mail* (17 December 1942)

November 1942

'Edith. *Edith.* You're daydreaming.'

'Sorry, Mrs Lambert.'

'I need you to go to your station. I've put you on roast potatoes with Marjorie.'

'Yes, Mrs Lambert.'

'Edith. Your hair. Put the net over *all* of it, please.'

Edith liked her blue tunic with its Red Cross beneath the left lapel, but the outfit lost its charm when teamed with a hairnet, or at least how Mrs Lambert insisted it be worn. How was she supposed to smile and wish the men a happy Thanksgiving when she could barely make eye contact for the embarrassment?

In the ladies' room, she tried pinning the net so it sat flush with her hairline. It didn't change the fact she looked like a pill.

The lingering heat of early summer had left a sheen of sweat over her face and neck. There was only a damp, grubby hand towel by the basin that she had no intention of using on her face. Searching for a box of tissues, she pulled the blind away from the window and found instead a tin of talc on the sill. It was warm as a cup of tea. She shook it and sprinkled the powder down the length of each arm before rubbing it in, then dabbed some on her face and neck. She liked how it lightened her complexion. Just like Scarlett O'Hara, she thought, pinching her cheeks to add some colour. It dismayed her how easily her skin tanned, even in spring.

Edith returned the tin to its spot on the windowsill. It was still light outside. She peered through the grimy window that overlooked Creek Street with the silly notion that she might see Frank on his way to the PX canteen. He said he might come to the dance tonight if he could wrangle a leave pass, but she expected he would stay with his buddies from the 81st after their lunch at the barracks. She didn't want to go herself and wished now she hadn't volunteered. It wouldn't be so bad if they didn't have to dance with whoever asked, which meant putting up with a lot of left feet, some dubious body odour (they weren't all smothered in cologne) and unwelcome hands on her derrière. At least dancing didn't require a hairnet. *Pretty is as pretty does*, she could hear Mother chime. Her sister had some other posh quote about vanity she'd forgotten.

Edith returned to find Mrs Lambert tapping her wrist, her caterpillar eyebrows so high they looked set to take flight. Edith squeezed in beside Marjorie and another girl who were both poised behind the serving counter with a set of tongs. Neither seemed to give a hoot how silly they looked. The aroma of roast turkey, vegetables and gravy was so heady you could almost see it. Her stomach rumbled like an army truck on a dirt road.

'I'm starving, too,' said Marjorie. 'I hope there's some leftovers.'

'Surely even MacArthur's hoards can't get through two hundred and fifty turkeys in one sitting.'

'I wouldn't count on that, but I'm sure they'll save us some. As long as I can try the pumpkin pie, I'll be happy. Have you seen it? Looks divine.'

The pumpkin pie didn't sound that appetising to Edith – the plum pudding was more appealing – but Frank said it was his favourite dessert. If she was going to become an American, she supposed she'd better get used to their food.

Mrs Lambert opened the dining room doors with the importance she believed the task required. Edith soon fell into a rhythm of issuing two potato halves apiece and forgot how ridiculous she looked.

They were alerted to the commotion at the intersection of Creek and Adelaide streets by the explosive sound of glass breaking. By then dinner was winding down and most of the men had been served. Those who'd finished had either drifted downstairs to the new recreational room to await the start of the dance or had gone elsewhere for entertainment. Some had stayed in the dining room, groaning like contented lions, their ample bellies on display.

Edith returned from a trip to the kitchen to find everyone gathered at the large corner windows. The brownout curtains had been pulled open and the ceiling lights turned off so they could see out. She asked Marjorie what was going on. A skinny, hollow-cheeked sailor with a Brooklyn twang answered for her.

'Some Aussies are trying to bust their way into the PX – a fair mob of them, maybe two hundred or so. They're in some kind of stand-off with our MPs by the looks. I'd put money on it being over cigarettes.'

159

'Typical,' said Edith to Marjorie. 'They're always bullying Americans for cigarettes. Frank and I were walking up Edward Street once and these three drunken Aussie louts stood right in our way and demanded Frank give—'

'I think this is a little more serious than that, Edith.' Marjorie walked off and started stacking the empty serving trays.

Edith would have followed to help take them away, but she was stung by Marjorie's tone. She could have her dinner, though she'd lost her appetite. They were expected to go downstairs to the dance after they'd eaten, but no one else was going anywhere. Even Mrs Lambert had taken up a post near one of the windows.

The thud of rocks and whatever else was being hurled against windows and concrete was escalating, as was the hooting and shouting. She was now glad Frank hadn't promised to come to the dance, even if she'd huffed a bit about it at the time. There was no way of warning him, but surely the police or more MPs were on their way and things would be under control soon. She wanted to see for herself what was going on.

The lock on the bathroom window was thick with dust and felt rusted into place. She broke a nail trying to coax it open. It eventually gave and she thrust the window up as high as it would go. Harsh noises tumbled in like the low thunder of an approaching storm, interjected with broad, nasal howls of: 'Come out and fight, you bastards!' In the dwindling twilight, Edith could see clearly enough a crowd intent on storming the PX canteen on the ground floor of the primary building. She couldn't have said how many men there were; it could have been five hundred or a thousand, perhaps more, all shouting and pelting the building with rocks, sticks and bottles. Some were smashing windows with uprooted parking signs. There was no traffic; even the trams had stopped running along the street.

The focal point of the riot was on the Creek Street entrance to the canteen. It was cordoned off all the way around to Adelaide Street by a small squad of MPs who were holding the mob at bay with batons. She saw the MP closest to the corner take half a brick to his face. He buckled like a ragdoll and was dragged into the crowd.

Edith was stunned. She'd never seen such unflinching brutality. She couldn't watch any more. With her back to the wall, she inched her way down until she was sitting on the floor tiles. Her hands were shaking.

She was eleven when her father had ignited in a way that made her guts feel like they were going to slither right out of her. He'd been fixing the car when he erupted without warning and threw his tools at the brick fence. He then kicked one of the tyres over and over again while shouting words that would have earned her a mouthful of soap if she'd so much as thought them. When he saw her sitting on the front steps he had yelled at her to go inside. That evening, he drew her into his arms and kissed her on the forehead, but said nothing about it.

The men were so angry. And, in some abstract way, she knew she was part of the reason. She thought she understood something about how the world worked then, or how men made it work, and perhaps why wars happened at all. It was more confronting than if they'd all been standing out there naked.

'Edith. Are you in here?' The hinges creaked as Marjorie opened the door. 'There you are. We've been looking for you. Are you all right? You're as white as a sheet.'

'Am I?'

'Why did you run off like that?'

Edith twisted the hem of her dress at her knees and shook her head. 'Have you seen what's going on out there?' she asked.

'Yes, I know. It's pretty scary. That's why I came to find you.

The American provost station rang. Some soldiers are coming to escort women from the area. They're not sure when they'll get here though, so we need—'

She was cut off by the sound of three gunshots. Edith's heart set off like a greyhound. She sprung up to look out the window, while Marjorie ran the length of the stalls to huddle in beside her. It was darker now and the scene outside was too chaotic to get any idea of how many had been injured or even killed. The centre of the action had moved around to the Adelaide Street entrance. From amid the fray one man scrambled to his feet; they saw a flash of his rifle as he brought the butt down on another man's head. The man with the shotgun then sprinted towards the entrance of the PX and was pulled inside. Another MP standing guard by the door was yanked away by the mob and subjected to a barrage of fists and boots. Edith looked away.

'Holy Mary, Mother of God,' said Marjorie. 'The world's gone mad. Do you suppose that's what it's like on a real battlefield?'

'They're animals,' replied Edith with a viciousness that surprised her. Up until then, she'd felt sorry for the Aussies with their scruffy uniforms and miserly pay cheques and their awkwardness around women. But right now she hated them. She was more determined than ever that Frank should ask her to marry him so she'd never have to marry one of them.

'Something's come over them, I'll say that much. But don't be too hard on them. They've been in some of the fiercest fighting of the war. And I'm not saying those MPs deserve to be hurt like that, but they don't do themselves any favours the way they lord about the place giving orders and throwing their weight around. And one of them did just fire off a shotgun.' Marjorie placed a hand on Edith's shoulder. 'We should probably head back to the dining room,' she said, though she made no effort to leave.

They stayed to watch the ambulances wade through the dark swamp of olive drab. The men moved like carp around them. There was a strange lull as the medics loaded up the wounded and injured from both sides. As they left, the waning, fat-bellied moon appeared above the silhouette of the Adelaide Street skyline. The crowd did not disperse, but instead drew more angry men into its ranks like fresh wood nourishing a bonfire. The humid night, heavy with dust and noise, felt peppered with gunpowder.

'Edith, I think we should go now. I just hope we haven't missed our chance to get out of here.'

'Yes, all right.'

'We'd better close the window and pull down the blind.'

Edith gave the window a good yank, but it wouldn't budge. It would be easier if she could press down on it. She asked Marjorie to pass over the chair by the door. As she went to step up on the seat, her elbow swung out and knocked the talcum powder out the window. The lid fell off on its way down. The tin landed on the sheet-metal awning one floor below with a resounding bang. A diaphanous cloud of white powder exploded into the strained night. Their initial shock and disbelief – mirrored in each other's wide-eyed, hand-over-mouth expressions – quickly turned into rib-pinching peals of laughter.

~

December 1942

Edith moved the heavy curtain aside and looked out at the dusk. It had been raining all week. The street was still and soundless. A single wreath of poinsettias on the neighbour's front door across the road was the only sign of Christmas cheer.

'That's not going to make him get here any sooner,' her father said.

Besides Edith, Hugh had been the most susceptible member of the Morton family to Frank's guileless Midwestern charm, due in no small part to the steady supply of cigarettes Frank provided him with. Frank's promise to bring a leg of ham for Christmas lunch, to which both he and his friend Corporal Danny Miller were invited, had also seen him make headway with Edith's mother. Even so, Clara Morton had taken the precaution of preparing a mock goose from a leg of mutton stuffed with breadcrumbs, onions, minced ham and kidney.

It didn't feel much like Christmas to Edith. There'd been no advertisements in the papers – not so much as a picture of the jolly bearded man in his red suit – and no decorations in the shops. Even their tree this year was more a totem to the family's fervour for austerity than the festive season. Following Prime Minister Curtin's edict to go about Christmas 'soberly, confidently and realistically', Edith and her mother had done their best with some mangy tinsel and a depleted box of glass baubles. In an inspired spurt of 'making do', Edith had cut out a string of angels from newspaper and added a few pinecones to the tree. She now regarded the angels with disdain and embarrassment and had a mind to remove them before Frank arrived.

She tried to consider reasonably why Frank might be late, because an unreasonable answer, such as having forgotten his invitation to Christmas Eve supper, was not something she could tolerate. Punctuality, to be sure, was not his strong point, but he'd only ever cancelled on her twice.

The first time he'd come down with a cold and said he didn't want to pass it on to her. The second had been the night after the 'Battle of the Canteens': a name that caught on like a brush fire in the following weeks and guaranteed its passage into local folklore. They had arranged to meet at the Lyceum Theatre on George Street that Friday night. *Wuthering Heights* had been playing and it was Edith's second favourite film after *Gone with the Wind*. She hoped it might stir in Frank romantic sentiments of the resolute rather than the 'here and now' kind he seemed inclined to. At her mother's insistence, though she didn't have to insist too hard, Edith had stayed at home the day after the riot to be doted on with cups of tea and many utterances of 'my poor darling'. Edith, deprived of her workmates to give her firsthand account to, imagined how she would tell Frank all about it that evening instead. She expected nothing less from him than abject concern for her wellbeing.

But when Frank telephoned to say his commanding officer had strongly urged the men under his command to stay in their barracks that night for their own safety, Edith had no choice but to agree with him. It was the sensible thing to do, she said, and she'd never forgive herself if something happened to him. It was a prescient piece of advice. Rumours started surfacing the next day of marauding Australian soldiers hunting down and beating to a pulp any Yank they found in the city that night, especially if they were in the company of a woman. Edith had no trouble believing any of it.

On hearing the knock, she bolted to the front door.

'It's only me,' June said. 'Sorry to disappoint. Here, can you take these?' She offloaded a box of meringues and a paper bag of something else, then shifted the stack of presents (quite obviously everyone would be receiving a book) in her arms.

Edith looked in the paper bag. '*Cherries?* How the blazes did you manage to get those?'

'A customer gave them to me as a Christmas gift.'

'An American?'

'Of course.'

'That sounds like my June bug,' Hugh called from the sofa. 'Come in here and give your old man a kiss.'

June entered the living room and greeted her father in the manner requested before arranging the pile of wrapped books beneath the tree.

'I see we have angels heralding news of the frontline this year,' she said while adjusting the drape of them around the tree. 'Not to mention product endorsements for personal hygiene.'

'Well, I like them,' said Edith. 'It wasn't easy to make things Christmassy this year, you know.'

'And I like them too, Edith. They're lovely. I'd kill for a drink right now,' she said. 'I swear every man, woman and dog left their Christmas shopping to the last minute. I haven't stopped from the second we opened until the moment we hustled the last customers out the door at closing time. Even Maclean earned his keep today. I'm absolutely beat. Anyway ...' She took a deep breath and looked around the room with her hands on her hips. 'I better go say hello to Mum. She's in the kitchen, I presume?'

June returned shortly with an empty bowl. She tipped the cherries into it, then popped one in her mouth. She looked as effortlessly elegant as always in a simple maroon frock with a white collar. She even had on a pair of nylons. If Edith were to ask where she got them, she expected the answer would be the same as the one she got for the cherries. June had gone over to inspect the walnut liquor cabinet, which was suffering since the restrictions on luxury items had come into force.

'There's half a bottle of brandy in here. Shall we?' she said.

'No argument here,' said Hugh. 'Now tell me, June bug, which of these is the better headline? *Wife Found In Truck With Yank* or *Wife Gallivanted As Husband Fought*?'

'I think it depends on which story has more legs. So to speak.'

'Really, I wish your father would stop reading that horrid scandal rag,' said Edith's mother, who had followed June into the room with a platter of devilled eggs. 'Is a little decorum on

Christmas Eve too much to ask? But if you want my opinion, the gallivanting wife is more intriguing than the wife in the truck. Where's the mystery in that? What's the gallivanting wife been up to? That's what we want to know, isn't it, June?'

'I think Mum's right. What exactly has the gallivanting wife been up to?' June poured a small glass of brandy and passed it to her father. 'Mum?'

'Oh, why not? It's Christmas, after all,' said Clara.

'Edith?'

'No, thank you.'

'Well?' Clara urged her husband.

'Well what?'

'You know well what. The gallivanting wife. Are you going to tell us what she did or not?'

'I thought you wanted some decorum?'

'I've changed my mind. Edith, darling, would you mind turning the wireless down?'

'Can we finish listening to this song first?'

'Just turn it down a smidge, then.'

Edith sighed. She hadn't grown the least bit tired of Bing Crosby crooning about his dreams of a white Christmas, despite it being played almost constantly in the Amcross rec room. Even without ever having seen snow, she had firm ideas about how glorious and magical a white Christmas would be.

'Shall I read, then?' Hugh waited until everyone consented, including Edith, who was now perched on the edge of an armchair picking at a piece of fruitcake like a myna bird and humming along to the refrain of 'may all your Christmases be white'. Hugh looked over the rim of his glasses at his audience before shaking out the paper and clearing his throat.

'*Brisbane's divorce court walls have heard some sorry stories, but surely none so shocking as those told by the procession of khaki-clad husbands in and out of the witness boxes, who relate tales of the infidelity of the wives they left at home, while they were fighting for them against the enemy at our very gates.'*

'Cut to the chase, dear.'

'We'd get there a lot sooner if you didn't interrupt.' Hugh gave his wife a look to ask if she was done. '*One of the most shocking of these stories was unfolded to the Chief Justice, Sir William Webb*' – he paused so they should all appreciate the gravity of the man's title – '*on Tuesday last, when it was proved that young Elizabeth Tones of Upper Edward Street, Brisbane, wife of AIF Sergeant Harold John Tones, newly returned from the hell of New Guinea, had been bestowing her love freely on a number of American soldiers and sailors, and was, it was alleged, pregnant to one of them.* Shall I read on?'

They all nodded, though Clara expressed a hesitant concern for Edith's ears.

'How are your ears, Edith? Are they troubling you?' Hugh raised an eyebrow at Clara. 'I expect it's not her ears that are bothering her. What time did your young man say he'd be here?'

'What?'

'Pardon, you mean,' said Clara.

'What time was Frank supposed to arrive?'

'Six o'clock,' Edith replied with a notable absence of personal injury.

'It's quarter to seven,' said June.

'Mum, do we still have that box of fake snow?' Edith asked.

'I have no idea. Wasn't it in the cupboard with the other decorations? We probably used it all up years ago.'

'I'm going to have a look.'

It wasn't in the box with the tinsel. Edith had an impression that she'd seen it under the house ages ago, perhaps among her father's tools, but was far from sure. It was not something she would have made a point of remembering.

She took her father's flashlight down the back stairs to have a look. Edith didn't like going underneath the house even in daylight. Everything was covered in thick gritty dust and there had been evidence in the past to suggest a number of mice made their home there. There was a definite smell of animal decay on top of the general mustiness as she shone the torch around.

When she felt confident enough of not encountering any type of rodent, she stepped inside and pointed the beam of light towards the shelves containing her father's tools. The book-sized box she was looking for was on the second shelf behind a wooden carton of rusted nails and screws, almost where she had pictured it. Edith picked her way, careful to guard her head against the low beams, between the lawn mower, a rusty fan and bicycle frame, a stack of suitcases, a dressmaker's dummy and some other general household items that had been demoted to the dark space beneath the floorboards. She could happily say the journey had been worth it when she inspected the box and found it more than half full.

Upstairs, Edith pronounced her find with glee. 'Look, I found it! *Asbestos Pure White Fire Proof Snow. Looks like real snow. Cleanest—Whitest—Best.*'

She held up the box, which depicted a bucolic snow-covered landscape of pine trees and a red cottage with a smoking chimney. She then tipped a pile of the fine white fibres into her palm and began sprinkling with largesse the branches of the Christmas tree.

'I'm making a white Christmas for Frank,' she explained. The overall effect when she was done suggested the snow had blown in as a heavy dumping rather than a light fall. 'So, what do think? Do you think he'll like it?'

'More to the point, are you going to like cleaning it up after Christmas?' said Hugh.

'Does it even snow in Kansas in December? Just because it's winter over there doesn't mean it necessarily snows,' said June.

'Of course it does.'

'Some places in America are warmer than others, you realise.'

'I'm sure he'll love it, darling. And I think the tree looks absolutely lovely. Where's Frank supposed to be taking you tonight?' Clara asked as though the answer was sure to be suspect.

'I told you. The Botanic Gardens. The American Red Cross has put up a big Christmas tree decorated with coloured lights. There's an army band playing carols.'

'You've got to wonder how they got around the brownout restrictions to do that,' said Clara. 'But I suppose the Americans can do anything they want in this town. You won't be home too late, will you?'

'At this rate I won't be going at all.' Now she'd finished whitening the tree, Edith's despondency over Frank's tardiness returned.

'I'm sure he'll be here soon enough. Why don't we finish hearing about Mrs Tones while we're waiting?' suggested Clara.

'Good idea,' said Hugh. 'Now where were we? Ah, here we go. *Nor did she draw the colour-line, for a number of Filipinos were included among her lovers! Mrs Tones tried to explain her physical condition in court by saying that when her husband returned on special leave – as a result of something he'd heard – he had spent the night of August 18 with her. Despite a particularly able defence by her counsel, however, his Honour found that Mrs Tones had committed adultery with men unknown about May 1942, during June, and on September 8.*'

Edith appreciated her mother's efforts, and usually she would have enjoyed her parents' banter. It was rare for her mother to be so light-hearted these days and, she supposed, indelicate, if that was the right word. Infidelity was not a trivial topic in the main. She suspected her mother had been helping herself to the sherry decanter while she'd been cooking, which was most of the afternoon. Her sister, on the other hand, seemed preoccupied. She visited much less than she used to, Edith had noticed.

'Is that it?' Clara asked.

'No, there's another two columns' worth. Perhaps I could just pick out the most salacious parts for you, Mrs Morton?' Hugh put the paper aside to help himself to a devilled egg.

'May I?' said June. She leaned across and took the paper without waiting for a response.

Edith watched her sister read the rest of the article. June regularly declared her contempt for *Truth* and those involved in its publication. She wasn't above chastising her father for buying it every now and again, either. Edith wished she were game enough to tease June for her sudden interest in it now.

'It says here that Mrs Tones said if she made the slightest attempt to defend her divorce, her husband told her he would cut her throat.'

'Well, it sounds like he had good cause if the rest is true,' said Clara.

June put her drink down and folded the paper over. 'I have something to tell you all before Aunt Judith and Uncle Jim arrive.' She looked at Edith before adding, 'And Frank.'

'Have you heard something about Peter?'

'No, it's nothing like that. I'm hoping, in fact, you might even think it's good news.' As no one offered any comment she went on. 'Yesterday, on my lunch break, I went to the new WAAAF recruiting centre on Creek Street.'

'You're not thinking of joining up, are you?' said Clara.

'I already did.'

'But what about your reputation? Girls in the services are not exactly known for their high morals. Aren't you worried you'll be tainted with the same brush?' said Clara.

'No, I'm not worried. And what a load of poppycock. I'm frankly surprised you would even buy into those ridiculous rumours, Mum.'

'It's mostly AWAS girls who have a reputation for getting themselves into trouble.' There was a pause in the conversation while everyone's eyes landed on Edith. 'Well, it's true,' she added.

'I'm not saying I buy into them myself, but it's what people believe. Isn't that right, Hugh?'

'Anyone who thinks our girls in uniform aren't worthy of respect for the job they're doing serving their country are no friends of ours, is what I think. And June's more than old enough to make up her own mind about what she wants to do.'

'Yes, thank you for the reminder of my age, Dad.' June smiled at him.

'But I don't understand why, dear,' said Clara. 'You have a perfectly good job and there's no shortage of volunteer work after-hours, if that's what you're looking to do.'

'Because I want to get away from Brisbane and I'd like to do something different; something, hopefully, a little more challenging than selling books. I have no interest in packing parcels for the troops or making camouflage nets or sewing buttons on uniforms because, God forbid, men should learn how to operate a needle and thread.' June looked at Edith. 'Not that I'm saying that's not valid war work, it's just not for me.'

'We do a lot more than that, just so you know.'

'Of course you do, dear. And it's not every volunteer who ends up putting themselves in mortal danger for the cause either,' said Clara, going in for a second piece of fruitcake.

'Mortal danger? That's an exaggeration even by your standards, Clara,' said Hugh.

Without it being said it was assumed that when her aunt and uncle arrived, Edith's account of what happened outside the American PX on Thanksgiving night would command the conversational stage. Clara Morton could always take over if Edith grew tired of telling it. Edith had enjoyed a level of celebrity equal to a local vaudeville star when she returned to work at the Base Section 3 mailroom the following Monday. One of the girls, Lola, offered that she'd heard that American soldiers had opened fire on the Australians with tommy guns and at least ten had been shot dead and their bodies laid out in front of the General Post Office. Edith told her flatly that was ridiculous and not at all what had happened – disappointingly for some, what she witnessed more or less confirmed the article in the next day's paper, which reported one man had been fatally shot and eight others injured. Edith got the distinct impression that Lola's version was the preferred one, which was strange since most of the girls in the mailroom were enthusiastic daters of their employers.

June's decision to join the WAAAF was spared further scrutiny by a knock at the door. She went to answer it. Edith held out hope that it was Frank for as long as she could, but knew it was far more likely to be her aunt and uncle. They were coming down from their farm in Eumundi to stay until Boxing Day. The surprise none of them expected was the addition of their son Davey, who was home on Christmas leave from the Buna-Gona campaign. With no brother – Clara had two miscarriages and a stillbirth, a baby boy, between June and Edith – their cousin had slotted into the role instead. In her delight at his arrival, Edith forgot for at least ten minutes that Frank had not turned up.

When Frank still hadn't arrived by eight o'clock, his absence warranted spirited speculation and a kitty jar for everyone's two bob's worth. Even Clara could not conceive of Frank being deliberately rude and standing up her daughter, especially when he and his friend had been invited to Christmas lunch the next day. She admitted to her sister Judith, begrudgingly, that his manners were close to, if not, impeccable. He always offered to dry the dishes when he came to dinner. No, Frank would either show up or telephone at some point to explain himself. If something had happened – yes, he could have been in an accident of one kind or another, but let's not get carried away – then they would find out soon enough and there was no point worrying until they knew anything for certain.

For Edith's own good, it was decided that Davey should take her to see the fabled Christmas-tree lights at the Botanic Gardens – he had a hankering to see them himself – and if Frank called or magically appeared in the meantime they'd tell him where she was.

June left at the same time. Davey had suggested she should come along too, but she was exhausted, she said, and wanted an early night. She'd see them all around midmorning tomorrow. They took the same crowded southbound tram together, Edith and Davey changing at St Pauls Terrace for the city while June continued on to New Farm. Edith turned to wave as the tram trundled and clanged away, but June was busy retouching her lipstick.

They alighted at the intersection of Queen and Edward streets. 'MacArthur's headquarters are in there,' said Edith, pointing to the AMP building on the corner. It was Davey's first real visit to Brisbane since he'd shipped off to Syria the year before. Edith felt it was her duty to update him on the city's developments since then. She nudged him with her elbow.

'And those two' – she inclined her head sideways towards two girls standing on the opposite corner – 'are "pick-ups".' Edith said this with more knowing than she possessed.

Davey looked over in their direction. There wasn't much to tell about them without street lights. The moon, full only two nights ago and partially clouded, lit the street and its inhabitants like a black-and-white film.

'Well, they weren't wrong about the bloody Yanks being everywhere. It'd be easier to pick them off than the Japs, that's for sure,' he said as a trio of them passed in the opposite direction.

'You're not supposed to pick them off, that's why.'

'I'm only joking, kiddo. I got nothing against them, except maybe this fella of yours from Kansas. What if he takes you back there with him?'

'He hasn't asked me to marry him, if that's what you're suggesting.'

'But is that what you want?'

'I do, yes. And I know what you're going to say, so don't bother.'

Davey didn't respond straightaway.

'I'm just gonna say I'd miss you, that's all,' he eventually offered. 'Your parents would, too. And June.'

'June says I'm living in a fantasy world. That it won't be anything like what I imagine. Do you think that's true?'

'I really couldn't say about that. How did you meet him, anyway?'

'Well, on a street corner, actually. I was in the city to go shopping. It wasn't like I was there as a pick-up.'

'Right-oh.'

'Please don't tell Mother. I told her someone introduced us at a dance.'

'Your secret's safe, kiddo.' Davey patted the left side of his chest.

Edith slipped her arm around his and put her head against his sleeve. The coarse fabric itched her face, but she didn't mind.

She was proud, she realised, to be walking down the street with an Aussie. She thought she was used to the disapproving stares and rude comments when she was out with Frank – sometimes she even enjoyed her own defiance – but it was nice, for once, to be free of all that.

'What's it like, Davey? War, I mean.'

Edith felt him stiffen.

'I don't know how to answer that, Edie. It's not something I rightly want to talk about.' He paused before adding, 'Not anything you'd easily want to imagine.'

'No, I suppose not. I'm just trying to understand it, that's all.'

'Well, being there makes you understand it even less.'

At the end of Edward Street they took the entrance to the Botanic Gardens at the bottom of Alice Street and followed the path along the riverbank to the strains of 'Jingle Bells' down to the reach. It wasn't long before the coloured lanterns and the fifty-foot bunya tree strung with hundreds of coloured lights came into view. Edith sighed; it really was beautiful. She tried not to dwell on the fact she'd imagined sharing the moment with Frank. Groups of people – some families, but mostly servicemen and couples – sat scattered around the grassed area near the band.

'Let's see if we can find a spot by the tree,' said Edith.

They went around the back of the crowd, huddled into little islands of candlelight, to the other side. Edith was looking for a patch of grass to lay their blanket down when she heard someone calling her name.

'Edith. Over here!' It took Edith several moments to locate the owner of the voice. Marjorie was waving at her from about two dozen feet away. She was sitting with another girl, Doreen, who also volunteered at the American Red Cross. 'Come and sit with us. There's plenty of room.'

They wended their way through the maze of legs and blankets and Edith introduced Marjorie and Doreen to Davey – 'My cousin,' she said to freeze any speculation. 'He's back from the Buna-Gona campaign, but just for a couple of weeks,' she added with pride as she sat down next to Marjorie.

'Nice to meet you both,' Davey greeted. His eyes fell immediately to his feet when the women – and it seemed to Edith, Marjorie in particular – returned the sentiment. He stood there as a monument to awkwardness until Edith urged him to sit beside her.

'What's Frank up to tonight?' asked Marjorie.

'I'm not entirely sure.' Edith glanced at Davey. 'He's joining us for Christmas lunch tomorrow.'

'So, even without Frank, you still manage to bring a good-looking bloke along with you.' Marjorie nudged Edith. 'And he's dinky-di to boot.'

Edith could sense Davey blushing. He wasn't used to being teased by women, with the exception of her and June. The girls joined in the singing as the band eased in to 'Silent Night'. Davey, Edith noticed, wasn't singing, but he seemed content. She hugged his arm and he turned his head to give her a reassuring smile.

Edith spotted Frank a quarter of an hour later, searching the sea of candlelit faces as the first swell of 'O, come, let us adore him' began to rise. Even with his face in shadow, Edith knew it was him. She hurried down as fast as she could without bowling into or tripping over someone. He waved when he heard her call his name. She should have been angry with him, but she could only think that he'd come to find her and that's all that mattered. To show she'd forgiven him, she would fall into his arms and let him kiss her in front of everyone. It would be the first truly cinematic moment of her life.

His face, when she saw it clearly, stopped her short, the shock caught in her throat like a fishbone. His left eye was completely closed over – the lids like bloated lips, the socket darkly purple. A piece of gauze was stuck over his swollen cheekbone. His nose was bandaged and skewed in such a way to hint at grotesque and permanent disfigurement. Green, blue and red light from the tree cast his features into ghoulish relief. The question was writ large in her horrified expression, but she asked it anyway.

'What happened?'

He kicked at the grass before answering. 'I ... we ... got into a fight, is what happened.' His voice was blunt and muffled as though he had a cold. He winced as he spoke.

'Let's go down here,' she said.

Edith could sense the interest of those sitting close by. Frank walked behind her down the slope of the riverbank where they couldn't be observed. The white glower of the moon had clouded over and their reflection was swallowed whole by the silky blackness of the river. His being there meant he was okay, Edith concluded, before she stopped walking – he wasn't in a hospital and he didn't have any broken bones. She felt some instinct to squawk like a mother hen over his injuries, but was far more consumed by the need to ask more questions.

'What do you mean a fight? But where were you? Are you saying some Aussies did this to you?'

'Not really, honey, no. I mean, there was an Aussie who got involved – he's the one who gave me this black eye – but he wasn't the main cause of what happened.'

'What on earth do you mean?'

'Well, me and Danny and a couple of other fellas from the squadron were having a beer at this hotel tonight and this coloured man got uppity at something Danny said. Danny's from Alabama, you see, and they got pretty set ideas about Negroes down there. So then Danny said something else that got him so

178

riled up he went straight at Danny with his fists and that's how it got started. I tried to pull him off Danny and all hell broke loose. His two friends joined in – another coloured man and the Aussie they were drinking with. By the time the MPs came along we were all pretty roughed up. It's just lucky that nigger didn't have a knife. We done him in pretty good with a broken jaw so he won't be giving sass to anyone for a while.'

Edith jerked her head towards him. That word, said out loud, even in the offhand way Frank had used it, curdled in her stomach. For Frank's sake, she was willing to doubt her own conviction that it was not a word used in polite society. It puzzled her why he would have been at a bar where there were coloured troops in the first place. She'd hardly have even known there were Negro servicemen in Brisbane at all if she hadn't seen them around the Base Section HQ at Somerville House.

'What hotel were you at?'

'That one over the other side of the river. The Victoria Palace, you know the one.'

She nodded, her chin stiff and unyielding.

'I guess you're wondering what we were doing there.'

'You had an invitation to supper tonight.'

'And I was planning on coming. But Danny asked me to join him, and I told him I couldn't at first, but he said surely I had time for just one beer ...'

Edith believed him, that wasn't the problem. She believed he hadn't meant to be late. Frank's problem was that he was always well intentioned – to everybody, not just her. She felt wilted, without being able to identify why precisely.

She turned her back on him and started up the bank towards the tree. Its lights glowed as pretty and bright as before, but for Edith they'd lost their lustre, whatever it was about them that made you feel like a child again.

The band was playing 'White Christmas', their final song of the evening and, by popular request, its second outing. Some people were already heading off to get ahead of the queues for the trams. Edith was hesitant to go back to the others on the bank; they would expect an explanation. She could see Marjorie had moved closer to Davey and they were talking. There was no hurry to join them. She sat down at the top of the riverbank.

Frank had disappointed her, but not in the way she'd expected. He was no different to the men she'd seen outside the Red Cross building that night. She had a hard time accepting her own conclusion, though the truth of it was now obvious.

He came up and joined her on the grass, picking up a stick to fiddle with.

'Edith, honey. I'm real sorry about what happened. I shouldn't have gone with Danny – I know that now. And by the time we got stitched up at the hospital and gave our statements at the provost station it was after eight o'clock. So I don't blame you for being mad at me. Not one bit.'

'I'm not mad, I'm just—' A puff of air shot through her nose. She shook her head; she didn't have words to neatly sum up what she was feeling.

'I know this isn't the best time to be saying this, but when I saw you tonight, when you smiled at me and called out my name, well, I just knew then that I wanted to ask you to marry me.'

'Oh, Frank.' Edith sighed and got to her feet. 'We can talk about that tomorrow.' She wanted to cry. Everything was so utterly wrong. She noticed that Marjorie was waving at her.

They headed back, Frank stuffily humming the final bars of the song.

Beauty, comfort and dignity – the triple note struck by the Vestibule – sets the key for the whole hotel. Fluted columns of gold-veined marble support the lofty ceiling. The walls are panelled in bleached maple, and the reception desks have a rhythmic line which is continued in curved seats upholstered in terracotta hide. From the threshold onwards, thoughtful service surrounds you.

—Lennon's of Brisbane Brochure, 1941

Olivia had never been inside Brisbane's Next Hotel. They were to meet in Lennons Restaurant & Bar on the first floor. The name, so far as Olivia could tell, was the only trace of the hotel it had replaced at the top of the Queen Street Mall, which in turn had supplanted the original on George Street. Time, along with the Bjelke-Petersen government: the great demolisher of landmark hotels and ballrooms. Olivia stood outside the high glass frontage, delaying the moment of no return: the one in which she stepped inside and onto the escalator. For surely he was waiting up there – she was already ten minutes late – and would see her as she emerged, like the Lady of the Lake, breaking the surface of the foyer. Passers-by rippled in the glass. Her own reflection was dim and flat, unreadable even to herself. With the sensation of having swallowed stones, she plunged in, the glass doors sealing shut behind her.

She saw him first, at a table by the window. Even as a silhouette against a canvas of harsh, white light, she recognised her father, Trevor, immediately. He'd aged, yes, but looked good – too good, by Olivia's reckoning. He should have gone to seed. Instead he was trim and remarkably well-dressed in smart grey trousers and a teal blue shirt, the top button undone. He was clean-shaven, his salt-and-pepper hair short and tidy, no sign of thinning on top. His skin was still a burnished olive that a vainer man might have tried to emulate with a spray bottle. There was a gold chain around his neck and a gold band on his wedding finger.

'Livvy. You're here. I was startin' to think you'd changed your mind.'

The sound of her name – his name for her – felt like the burr of velvet rubbed the wrong way.

'Yes, I'm here,' she said.

He stood up, pausing a fraction too long before pecking her on the cheek. 'I'm real glad you came. Sit down, sit down.' He indicated to the chair opposite. 'You wanna drink?' He waved the waitress over with an assuredness of his right to be in a restaurant that charged in the double digits for a glass of sav blanc.

Olivia scanned the wine list for the cheapest one. She doubted, even if she ever did get a job with a regular, robust income, she'd be cured of this particular poverty reflex.

'Lunch is on me, Livvy. Order what you like.'

'You don't have to—'

'I got an expense account, don't worry.'

She still ordered the least expensive white; she liked a crisp pinot gris, anyway. Her father's eyes, she noticed, did not linger on the waitress as she walked away. Olivia was looking for evidence her father was a womaniser. It was her mother who had cultivated the impression, though not without cause. The straw that busted the camel's back, as her mother put it, was when she found him *in flagrante delicto* with her cousin at her uncle's wake. Grief makes people do crazy things, had been the cousin's excuse. Whatever her father's excuse had been, Olivia's mother didn't buy it.

'You're married,' Olivia said, trying to keep her tone natural. She simply didn't have the stomach for the small talk he probably thought necessary to grease their way into things.

He cleared his throat. 'Yes. I was going to tell you, obviously.'

The details landed like clumps of pelted sand: twelve years, two children, ten and seven, a boy and a girl, Charlie and Evie. They lived in a beachside town on Sydney's outer reaches. Each gritty particular of his new life accumulated like teaspoons of salt in a glass of water, the brine dripping down her throat. His wife's name was Felicity. The expense account was care of his position as the NSW branch manager for a company that sold solar technology to agricultural industries. Business was healthy. They took the kids to Disneyland last year. He did not fill her in on the years that lay, like a wasteland to Olivia's mind, between his old life and the one he now led with job security and married respectability. Perhaps that would come later, perhaps with an apology. On her mother's behalf, mostly, she felt a surge of anger; the sort she'd denied herself for years.

The waitress came to take their orders. Olivia requested the ocean trout with fennel and leek.

'So,' said her father when the waitress left, 'your mother, what did ... Did she tell you why ...'

'She said you'd been in touch with a half-sister you didn't know you had.'

'That's right. Julie her name is. I've got a half-brother Richard, as well, but I haven't met him yet. It was real strange, I don't mind saying.'

'Your birth mother then – she married and had more children?'

'That's right. She's dead now, though. Her name was Noelene. Julie had no idea I existed until a year or so ago. When she found out she went about tracking me down.'

He paused, as if waiting for Olivia to prompt him, but the question was implicit and she didn't feel it was up to her to ask it.

'So, yeah, meeting my sister, it got me thinking. She asked about my life and everything, and I told her about you, and my other two, of course. She was interested to know more about you and, and I … I couldn't tell her much. It was Julie who sort of suggested I get in touch with you and … yeah.'

'So this' – Olivia waved her arm between them – 'was her idea?'

'That's not what I meant, Livvy. She encouraged me to contact you, that's all. But I wanted to, anyway. For a long while, actually.'

She muffled an impulse to tell him not to call her that, aware at the same time that she liked his assumption of their old familiarity.

'Your birth mother, that must have been … What did you discover about her?'

'Yeah, well, that was interesting. Julie found out about me when she was going through her mother's papers. She came across some medical records. They showed she gave birth to a baby boy, me, when she was sixteen. It was stamped BFA. Know what that stands for?'

'No.'

'*Baby For Adoption*. Julie showed it to me. She reckons for certain her mother was forced into it.'

'But she never told anyone? Not even her other two children?'

'Nope.'

'How old was she when she died?'

'Seventy-two, I think. Heart attack. Right out of the blue, apparently. Livvy …' He leaned in and crossed his arms on the table. His bid for eye contact had the studied sincerity of a car dealer. 'I'm gonna be honest with you. Finding out about my mother and what happened to her, it got me thinking about how stuff like that affects people. You know what I mean? And I've thought of how my leaving all those years ago might've affected you. At the time I thought I was doing the right thing.' He turned his head towards the window and squinted against the harsh light. 'The thing that I'm trying to say is I've wanted to get in touch with you for a long while now. And I had this idea that, as a way of us getting to know each other again, you could help me find out more about ... Maybe find out who my father was.'

So there it was. The speech he'd prepared earlier. She took a slow sip of wine.

'That's a strange thing to be asking of me. Didn't Julie apply for your adoption papers?'

'She did. That's how she found me. Guess what my mother named me?'

'I have no idea.'

'William. Can you imagine me as a William?'

'You'd probably get called Bill.'

'Don't think I'm much of a Bill, either. But anyways, I thought seeing as you're an expert at this kind of thing, it might appeal to you to help me learn some more.'

'What makes you think I'm an expert "at this kind of thing"? I'm not a genealogist.'

'I reckoned on you asking that so I'm not gonna lie. I searched you up on the internet. You can't blame me, can you? I wanted to know how you'd gotten on, what sort of person you'd become. I saw you got a double degree in history and English literature – I always said you were a smart cookie. And I also found some stuff you wrote. It was an article of some kind. I won't pretend I read it all, but it gave me the idea you know about researching history and that. People.'

'You mean the Maureen Meadows conference paper?'

'That sounds right. She the woman who worked for the Yanks during the war and wrote a book about it?'

'She wrote a memoir, yes. *I Loved Those Yanks* it was called.'

'That was it. So I thought maybe you'd be interested in helping me with this project. Because it's your history, too.'

'Well, you're right about the research part. The difference is, for that paper, most of what I was looking for wasn't that difficult to find. What you're asking—' Olivia stopped as the waitress set down their meals.

The dish looked appetising, but she felt self-conscious about eating. She was uncomfortable at the implied intimacy of sharing a meal with him – the unremarked upon resumption of such an everyday act when they hadn't eaten together for over seventeen years. Her father had no such qualms and was already tucking into his roast Berkshire pork. Olivia picked up her fork and nudged a sprig of fennel to the side.

'Well, it was just a suggestion,' said Trevor between mouthfuls. 'There's no hurry – I know you're probably busy with your, you know your … your mum told me about it.'

'My doctoral thesis?'

'Yeah, that's it. So just think about it for a bit and get back to me when you're ready, hey?'

'Sure, okay. I'll think about it.'

'So, um, tell me what else is going on with you. I want to hear everything. What about a boyfriend, you got one?'

'No, no, I don't. Would you mind if I ordered another glass of wine?'

~

Olivia let him escort her down the escalator and out onto the Queen Street Mall, now slung with the lengthening shadows of mid-afternoon. It was an oddly solicitous gesture in the face of so many years of silent neglect, but amends, she supposed, were painted in minute, exacting brushstrokes, as well as bold, splashy ones. Of the latter was a bank cheque for $20,000. Her reluctance to accept it was swept aside by a memory of her mother sobbing at the kitchen table one night, bony shoulders racking up and down, over a $300 car-repair bill. There had been an age, though Olivia couldn't pinpoint it, when she stopped sulking at her mother's refrain of 'I'm sorry, sweetheart, we can't afford it' and instead would nod with a sad little smile to her own refrain of 'That's okay, Mum, I understand'. She would do something nice for her mother with the money, maybe surprise her with a holiday at a resort somewhere.

Sometimes it was easy to forget the constant her mum had been in her life; Olivia could be as guilty as the next child of taking their mother's love for granted, as unheeded as the air she breathed. She loved her mother, fiercely. Seeing her father had reminded her of that fact.

After saying goodbye to Trevor – another awkward cheek-kiss and a promise to call soon – she decided to linger in the mall rather than head home. It was a warm afternoon, too warm to enjoy the walk back to the apartment. She would wait until the sun curtailed its head-on blaze before hiking across the Victoria Bridge. She meandered down the mall, pausing at a window display if something caught her eye. She browsed racks of new-season clothing and shelves of shoes with little enthusiasm, despite the fact she could, for the first time in her life, buy whatever she might have liked with no deficit in the financial guilt column.

Her thoughts were still on lunch with her father, trying to process the occasion, particularly his conception of her as the host on his own episode of *Who Do You Think You Are?*. Even·

if it were possible to find out who his father was, a mere name, Olivia couldn't help feeling, wouldn't mean much to either of them. He'd promised to send her copies of his adoption papers, and the hospital records, plus some photos and newspaper clippings his sister Julie had given him about Noelene.

But her father's ancestry project would have to take a number. Tomorrow was set aside for a trip to the Queensland State Archives to search police case files from the war years. The day after, she was meeting with Mandy to discuss the stagnation of her thesis. She would tell Mandy about Gloria Graham's letter, though she was still shadowy on how, exactly, it would reinvigorate things. Did she actually hope to solve the River Girl murder? It was a long way from her original research proposal, but these things change. Olivia could picture Mandy's mask of congenial politeness cracking with alarm and scepticism.

Her phone was vibrating. She retrieved it from her bag and left the clothing store she'd been aimlessly circulating to answer it.

'Hi Mum ... It was bizarre, to be honest ...'

Olivia wandered into the Brisbane Arcade, feeling the need for some yesteryear charm. There was a boutique on Adelaide Street, she remembered, that specialised in 1940s and 1950s reproduction clothing and accessories. She had in mind to buy Cheryl something. She still felt wretched about the painting.

There was a bunch of yet-to-bloom lilies on the dining table, along with Cheryl's handbag and keys. Olivia checked the time. It wasn't quite five o'clock.

'Hello? You're home early. Where are you?' she called in the direction of the hall.

Cheryl stuck her head out her bedroom door.

'Be there in a moment.'

'Who are the flowers from? Don't tell me Sam actually got you a "sorry" bouquet?'

'Huh! Not likely. They're for you, doofus. Look at the card.'

Olivia found the envelope with her name on it stuck to the cellophane. The card read:

What thing, in honor, had my father lost,
That need to be revived and breathed in me?
   T. x

Shakespeare, it had to be, but she didn't know which play. That her father could quote the Bard, and one of his more obscure lines at that, surprised her, but no more than anything else he'd said or done that day. The flowers were touching, in an off-key way, she supposed. And she did love lilies.

Cheryl came out tying the waist knot on a graphite-coloured dress with a metallic sheen Olivia hadn't seen before.

'What do you think?' She did a three-sixty, ending with a stagey hands-on-hips pose.

'Gorgeous. Leona Edminston?'

'Yep. On sale. Bought it today. I've got a date tonight. We're going to a show at the Judith Wright Centre. None of my shoes really work with it, though. Pity it's not cold enough for boots yet.'

'Well, I might be able to help you there. These should go well, I think. You're an eight and a half, right?' Olivia handed over the fancy rope-handled bag she'd placed on a chair.

Cheryl removed the box and held it up to peek inside the cellophane window on the side.

'Oh my fucking god. How much were these? They're bloody magnificent. But why? It's not even my birthday.' She sat down and took them out to try.

The 'Vixen Shoe' in red got the reception Olivia hoped for. She thought Cheryl would particularly like the crossover straps and widow peak's throat.

'It doesn't matter how much they cost,' she said. 'They're to say sorry for the paint—'

'That was not your fault! How many times—'

'Yes, I know, but—'

'Olivia.'

'Well, anyway. Just accept them. Did you find somewhere that can do the repair?'

'Sure did. There's an art restoration place in Bowen Hills. Turns out a girl I knew from uni works there. She offered me a discount, but I asked her to send me an invoice for the full amount, which I promptly emailed to Sam. I'm still waiting for a reply.'

'Don't hold your breath.'

'Oh, he'll be paying for it. Don't you worry about that.' Cheryl stood up and paraded across the living room. 'They fit well. Good job.'

Olivia wasn't worried. She hadn't spoken to Sam since she screamed him out of the apartment that day. He'd texted her two days later asking to talk. There was a single 'Sorry' (no emoticon) the next day, which had also been ignored. She didn't think she needed to end things formally – surely that was implied? Their break-up was going to stick this time, of that she was confident.

'*Soooo*, how did it go today?' Cheryl asked, now sitting on the couch and holding up a foot for admiration.

'It was … Well, he chased up the occasion with flowers,' Olivia upward inflected, gesturing at the bunch of lilies.

'Honey, they're not from your dad. Unless your father is a tallish, chiselled black guy who sired you when he was about six …'

'These are from Tobias?'

'That was him. I found him outside the building wondering where to leave them. I guess he was hoping you'd be here. And I do expect a full explanation of this Tobias, by the way.'

'Yeah, yeah. When was this?'

'Maybe an hour ago.'

'Damn.'

He'd rung the night before last to ask her to opening night of a Shakespeare play – one of the Henrys, she couldn't remember which, given an updated setting – he'd been directing with second-year actors. ('Think *My Own Private Idaho* but even grungier,' he'd said, which might have been helpful if she'd actually seen it.) She'd mentioned the reunion with Trevor, but had spared him any absent-father, woe-my-wounded-childhood tales. And from that he'd thought to buy her flowers? And quote (sort of) appropriate Shakespeare? She read the card again then showed it to Cheryl.

'What do you take it to mean?' Cheryl said.

'It means I've been with a self-absorbed jackass for three years.'

'You needed Shakespeare to work that out?'

She arrived right on opening at nine the next morning. Her mother had loaned Olivia her car for the trip to Brisbane's southside. She'd never been to the state archives before, a slightly damning oversight considering her research interests, but she had little enthusiasm for the bureaucratic side of history.

She registered for a researcher ID card then put everything bar her laptop, phone and cardigan in a locker before heading into the public search room: an ordered, no-nonsense area, with the attention to ergonomic comfort one might expect of a government facility. The long, smooth reading tables were equipped with additional overhead lighting, and there was metal shelving against one wall for storing requested items. The computer desks were clustered in a separate nook by the helpdesk.

Olivia sat down to request the items she'd looked up the night before. The biggest obstacle to her sleuthing, she'd discovered, was that murder investigations had a one-hundred-year restricted access period. She could, however, look through paperwork pertaining to other crimes including assault and sexual offences during the period, which could be accessed after sixty-five years. All search items relating to World War II had been helpfully collated on the QSA website, so it was just a matter of selecting them by description.

Item 319631: 'European war: American forces – sex offences by members of the US forces, c1/01/1943—c31/12/1945' was the first on her agenda. With some how-to guidance from a friendly archivist with, it had to be appreciated, a neat grey bob and stylish cat's-eye glasses, she requested Item 319631 and six others that included papers relating to World War II censorship and 'American provost corps, powers of, complaints regarding'.

What Olivia didn't expect, once the items were retrieved, was the packages to be all six or more inches thick. Rookie error. The archivist had kindly deposited the box that was Item 319631 at her preselected table. Inside were two thick dossiers of crumbling paperwork cross-tied with cotton bunting tape. The smell of age was fainter than she expected. The best strategy would be to take photos of everything she deemed even distant-cousin related and study them later.

Some cases, however, proved too irresistible to set aside. Like that of fifteen-year-old Norma Bamberry who 'hooked up' on seven documented occasions with twenty-four-year old Laurence Edwards, an African-American cook with the

192

US Navy. According to Edwards, they met at The Carver Club after he found her crying on a couch. She was upset, he said, because her boyfriend – Willie Pikes, another African-American soldier – was going away to New Guinea. A sexual relationship soon developed between the two with impromptu and scheduled rendezvous variously taking place 'in the scrub' outside the Mobile 9 US Naval Hospital in Camp Hill, a room on Hope Street in South Brisbane, then later on the beach and in a hotel room in Surfers Paradise that Edwards paid for.

As well as leading Edwards to believe she was nineteen years old, Norma had given birth the year before to Willie Pikes's baby. The 'male child', according to Norma, was 'an inmate of the Wooloowin State Children's Home'. Though Norma's mother, in her statement, declared she told Edwards of Norma's real age, it was she who bore the blame for Norma's proclivities: the girl was 'charged with having been a "Neglected Child", and was committed to the Salvation Army Industrial School for Girls at Toowong' until she turned eighteen.

Though the case was enlightening, it happened well over a year after the River Girl murder, and painted Edwards as no more than a young man with questionable judgement. Olivia sifted through the cases making note of the dates. She pulled out a manila folder marked '1942'. Odd that it should be grouped with what ostensibly were cases from 1943 to 1945 – clerical convenience or indifference, probably. If a serial rapist was responsible for the River Girl murder, then it made as much sense to look at cases before January 1943 as after.

Inside was a newspaper clipping glued to a sheet of paper the colour of a coffee stain, though no date had been included to indicate when the article was published:

U.S. Soldier Not Guilty of Rape

After sitting for nine hours a U.S. military court-martial last night found J.W. Floyd, 25, U.S. soldier, not guilty of rape, but guilty of assault and battery.

He was sentenced to be confined for six months with hard labour, and to forfeit 25 dollars a month for that period.

Floyd had been charged with the rape of a young woman near an air-raid shelter between Grey and Stanley streets, South Brisbane, on May 16.

Beneath it was an order, approved by the Commissioner of Police and handed over to the Division of Laboratories and Microbiology, for the Government Bacteriologist. It was a request to examine the bloodstained pocket from the offender's shirt, hairs found at the scene and on the offender's trousers that appeared to match those taken from the complainant, and 'a smear taken from the vagina of the complainant'.

The paper was as thin and brittle as a sheet of dry filo pastry. Most of the right edge had flaked away, including a bite-shaped chunk of the first paragraph, though its gist was readily gleaned. It was dated 18 May 1942 and was headed: 'An American Negro Soldier named J.W. FLOYD has been arrested on a charge of committing Rape upon one Rae Jane MASON, at South Brisbane on the 16 May 1942.'

This was followed by a description of the assault. Mason had been walking through a vacant allotment from Grey to Stanley Street when Floyd 'grabbed her by the right arm' and pulled her into the air-raid shelter. They struggled through the shelter and out the other side where Floyd 'threw her to the ground and committed rape upon her'. Mason struck her attacker in the face with a torch she'd been carrying and cried out for help ('whilst the offence was being committed'). She was heard by a passing 'Police Wireless Patrol Car'. The offender, on seeing the police car, ran away and 'made good his escape'. He was eventually found at the Redbank Military Camp 'with an injury to his upper lip, which he later admitted was caused by the complainant striking him there with the torch'. The final paragraph contained the request to have the evidence examined. It was signed by one Det. Constable J.F. Hammond and stamped as 'submitted' by a Det. Sergt. Lloyd.

The only other item pertaining to the case was a second newspaper clipping: 'Serious Charge; Man Remanded.' There had to be something between Floyd's arrest by the Brisbane CIB and his 'not guilty of rape' by an American court-martial that was not in the file. Olivia opened her Mac. Oddly, there was no wireless at the archives, so she hot-spotted it to her phone: if anything else had been reported in the papers about the case, it should be easy enough to find on the National Library's Trove site.

Sure enough, there was a piece in *The Courier-Mail* from Wednesday, 20 May 1942: 'U.S. Army to Deal with Rape Charge.' In addition to an account of the assault that matched the letter, the article reported that Floyd had been handed 'into the control' of the US military authorities at their request. An American officer, it said, told the magistrate 'that the penalty for the offence was, in time of war, life imprisonment or death by firing squad'. That the US Military desired to trial and punish their own was certain, but could they bypass the local CIB altogether?

Floyd had somehow avoided the firing squad and was 'confined for six months with hard labour'. It made sense that the US Military would be keen not to have him named in the papers as the River Girl rapist and killer if they were the ones responsible for not keeping him 'confined' for longer. But when was he sentenced? She searched Trove for the headline of the original article.

It was dated 31 July 1942, which meant Floyd would have been freed no earlier than 31 January 1943. While it didn't cork her theory entirely, the timing was an inconvenient spanner. And was Floyd the type of rapist who would bother with a nylon stocking as a perverted finishing flourish? Going by the description of the attack on Mason, it seemed unlikely.

Rae Mason was no anomaly. As Olivia pressed on through the files she found other cases where a woman going about her own business, usually walking home at night, was attacked and raped by a member of the US Armed Forces. The locations and the particulars varied, including the racial profile of the attacker, but the rapists' brutality and disregard for their victims had a disgusting, heartburning sameness. There was an unnerving intimacy she hadn't prepared for in learning the details, which included victims' names, descriptions of what they wore, where they lived, and what, in precise, clinical terms, had been done to them.

One case from November 1943 suggested some parallels to the River Girl murder. Followed by her rapist from the Oxley train station, the rape victim, a twenty-five-year-old nurse, told police the perpetrator 'looped his web waist belt around my throat and threatened to choke me to death'. The investigating officers, with some assistance from the American provost, did the fastidious work of tracking down and interrogating the perpetrator at the Ascot Base Camp. Once identified, Earl George Jones was handed over to the US authorities for court-martial.

That much was consistent across all cases involving sex offences committed by American servicemen. To their credit, Jones was sentenced to life imprisonment, though had he been black the sentence would probably have been death. Olivia couldn't find any mention of the assault or Jones's sentence in the papers, which at least proved not every heinous sex crime perpetrated by a Yank (even white ones) made it into print.

Whether Jones had raped *and killed* another woman ten months earlier was pure conjecture. That the police had been thorough and dogged in their pursuit of the men who'd committed these horrendous assaults was evident. It was there, in duplicate, documented in page after page of single-spaced typewriter font, passive voice and occasional grammatical errors notwithstanding. These were the cases, however, that the Brisbane CIB *had* actually investigated.

She'd been assuming River Girl was a random victim, but sexual offences of the 'closer to home' variety, like Norma Bamberry, made up the bulk of the files. They also invariably involved 'carnal knowledge of a girl under 17'. That the girls in these cases were, more often than not, described as being 'backward in [her] mentality' or having 'the mentality of a child of 12', probably said more about the Mariana Trench-depth sexism of the time than the girls themselves.

The next case involved a fifteen-year-old girl. The file included an extract from her birth certificate as proof of her age. Olivia read through the girl's statement, fancying she could hear her intonation in its careful formality, her pauses and hesitations in the stilted sentences.

6/12/43

S T A T E M E N T.

Elaine Mary CLANCY states:– I am a single girl, 15 years of age, and I was born at Brisbane on 15 November 1927. My mother is dead and I reside with my grandmother, Mary Ann CLANCY, at 57 Longhurst Crescent, Oxley. I know an American soldier named Elmore Jackson, who was attached to the 636th Ordinance Co.

Archerfield Road, Darra. This company, as far as I know, is now
in New Guinea. I first met Jackson at Nancy Little's residence, at
Archerfield Road, Darra, about August 1942. I became friendly with
Jackson, and he often visited my home, and brought his washing
to be done there. About the beginning of January 1943, my sister
Florence Pane, Jackson and I started going to the pictures together
at the American Camp at Archerfield. The three of us went together
to the pictures on several occasions, and about the end of the month,
Jackson and I started going alone in a truck, and sometimes we
would walk. He often kissed me, and tried to have intercourse with
me. I did not stop him from kissing me, but I would not let him have
intercourse with me, and I told him that I was only fifteen years of
age. I remember one night about the end of January 1943, I can't
remember the exact date, but it was about the third time that Jackson
and I had been out alone together. On this night we were walking
home together from the pictures. He suggested that we sit down,
and when near the corner of Ipswich Road and Darra Road, we sat
on the grass. He again started to kiss me, and then pushed me on to
my back. After a short while, he lay on top of me, and he pulled my
bloomers down and took one leg out. I did not struggle with him on
this occasion, I thought I would give in to him, as he had been trying
to have intercourse with me for some time, and he told me he would
look after me. Jackson then undone the front of his pants, and pulled
his private out. He then pushed his private into my private, and
worked up and down for several minutes. It hurt, as no one had ever
done anything like that to me previously. Then he stopped, and I felt
all wet. He took me home, and afterwards he continued to take me
to the pictures. I did not tell my grandmother what Jackson had done
to me. On about ten or twelve occasions from then, we would stop
alongside the roadway, and I would allow him to have intercourse
with me. In February, I knew I was pregnant. I told Jackson and was
worried as I was only fifteen years of age. He told me not to worry,

that he would help me. I asked Jackson whether he was married or single, and he told me he was single. I have since heard that Jackson is a married man. He continued to have intercourse with me after I was pregnant. The last time he had intercourse with me was about the beginning of July 1943. It was the night before he left on transfer to New Guinea. On 7 November 1943 I was admitted to Brisbane Women's Hospital, and on that date I gave birth to a male child, which has since been registered as Jonathon William CLANCY. Jackson is the father of my child and he is the only person who has ever had intercourse with me.

In an accompanying memorandum to the Inspector of Police, it stated that Jackson had been arrested and, predictably, handed over to US Army authorities for trial by court-martial. The sentence: five years and a dishonourable discharge. 'Although the home where this girl and her infant are living is clean and well kept,' the memorandum went on, 'the fact that she has associated with negroes [sic] at Darra, which is the principal [sic] camp for coloured Allied Servicemen, shows that she is not living in desirable surroundings and this fact, I suggest, could be brought under the notice of the State Children Department.'

Enough. Olivia snapped the manila folder closed and put it on the 'done' pile.

Item 319631 should have been labelled 'Pandora's Box'. *Warning: Contents may cause distress and anger, and once read can't be unread.* She was done with rapists, child molesters and serial flashers. Not to mention the manifest racism and sexism of the 1940s. She bundled up all the sex offences by members of the US forces, tied them together again and put them back in their box.

It was already twelve-thirty: no more getting sidetracked or there'd be no hope of working through all the items she'd requested. At the shelving cabinet, she exchanged the box for a new bundle wrapped in thick, tear-resistant paper, checking the number written in black marker against her request receipts: 'European war: misconduct by Australian soldiers.' That should be good. She would tackle it right after she fortified herself with coffee and lunch.

There were two missed calls from Cheryl. She'd rung while Olivia was driving home, her phone on silent in her handbag. Olivia called her back while trudging up the road to their apartment block. At least she'd found a park on the same street. The first leaves of a belated autumn had only just tickled the ground, not quite crisp enough to make a satisfying crunch underfoot. Cheryl was taking her time to answer.

'Sorry, I was in the loo,' she greeted. 'Where are you?'

'Almost home. Walking up hill now. You there?'

'No, I'm still at work. Look, Sam's had an accident. Now don't panic. Caitlin rang and asked me to let you know. He was working on a new sculpture, doing something with a buzz-saw and it slipped, or he slipped, or something. I don't know specifics. Anyway, basically, he almost sliced his hand in—'

'*Jesus Christ.*' Olivia could feel her face bleaching. She had no intestinal or psychological mettle for anything involving the slicing or severing of body parts. She'd never moved on from the ear in *Blue Velvet*.

'I know. I can't … Anyway, he's in surgery and apparently the doctors are optimistic about, you know, sewing it all back together again … You okay?'

'Yeah. No. I'm just …'

'I'm sure he'll be fine, really.'

'Should I go to the hospital?'

'I guess that's up to you. Do you want to?'

'I don't know. Is that appropriate?'

'I'm not sure I know what the protocol is for this situation.'

'I don't either, but I think I'm going to go.'

'Well, he's at the Mater, so at least it's close.'

She had her mother's car so she could drive, though trying to get a park in the vicinity of the hospital suggested walking would be the easier option. It was getting close to six o'clock. The play started at seven-thirty. If there was any chance of making it, she'd have to drive straight from the hospital. But that meant she'd have to shower and change now, which also meant she was prioritising her appearance over her injured ex-boyfriend.

Olivia stood rooted to the pavement, the same circuitous argument doing lap after lap in her already fried head. Cancel. She would have to let Tobias know she couldn't make it tonight. But she so wanted to go. Andrew would be there and she planned to ask him about perhaps interviewing his grandmother. And Clio. Crazy, darling Clio. Olivia had looked forward to seeing her, too. But no, Sam was in the hospital, that had to take precedence. What was she thinking? Yes, they'd broken up, but he'd almost cut his bloody hand off and she was standing there lamenting the loss to her social life. It was the right thing, the good thing to do. It had to be. It wasn't about forgetting, or excusing, what he'd done, it was about her being a decent human being. She headed back down the hill. And, damn it, she would drive.

She found Zach in the emergency waiting room. Caitlin had just left. Olivia sat on the rim of the hard plastic seat opposite as though her stay was to be measured in moments rather than possible hours. Without actually asking what she was doing at the hospital, there was a detectable coolness in Zach's demeanour towards her. When prompted, he filled her in on what happened. He was the one who called the paramedics. She asked him whether someone had called Sam's mother.

'Caitlin did, yeah. She's on her way, might take her a bit to get here, though.'

Olivia nodded. She liked Sam's mum. Meredith had lived in Mullumbimby for the last ten years as a born-again earth mother: a loud, bear-hugging, no-fucks-giving one who wore Doc Martens or no shoes at all, grew vegetables, raised chooks, smoked 'medicinal herbs', and, much to Sam's chagrin, talked a lot about sexual healing and the power of tantric sex. Before that she worked in the publishing industry as a literary agent and was known as 'the bull terrier'. Olivia wondered if Sam had told her they'd broken up.

'Hey, do you mind if I go for a walk and get something to eat?' said Zach, rising from his seat. 'I don't think Sam will be out for a while yet. And he'll probably be out cold afterwards, anyway.'

'Of course not.'

She hadn't considered the actual waiting part when she'd made the decision to come. Leaving now wasn't an option. She pulled out her phone and scrolled with disinterest through her Facebook feed. Was it just her, or was social media getting duller, inaner, and depressingly repetitive? She opened Words with Friends to play her turn with Cheryl, sighing loudly because she had five 'I's, an 'A' and an 'O', and there was shit all to be done with that. She was the only one basking beneath the overhead fluorescents not in thrall to her phone. There were over four hundred images of archival documents on it, though, that weren't going to read themselves. Misbehaving Australian soldiers it was.

She put the phone face down on her knee and squeezed the back of her neck. She could feel a tension headache coming on. US court-martial records, that's what she needed. Trickier, but probably not impossible to obtain in the age of digital archiving. Tomorrow, after her meeting with Mandy, she would investigate the possibility online.

She checked the time – 7.15 pm – and saw she had a text message alert:

> That's cool. Understand. Come closing instead & join us for afterparty. Andrew can't make it tonight either, so that's his plan. Call you tomorrow. Tx

Olivia texted back her thanks and a 'will def make it for CN ☺'. She felt better about missing the thing now, not that she had a searing desire to sit through an obscure Shakespeare performed by student actors. Zach was outside having another cigarette. If he was back on the cancer sticks full-time, Sam would be too. She was no longer obliged to care, but sighed as if it were a problem to fix anyway. It begged the question of what she was doing there now the initial shock of Sam's self-inflicted injury had worn off.

Was 'because she cared' a sufficient reason? Cheryl cared and she wasn't there. Olivia hadn't examined her motives too closely. Her presence would make no difference to the outcome of his surgery. His hand would come out intact or it wouldn't. She thought about the last time he touched her. The pressure of his fingers had broken capillaries and left a pebbled trail of burgundy stains down the side of her neck. They had faded within a week, giving way at the edge like a waning moon, and taking her outrage and hostility with them. She didn't want to test her susceptibility to a slurring, morphine-induced 'Sorry, babe, you know how much I love you ...'

She got up to find Zach and tell him she was going.

At the main entrance, she heard someone call her name.

'Olivia. Over here.'

Meredith was waving at her from the reception window. She

said something to the woman behind the counter then moved towards her. Olivia met her halfway, ready for a meaningful and extended embrace.

'Hello, darling girl. Come here.' Meredith wrapped her arms around Olivia and kept her cocooned for a lengthy few moments. On release, Meredith asked if there'd been an update on her son. 'Came a cropper with a buzz-saw, did he? Well, colour me surprised.'

'Nothing yet. We think he's still in surgery, but he'd have to be out soon. He's been in there a while.'

'Geez, it is bloody serious. Who else is here?'

'Just Zach, but actually I was … Well, I decided it would be better if I left. I'm not sure if Sam told you, but we broke up, so …'

Meredith was nodding in that intent way she had, pupils like twin drill bits zeroing in on Olivia's face.

'He tells me nothing, that boy. And I'm sorry to hear that. I really am.'

Olivia inched back to regain some personal space. Meredith didn't use deodorant, either.

'Well, anyway. I don't think it's appropriate for me to be here. Not after—' She shrugged and looked over her shoulder.

Meredith's eye contact, though shot through with kindness, was unrelenting. 'Hmm. Do you want to tell me what happened?'

'Oh, it was just, you know, it wasn't working anymore. I've known that for a while.'

That Meredith would be horrified by Sam's actions was an understatement. Where Olivia could downplay and diminish, without going so far as to justify, Meredith, like Cheryl, did not deal in a single shade of grey. Sam's father had been violent and Meredith was now a volunteer counsellor for a DV hotline. And even if there was a time to tell her, this wasn't it.

The cast-iron feeling in her ribs spread from her throat to her jaw. It really was over with Sam. Telling his mother had somehow cemented the fact and planted a flagpole with it. For the first time since it all happened, she felt the swell of a good cry coming on. Meredith did that to people.

Meredith took hold of Olivia's upper arm and lifted her chin, bringing her face square with her own.

'Now, honey, you listen to me. I've always said my son doesn't deserve you. So I want you to promise me you won't take him back. Not next week, not in a month's time, not in three months' time, not ever. He's got some growing up to do and I don't want him doing it on your time anymore. You hearing me?'

Olivia grimaced in consent. Meredith could be overbearing, but she was like a second mother. It was something she'd always listed in the 'pro' column in her debates over getting back with Sam.

'I'll miss you, though,' she said.

'Don't be an idiot. You can come stay with me whenever you bloody well like. I'm waiting to read that thesis of yours, don't forget. Now, come here and give me another hug before I go razz up these doctors and find out what the hell is going on.'

It was lightly sprinkling when Olivia arrived home. She'd snagged a park outside the apartment this time, but stood by the car door anyway, letting the haze settle like dew on her bare arms. That intoxicating earthy before-smell of rain was in the air. *Don't be an idiot.* She'd been an idiot about a few things and tomorrow she had to prove somehow to Mandy that her idiocy didn't extend to her thesis.

What would Gloria Graham do?

She laughed. What a hokey question. Still, maybe that's where the answer lay.

Cheryl was waving at her from the kitchen window. She pointed to the wine glass in her other hand and beckoned Olivia to come in.

12

At the City Hall where the U.S. Army held its dance for servicemen and their friends, the floor was packed. It was estimated that 2500 were present ... An American Army band played swing music and the programme embraced every type of dance from waltzing to 'jitterbugging'.

—*The Courier-Mail* (25 May 1942)

September 1993

'Correspondence? Margaret?'

'Yes, we've got two letters. Shall I read them?'

The six women murmured their assent.

'Yes, please, Margaret,' said Lenore, who never missed an opportunity to assert her standing as president.

'Well, the first is an invitation by the Australian Women's Army Service Association of Queensland to participate in their Christmas charity fundraiser. They're raising money for Meals on Wheels this year.' Margaret scanned the faces around the table.

'I think that's a marvellous idea,' said Evelyn, landing her beatific smile on each of them in turn.

Val was of the opinion that if it weren't for Evelyn, their little Brisbane branch of the World War II War Brides Association would have snapped off the host tree long ago. Her fingers itched to take the last Monte Carlo. It was the biscuits that really drew her to the meetings.

'We can vote on that later. What's the other letter about, Margaret?'

'Yes, okay. Well, it seems' – Margaret adjusted her glasses and the angle of her nose – 'there's a woman, I think, who, if I've got this straight, wants to make some sort—'

'Why don't you just read it?'

'Yes, good idea. *Dear Members of the—*'

'I think you can probably skip that part.'

'Um, yes. Well, she's a … *Brisbane-based filmmaker … and she's making a documentary about Australian War Brides of the Second World War to be released next year in time for the planned fiftieth anniversary commemorations to mark the end of the war and I'd like to conduct some interviews on camera regarding your experiences as war brides. If any of your members would be—*'

'Thank you, Margaret. We get the idea. Who's the letter from?'

'It's from a … *Ms* Gillian Stretton.'

'Well, I'd certainly be happy to do it. I think it'd be tremendous fun.' Evelyn beamed again, her cheeks lifting to resemble two plump apricots. She reminded Val of Betty White from *The Golden Girls*.

'What about you, Val? I think you've probably got the most romantic story of us all.'

Val was only half listening. She'd been thinking about diabetes, her distaste for needles, her doctor's warnings, and that Monte Carlo no one else seemed to want.

'Yes, well, if people are interested we can work that out later,' Lenore said. 'We really do need to move on. The next item on the agenda – and the reason for today's meeting, I might add – is what we intend to do ourselves for the fiftieth-anniversary commemorations. Submissions close at the end of the month if we want to be included in the council's official program of commemorative events, so we need to draw up a proposal today. I was thinking an exhibition of some kind might be rather nice. Has anybody still got their wedding dress?'

~

December 1993

Val's right hip was playing up again. She'd need that replacement sooner rather than later. Age was a bitch and Val didn't like her much. She could cop the tree-trunk waist, the chin bristles and grey hair the texture of wire, even the sunspots that stained her increasingly papery skin, but she got cranky about it when she couldn't take the dogs for a walk. She tossed the quilt aside anyway and, with some leverage from her arms, spun her legs round to the side of the bed, slipping her feet into a pair of worn fuchsia slippers. Tea first – one sugar only, she'd been told to cut down – then a bowl of All-Bran, then her blasted medications. How she wished to throw a cigarette into the mix.

It was a beautiful morning. A confident early sun fixed on warming the rest of the day ahead. The humid air was already spiced with honeysuckle and jasmine. She never tired of the view from her kitchen window. The jacarandas were past their prime, their brief, show-offy burst of purple flame now well into recession, but the rhododendrons and azaleas still held their own along the fence line. As, too, did the frangipani beside the verandah with its yellow and pink-tinged hybrid blooms. The branches of the mango tree down the back were drooping with their new summer bounty.

Minnie and Alfie were scratching at the glass door. She slid it open and the two elderly Chihuahuas scampered cautiously around her feet, their toenails tapping the floorboards like the click of typewriter keys. She took her tea outside to the patio swing installed on the verandah. The dogs followed, happy to sit by her feet for the time being.

They'd looked for him those first few weeks, going room to room when they came out of their kennel in the morning. For her, the ache was still there, but duller, diffused most days. Today, though, she expected it to come roaring back: the swell of an incoming ocean tide urged on by a northwesterly that would crash again and again until the tide inched out, leaving only the flotsam of her almost fifty-year marriage for her to scavenge over.

The dogs beseeched her with their black marble eyes. 'Later,' Val said. 'We'll go for a walk later, I promise.' By the afternoon the pain in her hip would have subsided. They could take a stroll around New Farm Park after they scattered Arthur's ashes on the river. Andrew would be up for that.

She sat until the last few mouthfuls of tea were stone-cold. The gentle rock of the patio swing had a way of lulling her into wanting to do nothing. But it was not a day for doing nothing. Lenore had rung yesterday to remind her about the meeting tomorrow. What would she be contributing to the war brides exhibition? Val rocked herself out of the chair and went back inside, the dogs tip-tapping behind her.

'What do you suggest, Arthur? Any ideas?'

At least she wasn't mad enough to think he might answer. Val had the same thought every time she posed a question to Arthur's urn, which had been sitting on the mantel over the fireplace for exactly a year now. His silence was about as useful as any answer he'd given when he was alive. 'Whatever you think, darling girl,' she could almost hear him say with his southern twang that had never disappeared.

'Oh, Arthur, I don't know.'

Perhaps it needn't be anything big. She never had a proper wedding dress. There was an old MacRobertson's chocolate box of mementos with photos, trinkets and letters in a cupboard somewhere. There could be something in that. Val hadn't looked through it in years. She had an idea it contained the garter Vera gave her, and perhaps even the hairclip with ceramic blue irises she'd worn on the day of her wedding.

She went to the guest room where the wardrobe had become a receptacle for all the things they'd ceased to use but hadn't had the sufficient will to part with. The first thing she saw on sliding open the mirrored door was Arthur's coats and shirts. The smell of him, overlaid with notes of his signature bergamot aftershave, struck her like a slap, rimming her lower lids with a briny film. The ache gave way to a fierce craving. She buried her face in one of his shirts and inhaled until her lungs were full.

The tin container was in a larger cardboard box of things she'd long ago forgotten they owned on a high shelf of the wardrobe. Common sense said she should have waited for Andrew to arrive, but with tenacity, a chair and a pile of old telephone books as a step, she managed to retrieve it without breaking any bones.

A second cup of tea, this time with two sugars, was in order before she opened it.

Val settled her mug on a coaster and adjusted herself at the table. The lid took some coercing, but eventually relinquished. The garter, now crusted yellow, and the hairclip were sitting on top. She removed them, along with the bundle of letters and cards underneath. The postcard was on the bottom. She snatched it up, noticing the slight rhythmic change to her heartbeat. The black-and-white picture was exactly as she remembered: a snapshot of a river and with a knob-shaped mountain in the background: *Maroochy River, showing Ninderry, Yandina.* She'd always thought Mount Ninderry looked like a woman's breast

211

lying flat with a distended nipple on top. Already knowing, almost word for word, what was written on the back, she turned it over to read. She was curious to know what effect it would have on her, fifty years later. Even with glasses on she had to squint to read the tightly packed, slanted handwriting.

Dear Val,   *June 18, 1944*

Congratulations on your wedding – I was very pleased to hear of it and sorry I couldn't be there. I am sure Rocko will make a good husband. When do you sail for America? I'm currently working on a ginger farm in Yandina as a Land Army girl (hence the postcard). It's hard work, but I don't mind it. Much prefer it, in fact, to waiting tables. It seems I really am a country girl. As you know I went home to Kingaroy and helped out on the farm there for a bit. Mother still hasn't forgiven me for leaving again to join the Land Army, but I just couldn't live at home anymore. Do you remember my (half) brother Jack? You met once, briefly. He was invalided out of the army about six months ago and came back to live on the farm. He lost his right arm in New Guinea, all the way to the shoulder. From a gunshot wound that went gangrenous. Anyway, he's been beastly since he came back, and I should have been more sympathetic, but I couldn't bear it. His friend Kanga came to visit and asked me to marry him. I haven't given him an answer yet and that was three months ago. He's nice enough, I suppose. Perhaps you had the right idea marrying a Yank, after all. Love, Alice

Val couldn't have said exactly what she felt. Her heart wasn't doing a frenetic jitterbug and her breathing was slow and even. The hot curdle of shame she also expected had cooled to something she didn't recognise. Forgiveness? No, and it wasn't righteous anger or even the sweet, sharp triumph of revenge. Not anymore. Time had done the job of rounding out the

212

edges of that. It was, though, something like triumph. She had triumphed. He had tried to destroy her and she'd won. She'd won herself a good life, forty-eight years' worth, with a man who would have tried to part the ocean if she'd asked him to.

She got up to answer the phone.

'Hello, Valerie Billings speaking.'

'Hey, Nan. It's me, Andrew. I've just landed. You're still expecting me, I hope.'

'Of course, dear, I'm not senile.'

'I was just calling to say I'm about to jump in a cab and come over.'

'Wonderful. Did you have a good flight?'

'It was okay, but it's bloody long. I'm in no hurry to do it again, so you better get used to having me around.'

'There are definitely worse things to get used to.'

'You ready to scatter Pop's ashes?'

'Yes, I think so.'

'Let's do this thing, then. Be there soon.'

She had promised Arthur she'd lay him to rest on the river. Down by the old submarine docks at Teneriffe where he'd first come ashore as a cocky, young submariner from Arkansas. She'd kept him for a year, but it was time to let him go. Give him back to the ocean that brought them together. As to his urn, she had an idea it would make a provocative contribution to the Brisbane War Brides 50th Anniversary Commemorative Exhibition.

- 13 -

Brisbane, with its servicemen of all kinds, its war workers, and all the rest of the population of a garrison town superimposed upon a once normal Australian city, is the most picturesque capital in Australia. It is also the most uncomfortable ...

—*The Sunday Mail* (5 December 1943)

The cover photo on the order of service for Mrs Billings' funeral was from her ninetieth birthday ('90' was writ large on the cake in red icing), not as recent as it might have been, but at ninety-four what constituted 'recent'? It was an increasingly slippery concept to Olivia in her not-quite mid-thirties. May felt like yesterday, yet here they were in late November. Inside the folded A4 sheet was a picture of Valerie on her wedding day; she'd been a tiny thing, though perhaps that was just in contrast to her US sailor husband who could have dented a tank. She looked genuinely delighted, too, with none of that 'posiness' that seemed to characterise formal pictures from the era. The difference between the two photos was stark. Age was a bitch, as Mrs Billings had said herself, while shakily dunking an arrowroot biscuit in the weak sugary tea she'd made when Olivia had visited her in June.

Olivia wouldn't have described the old woman as irascible, but you weren't sure where you stood with her, either. She seemed to delight in contrariness, though she was polite and hospitable in that reflexive way of her generation. She'd lived in a residential-care facility, but was largely independent, managing most things on her own with the help of a front-wheeled Zimmer frame.

The service was due to start in ten minutes. Andrew was still greeting people by the door. Olivia lingered on the concrete forecourt outside the chapel. Clio would arrive soon, hopefully. The small chapel was attached to a recently restored colonial-era building with a double verandah, corrugated-tin roof, a triple-pot chimney and the ubiquitous white cast-iron balustrades. Everything else, bar the oak doors, was painted a soothing, sanitised cream.

Olivia eventually gave up on Clio and went in. She chose a spot at the back close to the aisle. The chapel was almost full. The Billings', she'd been informed by a stranger on the way in, had been 'active in the community'. There was even a troop of neat little girls in pink leotards with matching chiffon wrap skirts and one boy in black pants along two of the rows. According to the leaflet included with the program, they were from a Salisbury dance school. There was a picture of the school from the outside, which Olivia recognised as the old munitions factory building. The girls and boy would be performing 'a small tribute dance' in honour of Mrs Valerie Billings. Small being the operative word, given the space they had to work with. As well as being a 'beloved teacher for many years', Valerie had also been an eisteddfod adjudicator and a 'dedicated ballet examiner well into her eighties'. She would have been terrifying, in other words, Olivia thought. The prelude song had just begun when Clio slipped in beside her.

'I'm not too late, am I?' she mouthed. She looked savagely elegant in a plain, sleeveless navy dress with a high gathered neckline, cinched in at the waist by a matching belt, and finished with beige rope wedges.

'You're fine,' Olivia whispered. 'It just started. You okay?'

Clio took a bracing breath in through her nostrils. 'Yep. Tell you about it later. It's nothing bad, don't worry.' She squeezed Olivia's hand and pecked her on the cheek.

They didn't stay after giving their condolences to the family. Some of them had flown in from America. Olivia hadn't expected to be so *affected* by the service. The soggy tissue was hardly a mystery, though. *I've never told anyone the whole story before. You do whatever you like with it, dear. It's your story now. Just be sure to mention what a good dancer I was.*

Outside the temperature had climbed from summery fresh to uncomfortable and sticky. November's promise of a sultry summer to Brisbane. Olivia wished she hadn't worn a black polyester dress with elbow-length sleeves. ('Polyester doesn't *breathe*,' she could hear her mother say.) It was Clio's suggestion they go get lunch somewhere.

'I'm bloody starving,' she said as they reached the car. 'What about Paddington?' Clio slumped into the driver's seat, making ouchy noises over the hot seat, and reached over to unlock the passenger side door. 'I was thinking the Java Lounge. I haven't been there in years. You happy with that?'

'Sounds good to me.'

Olivia played down the twinge of anxiety that came with even half a day away from her keyboard. If 'breathing down someone's neck' was sending daily six o'clock emails with the subject heading 'Where is it?' then Mandy was a neck breather. Olivia's original deadline had been and gone. Her father's 'scholarship' had enabled her to reduce her teaching hours for the semester, at least. What she needed to finish her thesis was the service record of Lance Corporal Jack Brennan she'd ordered from the National Archives in Canberra almost four months ago, which would include, crucially, the dates he took leave.

He had been in Brisbane in September 1942; that much was certain. But Mrs Billings, when Olivia had interviewed her, hadn't known whether he'd returned to Brisbane in January 1943. She had moved from Archibald House by that stage and wasn't in touch with her old roommate, Alice, during that time. Olivia hadn't wanted to tell Mrs Billings why she wanted to know, but she'd guessed anyway. *He did it to someone else, didn't he? I carried that with me my whole life. The guilt, you know. That he'd do it again. That I could have done something.* Olivia had told her she knew nothing for certain and she was not to blame herself for anything.

'I got a Facebook message from Tobias the other day,' said Clio, breaking in to her thoughts. 'Says he's missing Brisbane already. I think he really means he misses you. He said he's working on you to come visit him in LA. You reckon you might do it?' Clio beeped the driver in front of her. 'Green for go. Come on, buddy. He's looking at his bloody phone.'

Obstacle cleared, she turned left down Gregory Terrace in the direction of the Old Museum Building. 'Jesus, this air conditioning. Why won't it work?' She banged on the vent as if that might fix it.

Olivia wound down the window. 'Not a chance in hell at the moment. I've got at least two more chapters to write. Then there'll be revisions and rewrites. I have no capacity to think about anything else right now. And in the words of the man himself' – here Clio chimed in with a deep-voiced LA twang – '*Long distance doesn't work, babe. You know that.*'

Tobias. He'd been a worthy and profoundly enjoyable distraction while he was here. After Sam became an ex-boyfriend, Olivia had picked things up with Tobias where they'd left them

218

in the South Bank pool, but neither of them had raised the possibility of it being something more permanent. Now she was paying (in sleep mostly) for all the hours she had so willingly frittered in his company the past six months. It took her a week to admit it, but the end of his visa was a relief. She hadn't even the mental space to know if she missed him yet.

'But you're getting there with it, aren't you?' Clio asked.

'I suppose you could say that. I've got your box of letters here, by the way.' Olivia bent forward to remove the old tin she'd been carrying around in her bag. 'I think I'm finished with them,' she said, giving it a jiggle. 'I've also been meaning to say, did you know there's a key in there? It was wrapped in a square of calico inside an envelope.'

'Huh. I can't say I did.'

'Do you know what it might open?'

'No idea. What sort of key is it?'

'Like a chunky, old-fashioned one.'

'Well, fancy that. Dad might know. I'll ask him.'

'So, are you going to tell me what happened that made you late to the funeral?'

'When we get there.'

They chose a window table, though the wooden bench seats weren't the most comfortable option, and both ordered the vegetarian bagel. Olivia also requested a flat white, while Clio went with a frappe blended from a Carmen Miranda headpiece. That the cute waiter was flirting his pin-up girl tattoo off at Clio went spectacularly unnoticed by her.

'So?' said Olivia once they were shot of him.

'Sooooo, this is pretty crazy, right. This film production company got in touch with me because they want to turn *Apron Strings* into a screenplay.'

'Don't they need, like, rights to do that?'

'Well, exactly. And who do you think owns the rights to it?'

Olivia shrugged. She hadn't given the matter a single thought. She actually, shamefully, had no idea who owned the copyright on Graham's work.

'I do. Well, no, technically Dad and his siblings do, but that basically means I do. That's how I was able to do the play. Without paying a copyright fee.'

'But hang on, how does that work?'

'Because June was the beneficiary of Gloria's will, which included her intellectual property. June then bequeathed her estate to her sister, Edith, my grandmother, which her children inherited when she died.'

'Okay. But how do you prove that?'

'Well, that's the tricky part. So, this production company didn't actually know I had the rights. They just wanted to know where I got them from because they couldn't find anything online. The woman who wants to produce it saw the play when she was up from Sydney and really loved it. She was pretty chuffed when I told her I, we, owned the copyright and, yes, I was interested in letting her option the film rights. With some conditions, which I'll get to, and that was all fine, until their lawyers got involved. Long story short – and the reason why I was late for the funeral because I was on the bloody phone all morning – they need "substantive" proof, like legal documents, that we in fact own Graham's intellectual property.'

If Olivia had ever thought of Clio as a ditz (had she?) she made a mental note to retract it. 'Wouldn't you just need a copy of your grandmother's or June's will?'

As Clio explained it, that wasn't enough because Edith had not mentioned any matters of intellectual property in her will *at all*. And though copyright is inherited according to intestacy laws, which most often apply when someone dies without leaving a will, in this case, because Edith was not a relative or descendant of Graham, the lawyers were demanding irrefutable proof of copyright ownership. June had been more prudent about itemising Graham's intellectual property as an asset in her will (she also made Clio's father Gloria's literary executor), but what they wanted was proof that Graham both appointed June as her literary executor and made her the beneficiary of her intellectual property.

'What you need, then, is Gloria's will?'

'Bingo.'

'Here you go, ladies. One flat white and one watermelon, pear, mint, strawberry and apple frappe. Your bagels won't be too long now. Is there anything else I can get for you?'

'Some water would be good,' said Olivia.

'Water's right over there. Just help yourself,' he said with a helpful Usain-Bolt pose aimed at the half-empty glass dispenser on the counter. 'Hey, are you the girl on that Foxtel ad?' he asked Clio.

'That was me.'

'I knew it. I'm an actor as well so I notice that kind of thing. I'm studying at the Actors Mill in the Valley. You heard of it?'

'I don't think so. Is it new?'

Olivia got up to fetch some water.

It was after two when they wandered back out onto the footpath and into the broiling brunt of the day. Clio slung an arm around Olivia's neck and nestled her head against her shoulder. Olivia inhaled notes of coconut and pear mingled on her clammy skin.

'I guess you need to get on with your writing,' she said.

'I probably should.'

'Do you mind if we have a quick look in the antiques centre

first? I'll drive you home straight after. I seriously love this place.'

'Let's do it.' Olivia loved the Paddington Antique Centre enough to know there was no such thing as a 'quick look'. Call it another worthy distraction.

'Holy smokes. Would you look at that thing.'

A headless mannequin in a V-necked pink, green and yellow hibiscus-print evening dress was strategically positioned about six feet from the entrance. It had an empire bodice that slightly gathered and pulled up on one side, with a bias-cut skirt that draped over the hips and wrapped around to create a soft flounce at the front.

Clio inspected the handwritten tag. 'Beaded vintage rayon evening gown. 1940s. $550. Jesus. It is in bloody good condition, though. You know, people were definitely smaller back then.'

'It's a bit like the one you wore in the play.'

'This is much nicer. And it's the real deal.'

'Why don't you try it on?'

'Nah. It's a collector's item. It's not like you could actually wear it anywhere. Unless it was purchased for a period film with a generous costume budget – I didn't tell you that part yet, did I? We got waylaid by Brisbane's Ryan Gosling.'

'I can't believe he asked you how much you got for that ad. Is that an actor thing?'

'It can be. Anyway, I lied. I made double what I told him. But it is true that ads don't pay even a fraction of what they used to.' Clio let go of the front drape of the dress she'd been caressing between her fingers and went to peruse the antique jewellery across the aisle.

'So, tell me the bit you didn't tell me.'

'I told the producer that as part of the deal for the film I want to be cast in the main role.'

'You know how to play hardball.'

222

'Not really. My agent usually does that shit. This producer just wants something I have, so I'm using it. But it's not that simple. She said – liberal sprinkle of the saltshaker here – that she *loved* me in the role and would, her words, cast me "in a heartbeat" if it were up to her. But it comes down to money, *of course*, and those putting up the dollars for the film will want, *of course*, "someone bankable". Hello Sarah Snook or Jessica Marias. Or even Kate bloody Winslet who does a bloody good Australian accent. Did you see her in *The Dressmaker*? Fuck, I love her. What do you think of that?' She was pointing to a teardrop emerald and blue rhinestone brooch.

'It's nice. So, there's a bit at stake with finding this will, then?'

'I can't negotiate anything without it. And I've been waiting my whole goddamn career for an opportunity like this.'

They wandered through the narrow aisles, losing and finding each other several times among the rabbit warren of stalls groaning with yesteryear. There were racks of vintage clothing to be inspected, shelves and cabinets of bric-a-brac, silverware and collectibles to be perused, 'chic nana' hats to be tried on, and original art-deco light fixtures and lamps to be coveted. Clio picked herself out a pair of retro ceramic red cats intended as salt and pepper shakers, while Olivia settled on a February 1942 edition of *Australian Home Journal*.

Such was the compact busyness of the floor, it was easy to miss if you didn't look up that the building was an old 'atmospheric' picture palace built in the interwar period. The vaulted plaster ceiling of Reckitt's blue was badly deteriorated and hadn't felt the caress of a paintbrush in decades. At the far end was an ornate proscenium arch with orange and jade faceted columns and bronzed scrollwork on the supporting corners. The roof edge was decorated with vibrant Spanish-style mission tiles and carved corbels, and hanging from the arch was a gold-fringed, blue-velvet valance with the word *Plaza* in the centre. Olivia hadn't noticed any of it in the past.

'Hey.' Clio tapped Olivia on the shoulder. 'What do you think?' She'd put on a green top hat that was too big for her head and an equally verdant and oversized tailcoat. 'Suits me, don't you reckon?' she said, executing some adroit Astaire moves even in six-inch platforms. 'I just need a cane.'

'You look like Kermit.'

Olivia thought she just might be in love.

'Isn't this credenza like the one you've got?' She skimmed her fingers across the top. The polished surface had worn away and was splintery to touch. 'It's not in as good condition.'

The left-side door opened with some sticky resistance, revealing empty shelving and a locked drawer in top.

'I think I might know what that key is supposed to open,' said Clio, adjusting the hat, which had fallen over her eyes.

- 14 -

April 1943

Though women were 'allowed' in Lennon's private bar, their presence was discouraged, by attitude and design, which is why Gloria chose it over the Wintergarden lounge, even if it meant she couldn't sit down. Stifling a yawn, she resisted propping her elbows on the counter.

'Excuse me,' she called to the bartender who'd been creatively ignoring her for ten minutes. 'I'd really like a G&T when you think you can manage it.'

'Yes, ma'am. I'll be down your way in a moment.'

'Miss Graham. I almost didn't recognise you sans your jaunty uniform.'

Gloria didn't turn to greet the dimple-chinned US major who'd sidled up beside her.

'I'm not sure being readily identified as a sack of potatoes is a compliment, Major Mann,' she said. He reminded her of Claude Rains, though mostly in the hair, which had a slight bouffant. And the heavy eyelids, and brows that, when furrowed, looked

225

like a bird of prey in flight. He also had the touch of an English accent, which she knew came from having a British father.

'No, it probably isn't.' He laughed. 'Can I assume by the absence of a drink in your hands that the service is slow?'

'That or the bartender needs a written reminder of his job description.'

'Excuse me,' said Mann, pitching his voice to penetrate the barman's selective ear. 'Could I get a whiskey, neat, thanks and—'

'A G&T.'

'A G&T. Thank you.'

'Yes, sir.'

'Is this where I'm supposed to say thank you?'

'Only if you really, really mean it.'

'Well, I really, really want a G&T, so I suppose a thank you is in order.'

'Wouldn't you be more comfortable in the lounge?'

'I'm waiting for a friend.'

'I see.'

'A woman friend. I told her I'd meet her here.'

'Surely—'

'Yes, I know. And she'll probably suggest we move the moment she walks in.' Gloria tipped her crown towards the George Street entrance to the bar. 'That's her now,' she said of the trim woman in a WAAAF uniform.

'I should very much like to be introduced. Should I order another G&T?'

'Yes, do. But an introduction is all you'll be getting. We haven't seen each other in months.' Gloria lifted her hand high above her head and waggled her fingers.

'I'll take what I can get,' said the major.

June waved back before excusing her way past various shades of uniformed rumps stationed along the green, marble-faced counters that snaked down either side of the room. Gloria's outstretched arms awaited her at the other end.

After a satisfying embrace, Gloria introduced June to the major. 'This is Major John Mann,' she said. 'He frequently requires my services to get him home safe and sound of an evening. I practically tuck him into bed.'

'She exaggerates, but she's an exemplary driver nevertheless.'

'And this is June – Mrs Atkinson. Who is already looking uncomfortable in this noisy and soon-to-be overcrowded bar, as I predicted.'

'It's very nice to meet you, Major.'

'You too, Sergeant Atkinson.'

'Your drinks, sir.'

'Thank you, again.' The major slid a pound note across to the bartender who had an obsequious streak after all. Handing one tumbler to June, he said, 'I was told a G&T was your poison.' Filled almost to the brim, it sloshed over the sides.

'That's very kind of you. Thank you.' June took the glass with both hands. 'And, yes, I was going to suggest we find somewhere more comfortable. What's wrong with the lounge? You're welcome to join us, Major.'

'Oh, I don't want to intrude. It sounds like you ladies have some catching up to do.'

'Don't be silly,' said June. 'We'll have plenty of time for that.' To Gloria, she said, 'They gave me a whole week.'

'Come on, then,' Gloria said to Mann. 'But I expect nothing less than conversation that tap dances from you.'

'I've been told I do a very good Gene Kelly.'

They managed to snare a corner table by the ribbed-glass windows in the Wintergarden. They were impossible to see out of, but that was likely the point. Major Mann took the chair while Gloria and June sat at right angles to each other on the turquoise settee. Even at five o'clock the cocktail lounge was a chattering, chinking, cackling force of life, its breath foggy with cigarette smoke. It would be a sweating cauldron of booze, mostly bourbon and Gordon's gin, when Friday night really got its crank on and the evening-gown parade slinked in. Gloria found all the activity soothing for its consistency and the fact it didn't require her input to make it happen. Clamps of tension slowly relinquished their hold on her bones. She covered her mouth, but there was no holding it back; she yawned like a wild cat.

'Keeping you up, are we?' said Mann.

'Well, yes, in a manner of speaking. I've been on the nightshift all week in service to the US Armed Forces. This is my first night off.'

'Poor possum.'

'Watch it, Gene. I didn't ask for wisecracking as part of your routine.' What she liked about Mann was that sarcasm didn't whizz him by, like many of his compatriots who required a pin-up girl wink to ensure they knew she was 'just kidding around'. She asked June about the train trip from Sydney.

'Crowded. I was stuffed in a carriage with a gaggle of AWAS. Fresh Sigs right off the production line on their way north. The train stopped somewhere between Grafton and Lismore for over an hour for no discernible reason. I learned something interesting, though, but I highly doubt the truth of it.' She glanced briefly at the major. 'Apparently, women who live in houses that back onto the rail line hang their sheets out as a signal to American troop trains that their husbands are away overseas. Have you heard that one?'

The major snorted. 'I can't say I have, but it's a good one. Almost as good as the one about the train full of you WAAAFs supposedly in the family way being sent south with "return when empty" scrawled on one of the carriages.'

'Hilarious, Major. Though fascinating if it is true,' said Gloria. 'Archbishop Duhig probably started the rumour himself. Has all the makings of his alarmist propaganda.'

'Your politicians seem quite obsessed with that kind of thing. The, ah, what do you call him? Your minister for affairs of the home—'

'The Health and Home Affairs Minister. Mr Hanlon.' Gloria made a show of rolling her eyes.

'That's the fella. In the newspaper today he had told some other minister there were almost five hundred illegitimate births in Brisbane in the first half of 1942. Which, if you do the math, you can't blame our boys for – the first of them didn't even arrive until Christmas. The next fact given, incidentally, was the number of reported rape cases since July.'

'Do you remember what that was?'

'Well, it was a lot darn less than five hundred, which I think was the not-so-subtle point. Seven, I believe it was, and five or six attempted ones.'

Gloria pursed her lips and felt her nostrils twitch. 'Yes, that is interesting,' she said. 'We're talking about reported cases, though.'

'Did you get my last letter?' said June. She took a sip of her drink and darted her eyes again at the major. 'With the girl's name you asked me about?'

'Valerie, yes. I'd hoped you might remember her surname.'

'I don't think she said.'

'Well, it doesn't matter. I've decided to drop the whole thing anyway.'

'That's not like you. I thought, well, you seemed quite determined to ... to get to the bottom of things.'

'The bottom of what? I like bottoms, well, ladies' bottoms,' said Mann.

Gloria looked at June and sighed. She needed to pick her words prudently. Mann, for all she really knew about him, could be a noose-stringing stickler for things like confidentiality agreements.

'A girl was raped by a US serviceman last year, outside June's apartment,' she explained. 'She was on her way home after the late shift at the munitions factory. It was quite a brutal attack. He was interrupted by June and, ah, her companion, but fled the scene, unsurprisingly. As far as we're aware, he was never caught.'

'I see. That is ... alarming.'

If the mention of a 'companion' gave Mann the idea that he too might be a companion of June's, he kept it concealed. Gloria stole a glance at June, but she seemed unperturbed by any suggestion of marital impropriety on her part.

'She was adamant as concrete about us not reporting it to the police,' said June. 'I don't mind saying I thought she was an idiot.'

'I gather getting to the bottom of things, then, is finding the perp. You realise there's approximately sixty-six thousand US troops stationed in and around Brisbane alone. You should see the goddamn paperwork that goes with that.'

'Yes, I'm aware of the odds of such a caper, but there's a bit more to it.' Gloria shifted her gaze to June.

'I'm sure it's fine,' said June, her face a pinch of doubt.

'Major, what, if anything, might you know about a young woman who was found dead, strangled, in the mangroves by the river in South Brisbane? It would have been sometime in January.'

The major flicked his eyes between the two women.

'I would say it's news to me. And, ah, how exactly did you find out such a thing? Not via the press, I assume.'

'I'd rather not divulge that.'

'Yes, okay, I see. So, if I'm putting two and two together, you're suggesting that the man who attacked the girl outside June's apartment could be the same man who killed this girl?'

'It's a just a theory and, like I said, I have no plans to pursue it. I mean, what am I going to do? Put on a deerstalker, start smoking a pipe and go searching for clues? I guess we just have to trust the US provost got the right man, he'll be duly court-martialled and punished, and the girl's family will receive some justice. Beyond that—'

'A man has been arrested, then?'

'As far as I know, yes, but he's not the man who attacked Valerie.'

'How can you be sure?'

'Because *that* man was white.'

'And the man you're saying they arrested is not.'

'Correct. And I got the impression the evidence against him is on the flimsy and conveniently circumstantial side. But, as I said, due process and all that ...'

'Would you like me to make some inquiries? I've got a couple of friends in the provost corp. I might be able to, well, let's say put your mind to rest.' He reached over and touched Gloria's wrist. 'I'm guessing you'd at least like to know who the girl was.'

'Yes, thank you. We would like very much to know who the girl was. She at least deserves a goddamn name.'

There was an offensive blaze of sun through the lace curtains. It couldn't be that late, but the warmth of the room said otherwise. The blankets on June's side of the bed had been neatly pulled up and the pillow smoothed on top. Gloria could hear the clatter of crockery in the kitchen. Eliot wasn't on the bed, suggesting his allegiance lay with his owner after all. She yawned grandly before swinging herself out of bed and tossing on her robe.

'What in heaven's name are you cleaning the kitchen for? I know it's your house, but you're supposed to be my guest,' Gloria said, pulling a seat out from the table and angling a second one to put her feet up on.

'I'm just putting a few things away. I wanted something to do. I've already finished the book I brought with me. You must really have needed that sleep. It's after ten.'

'You have no idea. I'm perpetually exhausted. I can't keep up with this driving job and my one at the university at the same time. It's killing me. Would you mind putting some coffee on?'

'Toast as well?'

'Yes, thanks. You're bloody marvellous, you know. Are you sure you don't want to quit the WAAAF and come back and be my maid?'

'Quite sure.'

'So you're liking it? Not too tedious?'

'The rules and regulations aspect can be tiresome, though not as much as I anticipated. Work in the cypher office is routine, but isn't tedious. Most of the incoming signals are to do with aircraft maintenance, personnel postings and the like. But they still need to go through the same procedures as the top-secret stuff and the casualty reports. They're always grim, of course. Then there's the occasional prime ministerial signal, which causes a flutter around the office.'

Gloria watched as June measured out coffee, lit the stove, sliced bread and cut slim wedges of butter: her slight, bony wrists leading the charge as she crisscrossed the kitchen through angled patches of sunlight. She hadn't dressed yet and looked crisply elegant in an ankle-length ecru robe, though the satin fabric emphasised how thin she'd become.

'The food any good?' asked Gloria.

'Mess food? It's passable, I suppose. I'll be happy if I never see mashed potato again in my lifetime. But then I think of Peter, so that just makes me cranky when others complain.'

Eliot, bored with standing sentinel by the back door, trotted beneath the table and made a play for Gloria's outstretched lap.

'I'm not sure that's going to work, TS,' she said, letting him perform contortionist circles on her thighs in the hope he'd figure that out for himself.

'Oh, Eliot, no. Come here.' June scooped him up and held him to her chest. She planted several kisses on his face before giving him the scratch he so desired under the chin. 'Time for you to go outside, I think.' She opened the screen and plopped him onto the concrete landing. Eliot made sure to look nonplussed then stalked off to his spot beneath the climbing bauhinias along the fence.

'So, tell me,' said Gloria, picking fur off her lap. 'Karl. You've barely mentioned him in your letters. You still … seeing him?'

'I saw him when he was in Sydney last, which was maybe a month ago. He was headed back to New Guinea.'

'And?'

She paused and placed her fists on the counter, butter knife in hand, and looked up at the ceiling.

'It was fine. We spent a few nights together. Dinner at Romano's. Cocktails. His hotel room. We even went to a concert.'

'But? You feel guilty about Peter, is that it?'

'No, that's just it. I don't. I like it all a bit too much. Karl, yes, he's part of it, but not for a minute do I think I'm the only dalliance he's had. Not that I've asked. No, it's – well, I can't even put my finger on it, except to say I don't know how I'm going to go back to an ordinary life again, here in Brisbane, with my sweet, distracted husband. If he makes it home, that is.'

'It is something, isn't it? It's hard not to get caught up in the fever of having a common purpose. Uniforms everywhere and everyone feeling what they're doing is important and useful. And the Americans, let's not forget them. For all their braggadocio, they've certainly brought a touch of glamour to our little colonial outpost.'

'The glamour is relative, I think.'

'Can I assume you're referring to everybody's favourite farm boy?'

'You assume correctly.'

'So Edith's still—'

'Yes, she's *still*. You know, I did think perhaps she'd ... She barely spoke two words to him Christmas Day, yet he followed her around like a dopey Labrador. Then after lunch he got down on one knee, in front of that ridiculous Christmas tree she'd covered in "snow", and proposed to her in front of us all, and she burst into tears and ran from the room.'

June paused to place Gloria's toast and the butter dish on the table. Opening the icebox for the plum jam, she said, 'I felt sorry for him, to be honest. The poor kid was utterly bewildered, as were the rest of us. I mean, he did look frightful; whoever got stuck into him during that brawl really did a number on his face.'

'Her aversion to his rearranged features didn't last?'

'By New Year's it was like Christmas never happened. Frank's face was almost back to normal and she was parading about the place like ... I don't know ... she'd signed a contract with MGM or something.'

'You don't think she really loves him?'

Intent on pouring the coffee into two mugs, she didn't answer.

'That sounded like a sigh,' said Gloria.

'I don't know. Maybe she does. It's just ... Well, you've heard it all before. At least Mum and Dad have asked them both to wait a year. Frank's unlikely to go anywhere, unless the war suddenly finishes. And they won't sign anything or submit to any interviews with the US Army unless Frank and Edith both agree to those terms. So that's something, I suppose.' She brought their coffees over and placed one in front of Gloria. 'And I suppose you want sugar.'

'Please.'

'There's not much left,' June said, lifting the lid. 'I'll give you some ration coupons.' She put the canister on the table with a teaspoon, then surveyed the kitchen, fists propped on her hips.

'Would you sit down for Christ's sake?'

June sat and picked up her mug. She blew at the surface, rippling the hot liquid and directing the curls of steam like a snake charmer.

'Want to see a film tonight? Let's look what's on, shall we.' Gloria reached for the newspaper June had retrieved earlier. 'So flimsy these days,' she said, turning the back sheet over. 'There's a play on at His Majesty's. *The Man Who Came to Dinner*?'

June shook her head. 'No. Well, what about Paulette Goddard in *The Lady Has Plans*? That's at the Embassy, so it's close by.'

'Yes, maybe. I like Paulette Goddard. She should have played Scarlett O'Hara.'

'Oh treachery! Don't ever let Edith hear you say that.'

June took a cautious sip of coffee, placed her mug back down, and focused her smoky-greys on Gloria. 'I was thinking about our conversation with Mann last night,' she said. 'Specifically about Valerie, and me saying I thought she was an idiot for not wanting us to ring the police that night. We really should have ignored her and done it anyway. I admit I feel terribly guilty about that now. But it occurred to me, there must be a reason, and I mean a proper one, why she was so insistent about it.'

'Yes?'

'Well, if it happened to you, what would stop you wanting to report it?'

'I'd want to hunt down and kill the bastard myself.'

'Besides that. And we're not actually talking about *you*.'

'Well, I guess because the poor kid was terrified out of her skull.'

'Of course she was. So wouldn't it be comforting, in that case, to know the police were going to try and find him and put him away?'

'Ah.'

'Exactly,' said June.

'She knew him. And it took us this long to figure that out. Some detective I am. So what do you suggest?'

'There's nothing to stop you from talking to her. She lives close by, just around on Moray Street in the girls' hostel – or she did. The back entrance to it is at the end of our lane. Why don't you go round this afternoon? I'm going over to visit my parents and Edith, and it's probably better if I'm not there, anyway. She might find my presence ... Well, it could be upsetting for her.'

'All right, I will. But I'm going back to bed first for a few hours,' said Gloria.

'Good. Well, it's time for me to get organised.'

June stood, taking one more mouthful of coffee, then passed it over to Gloria to finish.

Gloria watched her sail out of the room, an ethereal, upright ironing board.

With no warning, the afternoon sky filled with low, dumpy clouds that looked resolved to hang around. The umbrella Gloria thought to take was gone from the stand beside the door. Gladys Atkinson, Peter's mother, had collected the last of her belongings two weekends ago after she'd decided to move permanently to Toowoomba. That was something else she needed to discuss with June: getting a boarder. Gloria thought she might have a candidate in Phyllis Gordon: a newbie driver who'd just moved from Melbourne to be closer to her husband when he got leave, but as landlord it would be June's decision. Gloria closed the door behind her, and stepped into the lightly spitting wind.

The other, harder thing she had to tell June was that her neighbour Mr Bellincioni had been rounded up and sent to an internment camp. June was most fond of him and would not take the news well.

Gloria headed down Sydney Street, one hand shielding her face, the other clutching her skirt, and took the first right onto Moray. She soon spotted Archibald House, which was not built to blend in. The front was dominated by double-storeyed bay windows, each overhung with a red awning and a creamy wooden valance. Lacey timber bargeboards skirted the crowning gable, while double verandahs, trimmed with white, cast-iron balusters and valances, ran along the front and down both sides. Ignoring the flutter in her chest – what was there to be apprehensive about? – she marched up the steps and knocked on the door. It was opened by a portly woman with tired eyes.

'Can I help you? If you're collecting for charity, you'll be disappointed, sorry. This is a church-run facility.' The woman's tone conveyed weary despondency more than hostility.

'I'm not after money. I was hoping to talk with one of your residents, if she's here.'

'And who is it you're after? Most of 'em are off working on a Saturday afternoon.'

'Her name's Valerie. I don't know her surname, sorry.'

'I'm supposing you mean Valerie Watts. She left here over

237

six months ago. Can't say I was too sorry, either. Difficult to manage, you might say.'

'Do you know where she went?'

'Can't say I do. She upped and left. Not even a week's notice, which they're supposed to give. She was a bit wayward, you know the sort. And this is not *that* sort of girls' hostel, but we took her in 'cause her mother died when she was young and her grandparents were Methodists who attended the local church. Also dead as dodos now. Not much I could have done. She's too old now to be worrying the Child Welfare about. Wouldn't surprise me if she'd made her way to the lock hospital, if you follow my meaning. Her old roommate might know where she took off to, though. You wanna ask her?'

'Yes, please, if I may.'

The woman stepped back to let Gloria pass. 'Up them stairs.' She pointed behind her. 'Turn left and it's the second door on your right.'

'Thank you very much, Mrs—'

'Ingle. You're welcome. Just as long as I don't have to climb them stairs. Her name's Alice, by the way. She's leaving herself come Monday. Heading back to Kingaroy.'

The door was ajar, but Gloria knocked anyway. A young woman – Edith's age, or maybe younger – with coarse dark hair and ungainly eyebrows opened the door.

'Hello?'

'Alice? Hello, I'm Rhia.' She greeted with her best smile, desperate to put the girl at ease. She put out her hand, but quickly retracted it. 'May I come in? I just want to ask you a few questions about your old roommate. Valerie. Valerie Watts.'

'I suppose that's okay.' Alice peered out into the hall. 'I don't know what I can tell you, but you can come in.'

The room was much simpler than the outside of the house

implied. Two single wireframe beds, two chairs, a desk and a wardrobe, no trimmings. There was a suitcase on one bed with folded piles of clothes around it.

'Do you want to sit on a chair? I can move the stuff off it.'

'No, that's okay. I won't keep you. I really just want to know where Valerie went after she left here. Did she leave a forwarding address with you?'

'I only know she was going to a boarding house in West End. That's all she told me. She found a room to share with her friend Vera. I told her to write me once she was there so I could send her some photographs I was getting developed, but … I never heard from her.'

'Oh. When was it that she left, exactly?'

Alice sat on the edge of the bed beside her suitcase and clasped her hands over her knees. Gloria felt a pang of tenderness for the girl.

'It was September, or maybe October. I remember because it was about a month after my half-brother was here on leave the first time.'

'Was there … Well, do you think there was a particular reason she left?'

'I thought …' She dropped her chin. 'I thought it was because of me, at first. Val liked to go out dancing a lot, having fun, but I'm not really like that. And maybe that still is the reason, but I think she just wanted to get away because of everything that happened.'

'Like what? If you don't mind me asking.'

Alice's head snapped up. 'Well,' she went on, a strange note creeping into her voice, 'first she got stood up by her fiancé, that American submariner, on the day they were supposed to get married, and then her father died a few weeks after that.'

'Oh. I'm sorry, I had no idea.'

'But aren't you her aunt? The one she went to visit after her father died?'

'No, that's not me, sorry. I apologise if I gave you that impression.'

'Then who are you? And why are you so interested in Val?'

Gloria felt like she'd been caught pilfering. She fidgeted with the house key in her right pocket. 'I'm interested because, well, she was attacked by a man not far from here, just round the corner, in fact, and I'd like to know a bit more about what happened that night.' She paused, then added, 'Did she not tell you about that?'

Alice's expression was inscrutable but for a small tightening around her eyes, which were trained, unblinkingly, on Gloria. They were an unusual shade of brown, Gloria noticed – a kind of peanut colour.

'No, she didn't,' she said eventually.

'I am very sorry to have bothered you in that case. Please forgive me.'

'Have you even met Val before?'

'No, I haven't, I'm afraid.'

Alice only nodded. She got to her feet and turned to face the bed. 'I have a picture of her if you want to see it?'

'Yes, please. I'd like that.'

Gloria inched a step back while Alice crouched to pull a large McWhirter's box out from under the bed. She moved a pile of clothes out of the way and placed it on the bed. The photo album was on the bottom and was less than half filled. Alice opened it to where she'd pasted in the most recent snaps. Gloria had to stifle a laugh. There was one of Alice in an oversized fur coat standing beside a cane chair, with an awkwardly angled pillbox hat on her head. She looked cringingly self-conscious.

'That's her,' said Alice, pointing to the adjacent picture. 'Another girl who lives here let us borrow her Box Brownie. We took them a day or so after she was jilted by her fiancé. It was my idea to do it. I thought it might cheer her up.'

Though wearing the same fur coat, Valerie was hamming it up in the mode of a Hollywood starlet. She sat with one arm draped over the side of the chair, the other propped against the back, a cigarette dangling insouciantly between her fingers. Her chin was thrust out at a modish angle, but her joyful mockery was most evident in the laughing smile she couldn't contain to cooperate with the rest of the pose. There were two other pictures of the girls together in which they took it in turns to wear the coat. On Valerie it looked like a bearskin tent. Where they got such a monstrosity, Gloria could only hazard.

'I've got copies of these to send to her. So, if you do find her, can you tell her and ask her to write me so I can post them to her? I'll give you my address in Kingaroy.'

'Of course, Alice. And thank you. You've been very helpful.'

The rain, when she left, was not the sort to be brashly fobbed off. Mrs Ingle needed her suspicions allayed, but she allowed Gloria to exit via the rear of the building and take the back gate. She still got drenched. The cane chair in Alice's photographs, she noticed, was lying askew on the lawn by an iron jardinière.

~

After seeing June off at South Brisbane Station, Gloria drove back to the garage, getting stuck behind a convoy of lorries as they lumbered off the Grey Street Bridge. Brisbane's newfound vibrancy had come at the cost of its artless countrified charm: air-raid shelters down every street, water pipes along gutters, sandbags lumped like sleeping seals against public building doors, boarded-up windows imprisoned in wire netting. It was still as ramshackle as ever, though, despite the khaki, concrete and grit.

Gloria pulled up beside one of the petrol pumps inside the double-storeyed brick garage, which had been built beneath the interstate railway line. Using the car for private purposes was not allowed, but on a quiet shift, and with a few fellow drivers enlisted to be cool liars if required, that could be got around. At day's end, she was supposed to sweep the car out, then dust and polish it, but the siren song of the camp bed in the drivers' retreat upstairs was a compelling wail.

Only Phyllis was in the sitting room, listening to the wireless and reading *Home Journal* magazine. Despite having no windows, it was comfortably outfitted in the manner of an English drawing room, with dark-red upholstered chairs and silky-oak panelled walls. There was even a green cut-glass vase of wild roses on the polished table beside the wireless. Somebody else, by the sound of it, was in the shower. You had to hand it to the Yanks: they understood the relationship between comfort and morale.

Gloria flopped into an armchair and loosened her tie.

'Tea?' said Phyllis. 'I was about to make a pot.' She spoke genially without being overfamiliar.

'Yes, thanks.'

Phyllis put the magazine aside, fixed Gloria with a polite smile and smoothed her skirt on the way to the kitchen. Gloria closed her eyes, the serial drama on the radio percolating cosily in her ears.

'Gloria. Tea's ready,' said Phyllis, her voice low and gentle. She clinked a teaspoon against a china cup.

'Thank you,' said Gloria without opening her eyes.

'Sugar? Milk?'

'That's okay, I'll do it.' Gloria sat up and forced her eyelids open. 'Are you still looking for a place to live?'

'Yes. It's impossible to find anywhere remotely suitable. I had no idea it would be this difficult.'

Phyllis melted with relief when Gloria offered her the second room in June's apartment.

'I told Ian I was going back to Melbourne if I didn't find anything this week. I can't keep living in a hotel room, and it looks like he'll be in Brisbane for a stint from next month. You don't know how grateful I am.' She settled back against the chair with her tea, relaxed in a way Gloria hadn't thought she had in her.

'And what does your husband do in the army?'

'Something to do with communications. I don't know the ins and outs of it, but it's a public relations role of sorts. Liaising with all the various divisions, and the Americans, of course. Information management is how he describes it.'

'And where is he now?'

Phyllis gave a lengthy discourse on her husband's various movements up and down the Eastern seaboard before explaining he'd been in Port Moresby for the last three months. A more permanent posting to Brisbane looked to be on the cards, though, she said.

'They want him to work more closely with the Americans on matters of – how does he put it? – "civilian perception of troop misbehaviour". Something like that. You should hear the things they *don't* put in the papers. Tip of the iceberg what they allow the public to know.'

'Brawls, you mean?'

'That kind of thing, yes. From the bits and pieces he tells me, the vile behaviour is fairly evenly distributed among both sides.'

'No doubt. Our boys do seem excessively punch-ready.'

'Yes, but the Americans carry knives. Though even on the Australian side it's not all just your usual hot-headed, fisticuff affairs with a few bruised eyes and egos. Ian told me about something in September last year that struck me as just plain cruel. This trio of Aussie soldiers were drinking in a park with some Yank they'd met somewhere, and after getting this fellow so stonkered that he passed out they stripped him naked as the day he was born and tied him to a tree with some rope. Then, as if that wasn't enough, they used the Yank's own knife to carve obscenities into the tree and left it stuck there so it looked like he'd been stabbed in the head. And to add injury to insult, they took off with his uniform.'

'How utterly craven. They were arrested, I take it?'

'I believe the MPs rounded them up about week later. The problem was the poor Yank's testimony wasn't particularly reliable, so they were let off on some technicality. They weren't even slapped with a dishonourable discharge.'

'Was this in Brisbane?'

'Yes, but don't ask me where. I haven't even figured out which way is north yet.'

The phone was ringing in the cordoned-off office space. Gloria made a half-hearted move to answer it, but Jan Jacobs, fresh out of the shower, got there first.

'Rhia?' Jacobs poked her turbaned head around the corner. 'Job for you,' she said. 'It's for Major Mann. He asked specially for you.'

Mann was waiting for her at the bottom of the stairs outside the entrance to Somerville House. He folded himself into the front seat, contrary to convention and official policy. His long legs peaked into an awkward A-frame at the knees.

'Don't start yawning on me, Graham.'

'You didn't see that. Home, I take it?'

'Thank you, ma'am. Look, now you've got me started,' said

Mann stretching his mouth to full capacity. 'Your friend June, she's gone back to Sydney?' he asked once his face contracted.

'Saw her off this afternoon.'

'A very handsome woman. Doesn't bother with unnecessary embellishment, I like that.'

'I would say so.'

'You're like that, too. Straightforward in every way. I admire that in a woman.'

'What are you angling at, Mann?'

'See? You just proved my point. But you haven't asked me yet why I made a point of asking for you tonight.'

'I thought it was because you wanted my scintillating company. Isn't that the usual reason?' She swerved to avoid a butcherbird someone had hit earlier.

'You got me. There is another reason this time, however.'

'No. You didn't really manage it?' Gloria bounced in her seat.

'It's right in here, my dear,' he said, tapping the leather briefcase beside him. 'And I had to make all sorts of grotesque promises to ensure its contents remain ...' He made a key-locking gesture at the side of his mouth.

'Well, for God's sake, are you going to tell me what it says?'

'You can read it for yourself when we get to my pad. Now concentrate on the road. It's like peat out there and I don't want you hitting a kangaroo or something.'

Mann's 'pad' was a luxury one-bedroom flat in St Lucia. The sort its owners knew they could bankroll themselves into retirement on by renting it out to the Yanks. Gloria had been inside a few times, and had even been a guest at a little dinner party Mann had thrown last month. The furnishings in the sitting room were as modern and tasteful as you'd expect. Anything with a whiff of the Victorian long expunged.

Gloria acquainted herself immediately with the leather settee once they'd walked through the front door.

'First things first,' Mann said, already at the drinks caddy with the whiskey decanter in hand. 'Let's get ourselves drinked up.'

'I better not.'

'Rubbish. Ice or neat?'

'Ice, thanks.'

Mann's serves were always generous. She took the drink from him, the ice tinkling prettily against the glass. He went over to his leather satchel on the dining table and retrieved a manila envelope. Holding it just out of Gloria's reach, he said, 'You never saw this, remember.' Envelope handed over, he made himself busy in the kitchen.

Gloria put her drink on a nearby coaster. What he'd given her, she saw on sliding it from the envelope, was a general court-martial order, as well as a transcript of the trial. She read the order slowly as if she were to be quizzed on it later, committing the details to memory. Olive. Her name was Olive Jeanne Moon. And she was eighteen years of age. There were two charges: Felony murder, and Rape.

The defendant was Grayson M. Woods. He pleaded not guilty to both charges and was found 'Of all Specifications and Charges: Not Guilty'. The order was date stamped '26 March 1943'. The transcript was more longwinded, and she skimmed it for the details not explicated in the order.

Mann returned with a plate of ham and tomato sandwiches cut into triangles and a dish of cocktail onions and olives.

'I thought you might be hungry.'

'I am, actually.' She put the envelope on the coffee table and took a sandwich. 'So, they didn't convict him. That's something, I suppose.'

'Not from want of trying, I was told. But his alibi was tighter than a—'

'Yes, it read that way.' She swallowed a mouthful of sandwich. 'No less than three men, including two Australian privates, accounted for his movements on the night she was murdered, from early in the afternoon to when he was back at Camp Freeman at Inala before midnight. And they didn't find any blood, dirt or incriminating hair of any kind on his clothing. You have to ask how he was arrested in the first place.'

'On the basis he was heard saying he gave her a pair of nylons as a present, I believe.' Mann, perched on the arm of the lounge at the other end, reached for a sandwich.

'Well, if that's a motive for rape and murder then you might want to put half the US Armed Forces under house arrest. Her body wasn't found for almost twenty-four hours, you know, so whoever did rape and kill her had plenty of time to—'

'Gloria. You're going to have to let it go. They'll get whoever did it, you're just gonna have to believe that, honey.'

She took in a rough, unsatisfying breath and reached for her drink. She was getting worked up. She was so bloody tired. Mann passed her his handkerchief, though her eyes had only watered a smidge. She wasn't crying.

'Gloria, you can't keep this up. The driving, I mean, while also working a full-time job.'

'I only work four days a week at the university.'

'You know what I mean. Do you like the driving work?'

'I do, but it can be a wretch doing it for nothing. Especially when they roster you on six nights in a row.'

'Come and work for us properly then so you can get paid for it. I can arrange it for you on Monday and have you on the payroll by week's end. It would mean quitting your other job.'

Gloria stretched out along the settee and cradled her head on her arm angled against the armrest.

'Can I think about it?'

'You can.' Mann patted her leg before strolling over to his satchel to return the envelope. He took out a copy of *The Courier-Mail* and waved it like a flag above his shoulder.

'They finally announced it today,' he said. 'My department's been pushing for something for months.'

'What's that?'

'A recreational club for coloured servicemen. It'll be run by Amcross. The Doctor Carver Service Club, they're calling it. Opens early next month.'

'Whereabouts?'

'South Brisbane. Grey Street.'

'P'rolly be the best club in town,' she said without moving her lips.

'Gloria?'

'Hmm … John, tell me stories about your childhood. About Oregon.'

'If you like.'

Gloria let her eyelids sink and her mind drift into a landscape of snow-capped mountains, holiday cottages by crisp, sparkling lakes full of trout, swimming and rowboats, and horses with silly names for riding on through meadows, pine forests and other idyllic terrains.

She woke briefly some hours later. She turned over, acknowledging the pillow under her head, her shoeless feet and the blanket draped cautiously up to her shoulders. Swiftly, easily, the dark and quiet tugged her back to sleep again.

A panicky need for air woke her the second time. Her tie was skewed around her neck and pinned beneath her shoulder. In her dream, the cause, though murky, had been more sinister.

She recovered her breathing, reassured herself, and released her tie. Before the sensation of being suffocated stole in, she'd been dreaming about an olive tree by a river that harboured in its branches broken birds that could no longer sing.

She lifted the heavy curtain above the lounge to check her watch in the moonlight. Had they noticed her missing car from the motor pool? It was too late now to worry about what sort of reprimand she'd receive, or the rumours her absence would inspire. She felt her aloneness, acutely, and not in a way she recognised and usually appreciated when by herself. She got up, taking the pillow with her, and felt her way through the black space to Mann's bedroom.

~

The American Red Cross had been unenthused when Gloria applied to volunteer at their new service club on Grey Street. Her skin colour was the main sticking point. Was she a light-skinned Aboriginal by any chance? Any South Sea Islander blood? What persuaded them in the end were her age, clerical experience and 'obvious' respectability. At thirty-four, they judged her as less susceptible to 'inappropriate relationships' with the clientele, though it would have been better if she'd been a teacher or a social worker. She could only manage one day or night a week, anyway, two at the most, which though she'd quit her job still had to fit around her new one driving for the Yanks. She preferred to come in on weekends, thus optimising her chances of crossing paths with Grayson Woods.

Two and a half months in, however, and with no result, she was less enamoured with her plan. Not to say she didn't enjoy her hours at the Carver Club where she was most often put to use serving meals in the cafeteria, or undertaking a bit of light administration. She'd also become an unofficial librarian of sorts, making recommendations from the small library attached to the reading and writing room, and establishing a loan register based on the honour system to keep tabs on who had borrowed what. What she politely refused to do was sew even so much as a button on a shirt, or dance. The former she hated and at the latter she was an embarrassment.

The club held dances twice a week and had its own swing band, as well as the occasional guest band or musical quartet. The US Fifth Air Corps Orchestra was set to play tonight. They were setting up and tuning their instruments on the stage: a cramped, pokey affair for a seven-piece outfit, but they made it work. Come night-time the dance floor would be more atmospheric with its blue ceiling and moonlight effects, but this time of the afternoon the 'ballroom' was dull and empty, with the men relaxed playing cards and billiards or table tennis in the lounge areas.

Gloria stopped on her way through to listen to the trombonist belt out a few riffs.

'Whaddya think?' he said, pausing to tighten his mouthpiece.

'Fantastic.'

'See you out on the dance floor tonight?'

'Not a chance in hell.'

She saluted him goodbye and went through to the reading room. Two men were ensconced in armchairs with books, while a third appeared to be writing a letter at one of the desks. In the library – a shelved closet, really – Gloria opened the loans book to see what had been borrowed and returned in the last five days. There was an encouraging page and a half of entries.

She ran two fingers down the columns checking names against books; there were always a couple of voracious readers. Right at the bottom, and about to turn the page, she almost missed the entry: G. Woods. *Farewell, My Lovely*. He'd borrowed it three days ago and had already returned it. Yesterday. But how many G. Woods were there likely to be? He could be a Gary or a Grant. Or a Graham. She flicked the page over and looked at the first entry. He'd also checked out *The Lady in the Lake*, another Raymond Chandler, also yesterday, which he was yet to return. She poked her head into the reading room; the two men there weren't reading Chandler.

At the club reception she asked to see the guest registration book. It was a big, hefty thing, but it didn't take long to find what she was looking for. The G did stand for Grayson, and he'd signed in on Tuesday for a five-night stay in a dormitory. He was leaving tomorrow morning. Feeling light-headed, she handed the register back to Rosie behind the desk and thanked her. It didn't seem possible he could actually be here.

He wasn't in the cafeteria; that much she established after asking around, although one man offered her a doughnut. Out in the lounge area, she asked a couple of soldiers playing ping-pong if they knew a Grayson Woods and, if so, where he might be.

'Can't help you there, ma'am. Sorry. Do you know a Grayson, Pete?'

'Name don't ring a bell, no. We only arrived here yesterday from Townsville.'

'Well, have you seen anyone reading a book somewhere?'

'Saw a fella head up to the balcony with a book about an hour ago.'

The fella with a book – it was Chandler – had chosen a spot at the far end of the empty balcony. The winter bite off the river had kept everyone else indoors. His feet were parked on a second cane chair, the book in his right hand, a cigarette in his left. The posture of a man who didn't want to be disturbed.

She'd had almost three months to plan what she was going to say but had failed to think past the moment of actually finding him. Heart on a steady but insistent pummel, she approached him from behind the tables and chairs that stood between them.

'Grayson Woods?'

There was a beat or two before he lowered the book and turned his head in her direction.

'That's me.'

'Good book?'

'Yeah. I like his style. You never know what's coming next. You read any of his?'

'A couple, yes. Not that one though, so don't spoil the ending.'

He waited for Gloria to explain her presence.

'Mr Woods—'

'Grayson will do. What can I do for you, Mrs …?'

'Rhia is fine. Mind if I sit down?'

He removed his feet from the chair opposite and gestured to Gloria to take it, before stubbing out his cigarette on the concrete.

'I … Well, I wanted to ask you about Olive Moon.' She put a hand on his knee when he made a move to stand. 'No, please hear me out. I know you didn't kill her.'

'Then what's this about?' He remained seated, but shifted back to a more upright position and crossed his arms, book still in hand, middle finger marking his place.

'I just … I really just wanted to know more about Olive. What did you know about her? Were you friends?'

'I was friendly with her, yeah. We went to the pictures a couple times, that kind of thing. She was a nice girl. Real sweet. She worked as a maid for some rich white family.'

'Friendly enough to give her stockings?'

Grayson tipped his head forward and shook it slowly.

'You kidding me, right? Yeah, I got her a pair of stockings 'cause she asked me to. She said how she really wanted some and, fool me, I boasted I could get 'em for her. It took some fandangling, but I got her some eventually. Stupidest thing I ever did.'

'And that was the last you saw her? The morning she was …'

'Yes, it was, and I don't know how many times I got to keep saying it.'

'Do you have any idea who might have done it? Did she associate with anyone else? Other soldiers?'

'No, I don't. Like I said, we only went out a few times. But I told them MPs when they hauled me in for questioning there was this Aussie soldier standing right across the street watching us when I gave her them goddamn nylons. She lived on Hope Street and he was outside Hamilton's Store right opposite, on the corner of Peel there.'

'What did the MPs say to that?'

'They weren't the least bit interested, so sure they were on doing me for killing her. But this guy, he had a mean look. He was looking me over when I went in the store to buy a soda. Nasty in the eyes, you know what I mean. Not like most Aussie fellas I know. Us black soldiers, we get on like a house on fire with your diggers 'cause we both hate them Yank white boys, especially them goddamn mud puppies.'

'Mud puppies?'

He smiled for the first time then laughed. 'MPs, I'm talking about. Anything else you want to know about Olive? I want to finish this book before the dance tonight. I'm leaving in the morning, back to that shithole Mt Isa. You ever been there?'

Gloria shook her head. 'Can't say I have.'

'They transferred me there after the court-martial. Thought they'd punish me anyway, even though I was found not guilty. You know where I'm from? Chicago. To get this leave pass I couldn't so much as fart out of turn for three months.'

Gloria rose and thanked him. The late afternoon had chilled sharply. Her breath had started to cloud. She was at the door when he spoke again.

'You know, Olive's sister comes here for the dances sometimes. She told me all about the Carver Club in a letter she wrote. She wanted to say she was glad they didn't find me guilty. She never believed it was me from the start. Her name's Lila. You know her?'

'The name's not familiar, no.'

'Well, now you know.'

Gloria helped clean up in the kitchen before leaving. Trumpet and saxophone notes were already reverberating through the walls. She felt strangely deflated. Whatever she'd expected from Grayson Woods had not materialised; she'd only exposed her own folly to herself. She could pursue his lead of the nasty-eyed Australian soldier – the theory didn't lack credibility – but what would it prove? Justice for Olive, if such a thing existed, was not in her power to deliver. Even if she could find out who the man was – and he was probably long gone from Brisbane – it wouldn't change anything or bring Olive back. She had to accept that.

Outside it was cold, the night still, the moon full, high and bright. Good for the walk over the Victoria Bridge into the city. On leaving the club, she asked a soldier for a cigarette; her first in months. Her lungs thanked her for the relapse, the old cough immediately barking back to life. Her second inhale, when she recovered, was more cautious. She headed off towards Melbourne Street.

'Excuse me. Excuse me! Hello!'

Gloria turned. By moonlight alone she recognised the young woman's face – she was a volunteer at the club – and had noted on previous occasions her wide generous mouth, and the smile that could melt glass.

'Are you Rhia? I'm Lila.'

The only thing Gloria promised was to do her best. And she would start by finding Valerie Watts.

– 15 –

September 1975

My Dearest June,
Enclosed ('forthwith') is my 'Last Will and Testament' — signed,
sealed, 't's dotted and 'i's crossed, etc. I'm sure you'll know exactly
what must be done with it. As to the matter of my unfinished novel,
the only thing of importance we have ever disagreed over, I have taken
it upon myself to have the manuscript burnt in order to spare you
the task to which I know you are so adamantly opposed but would
carry out anyway because it's what I wanted. My failure to finish the
novel (it even remains without a proper title) was the most profound
one of my writing career. You might say it was the first time words
failed me. I thought, with words alone, I could undo what had been
done to Olive; perhaps rewrite her story entirely. Write her a different
ending. At the very least, I believed, I would expose to history the
man who so callously and brutally stole her life, but I couldn't even do
that with ethical certainty. I never could prove it was him. There are
some evils that no art form can make better, fix or even soothe, though
Shakespeare, perhaps, comes close at times. One can only hope fate
caught up with him somehow.

I say all this in the hope you will understand my reasons and not hold
it against me in your heart for too long. That you were always my greatest
champion, best friend and a terrible critic of my work, I have never
taken for granted. You were, and will be to that day we know is coming

257

soon – and I apologise for the burst of sentiment – the love of my life.
   Love tautologically forever and always,
   Rhia x

~

Subject: Re: My manuscript
Cleo Manning <cleoedithjunemanning@hotmail.com>
To: oliviawells83@gmail.com

I <u>love</u> it. Don't change a word.
Cleo xx

PS. Why did you spell my name differently?
PPS. Do you really think I have a hoarding problem?
PPPS. I ~ think ~ I might be in love too.

Also, negotiations going v. well (got my agent on it). But not
done deal, yet. And bought (the) dress as lucky charm (Foxtel
ad rolled over).

Subject: Re: My manuscript

So glad you're happy with it.
Livvy xx

PS. https://en.wikipedia.org/wiki/Clio
PPS. Not really (maybe a little).
PPPS. Really? *Like really?*

Fingers & toes X-ed! Thoroughly approve of dress purchase.

With Cleo's approval, Olivia felt confident about finally sending her full thesis (*Meet Me at Lennon's: a narrative reclaiming of women's lives and voices from World War II Brisbane*) to Mandy. All that remained was to hope for the best. That and the email to Tobias she'd been putting off for weeks to tell him why she wouldn't be coming to LA after all. She'd hosted elaborate debates in her head over whether 'the why' was necessary, and, in the end, team 'you need to be honest' had won with its appeal to ethical behaviour and her better nature. The email could wait a little longer, though. First, she wanted to look at the documents her father had sent all those months ago. While she was still processing his re-entry into her life, cycling through feelings of forgiveness, indignation and even rage, she was still loath to disappoint him. Was it the need to prove herself to him? They were scheduled to catch up next week – at which time Olivia would also meet her half-brother and -sister for the first time – and she wanted to say she'd at least looked into things for him, in the knowledge that she honestly had, before she let him down with the news that what he wanted to know was simply lost for all time.

She retrieved the email from the 'Trevor' folder with its stockpile of attachments. There were a few family photographs of Noelene, her son and daughter, and what Olivia surmised were grandchildren. She stared at the pictures for a long time, trying to grasp, beyond an intellectual understanding, that the woman in the photos was her biological grandmother. Perhaps the feeling of that would come later. Among the scanned documents were the hospital record from Trevor's birth stamped 'BFA' and a newspaper article from 1994 on the closure of the Boothville Maternity Hospital in Windsor.

Olivia read through the adoption certificate Trevor had mentioned at lunch, skimming through the legalese, to establish he'd been adopted by Eric and Sonia Stephens, a coal miner and housewife respectively, 'domiciled' in Ipswich, Queensland, and 'not under the age of twenty-five'. Furthermore, they were 'desirous of being authorised under *The Adoption of Children Acts, 1935 to 1952* to adopt William Clancy Kidd an infant of the male sex, aged two weeks ... the child of Noelene Marie Kidd and [blanked] ... who shall henceforth be named Trevor John Stephens.'

William Clancy, for some reason, rang a bell.

– Acknowledgements –

I'd firstly like to acknowledge the Turrbal and Jagera people as the traditional owners of the area we now call 'Brisbane', and to acknowledge that key events in the novel take place on significant Aboriginal sites such as Meanjin and Kurilpa along the Brisbane River.

To Paul Slessor, Kenneth Slessor's heir, I'd like to express my gratitude for permission to quote from Slessor's seminal poem 'Five Bells'.

Meet Me at Lennon's was written as part of a Doctorate of Creative Arts, and involved extensive research across a wide range of primary and secondary resources. Many of these are held in collections at the John Oxley Library at the State Library of Queensland, the Queensland State Archives, the Australian War Memorial library, the MacArthur Museum, the Brisbane Tram Museum, and the National Library of Australia's digital newspaper archive, Trove. Through this research I uncovered many anecdotes, incidents, and stories about Brisbane's wartime history and the people who lived through World War II in Brisbane. Though *Meet Me at Lennon's* is a work of fiction, it draws on a number of personal histories adapted from these collections, as well as from commemorative publications, memoirs, popular and academic histories, family war stories and urban legends told to me by people I met at barbeques and other social gatherings. The details of Gloria's job driving for the Americans, for example, were borrowed from Molly Mann and Berth Foote's memoir *We Drove the Americans* (Angus & Robertson, 1944). And while the character of Alice is fictional, I took the idea of her purchasing and burning a fur coat from a small memoir account by a woman named Marjorie Stone I read in *Yandina Women Remember* (edited by Audienne Blyth, 1994). Like Alice, Marjorie worked as a waitress for the Americans at Lennon's Hotel and was generously tipped for her efforts. With the tips she collected, Marjorie bought herself a fur coat for fifteen pounds from McWhirter's 'and felt very smart indeed' until she 'realised that American servicemen bought fur coats for the girls who favoured them'. As such, Marjorie decided to burn the coat, but not without having her photo taken in it first. To all the women, including Marjorie Stone, whose wartime recollections and stories I borrowed and pinched from, appropriated and adapted for *Meet Me at Lennon's*, I am deeply grateful. You have my greatest respect and admiration, and I hope I have done your experiences justice.

To the Queensland Literary Awards judges, I'd like to say a very big thank you for selecting my manuscript as the winner of the 2018 Glendower Award for an Emerging Writer, and Jenny Summerson for her generous financial sponsorship of the award. None of this would have happened without their faith that my manuscript had the makings of a publishable novel.

My deepest gratitude also goes to the team at UQP who looked after me and shepherded this book to publication, with special thanks to my publisher Aviva Tuffield, managing editor Jacqueline Blanchard, and Rebecca Starford for her careful editing and attention to detail.

Finally, I'd like extend my warmest thanks to the following people who supported me through the, often bumpy, journey of researching and writing this book: My DCA supervisor, friend, and fellow UQP author Ross Watkins, whose way with encouraging words is an artform in itself. My co-supervisor Paul Williams for his contribution to my doctorate. Kate Elkington for her abiding friendship, over-the-top praise, critical insights, and letting me follow in her literary footsteps from the day we met. My mum, Patricia McMinn, for simply doing what mothers do. My daughter Katerina Gibson, who inspires me with her imagination for stories and storytelling. My other early readers – Annette Hughes, Nicole Stephens and sister-in-law Natasha Myers – for their observations, eagle-eyes, and suggestions. The sisterhood – Frankie, Jacobie, Rebekah, Kay, Danielle and Corinne – for their years of sisterly support, laughter and tears, wine and nachos, and simply being the most divine friends any woman could have. And, lastly, my partner Glenn Hunt, who not only takes flattering author pictures, but gave me the gift of space and time to write this book, and had zero patience for my self-doubt.